P9-DMW-882

THE
ONLY
ROAD

THE
ONLY
ROAD

ALEXANDRA DIAZ

A Paula Wiseman Book

Simon & Schuster Books for Young Readers

NEW YORK   LONDON   TORONTO   SYDNEY   NEW DELHI

SIMON & SCHUSTER BOOKS FOR YOUNG READERS
An imprint of Simon & Schuster Children's Publishing Division
1230 Avenue of the Americas, New York, New York 10020

This book is a work of fiction. Any references to historical events, real people, or real places are used fictitiously. Other names, characters, places, and events are products of the author's imagination, and any resemblance to actual events or places or persons, living or dead, is entirely coincidental.

Text copyright © 2016 by Simon & Schuster
Jacket illustrations copyright © 2016 by Rebecca Green
All rights reserved, including the right of reproduction in whole or in part in any form.

SIMON & SCHUSTER BOOKS FOR YOUNG READERS
is a trademark of Simon & Schuster, Inc.
For information about special discounts for bulk purchases, please contact Simon & Schuster Special Sales at 1-866-506-1949 or business@simonandschuster.com.
The Simon & Schuster Speakers Bureau can bring authors to your live event. For more information or to book an event, contact the Simon & Schuster Speakers Bureau at 1-866-248-3049 or visit our website at www.simonspeakers.com.
Jacket design by Krista Vossen
Interior design by Hilary Zarycky
The text for this book was set in Bembo.
Manufactured in the United States of America
0217 FFG

2 4 6 8 10 9 7 5 3
Library of Congress Cataloging-in-Publication Data
Names: Diaz, Alexandra, author.
Title: The only road / Alexandra Diaz.
Description: First edition. | New York : Simon & Schuster Books for Young Readers, [2016] | "A Paula Wiseman Book." | Summary: "Twelve-year-old Jaime makes the treacherous journey from his home in Guatemala to his older brother in New Mexico after his cousin is murdered by a drug cartel."—Provided by publisher.
Identifiers: LCCN 2015046179 | ISBN 9781481457507 (hardback) | ISBN 9781481457521 (e-book)
Subjects: | CYAC: Emigration and immigration--Fiction. | Refugees—Fiction. | Guatemalan Americans—Fiction. | BISAC: JUVENILE FICTION / Social Issues / Emigration & Immigration. | JUVENILE FICTION / People & Places / Caribbean & Latin America. | JUVENILE FICTION / Family / General (see also headings under Social Issues).
Classification: LCC PZ7.D5432 On 2016 | DDC [Fic]—dc23
LC record available at https://lccn.loc.gov/2015046179

Para mi familia, and for all of those for whom leaving their home was, or is, the only choice.

—A. D.

CHAPTER ONE

From the kitchen came a piercing scream. The green colored pencil slipped, streaking across the almost-finished portrait of a lizard Jaime Rivera had been working on for the last half hour. As he jumped to his feet, a wave of dizziness hit him, leftover from the fever that had kept him home from school that morning. It took a second for his vision to clear, his hand braced on the sill of the glassless window that no longer held the posing lizard. He took a deep breath before bursting into the kitchen. The wailing only grew louder.

No, no, no, no, please no, he thought. It couldn't be, couldn't. It had to be something else. *Please!*

"*¿Qué . . .*" Jaime stopped short. Mamá was slumped on the plastic table, crying into her arms. Papá stood behind her with a hand on her back. Despite his quiet stance, his broad shoulders were hunched, making him look as distraught as Mamá.

At the sound of Jaime's entrance, Mamá looked up. Streaks of black, brown, and tan covered her normally perfectly made-up face. She beckoned him closer, pulled him onto her lap, and held him as if he were two instead of twelve. Papá's strong arms encircled both of them.

For a second Jaime allowed himself to melt into his parents' embrace. But only for a second. Dread twisted his stomach into a knot. *It* had happened, something he'd feared for a long time. He had convinced himself with all his might that it wouldn't, couldn't happen, because he didn't have anything to offer *them*. But *they* obviously disagreed. *They* had made that clear two weeks ago. If only he were wrong, and it wasn't that at all.

The incident that had happened two weeks ago came back to him; his former friend Pulguita had called over Jaime and his cousin Miguel as they were walking home from school.

"What does he want?" Jaime had muttered under his breath.

"I don't know. But at least he's alone." Miguel looked up and down the dirt street before crossing it. Jaime double-checked as well. Good. *They* weren't around.

Miguel stopped a few meters away from the boy.

Jaime folded his arms across his chest, keeping more distance between himself and his former friend.

Pulguita leaned against a deteriorating cinder-block wall. His slicked-back black hair gave him the look of a little boy pretending to be his papá. Fourteen and unlikely to grow anymore, Pulguita was still a head shorter than Jaime and Miguel, who were two years younger. But his height wasn't the only reason he went by the name that meant "little flea."

"¿Qué?" Miguel asked, barely opening his mouth.

Pulguita threw his hands in the air as if he didn't understand the hostility and laughed. Even at Jaime's distance he caught a whiff of cigarette and alcohol breath. "Can't a boy say hi to his old friends?"

"No," both Miguel and Jaime answered. Not when the boy was Pulguita. Not when he had become one of *them*.

Until last year, Jaime and Miguel had played with the tiny, dirty boy. Then things started going missing—first bananas from the backyard and tortillas wrapped in a dish towel; later new shoes and Jaime's drawing charcoals that had been a birthday present. Jaime and Miguel had stopped inviting Pulguita to their houses, and the little flea had found new "friends."

Now Pulguita's clothes were immaculate. From his white sleeveless undershirt and blue *fútbol* shorts to his white socks stretched tight to his calves and white Nike high-tops, everything he had on was new and expensive. To prove it, he pulled out his flashy iPhone and twirled it around his palm, making sure the cousins noticed. Oh, Jaime noticed it. The only phone anyone in his family could afford belonged to Tío Daniel, Miguel's papá. He shared it with Jaime's family and other relatives, but there was nothing fancy or smart about it, just one of those old flip ones.

Pulguita turned to Jaime with a sly grin. "I saw your *mami* the other day, carrying a heavy laundry basket. Looks like that leg is still bothering her."

"You leave Tía out of this." Miguel took a step closer, his eyes glaring at him. Pulguita ignored the threat as he continued showing off the fancy phone.

"Sure would be nice, wouldn't it, if she didn't have to work so hard. If she could relax in front of *la tele* with her leg up. You two were always nice to me. I'd like to help you out, you know."

"We don't need your help," Jaime said, but in the back of his mind he was intrigued. Mamá had been a teenager when she had broken her leg and it had been set incorrectly. Her limp was barely noticeable when she walked, but the injury kept her from jobs that required standing or sitting all day. She earned next to nothing washing and ironing clothes for rich ladies. Papá made barely enough at the chocolate plantation to keep them fed and sheltered in their small house that consisted of two small rooms: a sleeping one and a kitchen. The outhouse was, well, outside.

If they had extra money, just a tiny bit more, maybe his parents wouldn't need to work so hard. Maybe they could live better. But not by earning money the way Pulguita offered. It wouldn't be worth it.

Right?

Pulguita's smile widened as if he were mocking them. "You'll change your mind. Someday you'll want our help."

Our help. The words pounded repeatedly in Jaime's head. His stomach twisted at the thought of what Pulguita and his new friends expected in exchange for *help*.

"Not until your farts smell like jasmine," Miguel assured him. Jaime nodded. He couldn't do anything else.

With a shrug Pulguita tapped a code on his phone before bringing it to his ear, stuffed the other hand deep into his pocket, and swaggered away.

Jaime had tried to put the confrontation with Pulguita out of his mind. Until now, in the kitchen, with his mamá wailing and both of his parents smothering him.

Something was wrong. Horribly wrong. And he had a feeling he knew what.

His body tensed up to break free, but Mamá's grip only got tighter.

"*Ay Jaime, mi ángel,*" she said between her cries. "What would I do without you?"

Mamá released him. Her dark eyes were puffy and red. Her black wavy hair hung in tangled, wet clumps around her face. Jaime brushed a strand away from her eyes, something she used to do for him when he was younger and feeling upset.

She took two deep breaths and stared into Jaime's brown eyes. "It's Miguel."

Jaime scrambled out of his mamá's lap. Papá reached out for him, but he jerked away. The dizziness that had almost overcome Jaime in the bedroom threatened to overtake him again.

Miguel just has the flu, Jaime tried to convince himself. After all, Jaime had been pretty feverish this morning too. *That's it. Just a bad flu.*

But that didn't explain Mamá's crying, why she looked at him like it would be the last time.

"What's happened?" The words choked him.

Mamá averted her makeup-streaked red eyes. "He's dead."

"No." Because even though he had guessed the possibility, it couldn't be true. Not Miguel. Not his brave cousin. Not his best friend.

"He was walking through Parque de San José after school. And . . ." Mamá took a deep breath. "The Alphas surrounded him."

Of course, *them.* Jaime wrapped his arms tightly around himself, desperate to stop the shaking that had taken over his body. His sore throat from this morning made it impossible to swallow or breathe. Parque de San José. He and Miguel cut across the small park every day, twice a day, on their way to school and back. At night it was filled with drunks and druggies, but during the day, with everyone else who walked through it, it had always felt safe enough.

Had. Not anymore.

"Di—did they—how—¿qué?" Jaime stumbled over the words. His mind had gone blurry.

A fresh wave of tears overtook Mamá. When she couldn't answer, Papá said the words she couldn't. "Six or seven gang members approached him. Including Pulguita."

Jaime cringed. Of course, Pulguita. If this was the puny, stinking pest's idea of "helping" . . .

Papá pressed his fingers against the bridge of his prominent nose before he continued, "Hermán Domingo was walking by. He saw everything. The Alphas told Miguel he'd be an asset to the gang and should join them. Miguel told them to leave him alone. That's when they started hitting him."

"Stop." Jaime didn't want to know more. He could see the Alpha gang members in his head—some big and burly, some lean and quick, and Pulguita, small enough to be squashed. All of them punching and kicking until Miguel fell to the ground. If only Jaime had been there.

"There was no stopping them," Papá said as if he'd read

Jaime's mind. "If Hermán or anyone had interfered, they would have put a bullet in his head. Like they did to José Adolfo Torres, Santiago Ruís, Lo—"

Jaime stopped listening because he knew the names. Older boys he'd gone to school with, grown men with wives and children. People who tried to stand up to the violent gang; people who were now dead.

Dead, *muerto*. Like Miguel. His cousin had come over that morning. His face, with its lopsided smile, ecstatic over his scholarship into the exclusive science *prevocacional* school in the city twenty kilometers away: he had always wanted to be an engineer. His disappointment that Jaime was sick and couldn't walk to school with him disappeared as Miguel counted all the people he had to tell his good news to.

Guilt blazed in Jaime's chest as he gasped for air. Why Miguel? Why not him? The room suddenly didn't seem to have enough of it even with the humid breeze coming in from the glassless windows. His fault.

The gang had a strong presence in their small Guatemalan village and other villages in the area. Kids younger than Jaime were addicted to the cocaine the Alphas supplied. Shopkeepers were "asked" to pay the Alphas for protection: the protection they offered was from themselves. Protection from being robbed, or killed, if refused.

Miguel.

Jaime crouched down on the bare dirt floor, hiding his face in his arms. If only he hadn't been sick this morning. If he had walked through the park with Miguel like always, could he have stopped them from attacking? Two against six was better than one against six. Except Jaime had never been good at fighting. Would it have been easier to give in? Become the gang's newest member? Sell drugs on street corners, demand "insurance" from villagers, kill anyone who refused or got in his way? No, he couldn't have done things like that, but he wouldn't have been able to stand up to the Alphas either.

He'd never been brave like his cousin.

"Here," Mamá's voice said softly. Jaime looked up from his crumpled spot on the floor. Mamá had put the coffee on the stove and cleaned herself up. Her eyes were still red, but now she just looked tired, and old. She offered him sweet and milky *café con leche*. Like it would help.

Still, he held the cup, wrapping his hands around the ceramic mug as if it were a cold day instead of a suffocating one. He took a deep breath; after all, he'd been with Miguel that day when Pulguita had made his "offer."

"Will I be next?"

His parents didn't look at him. Mamá started crying again and Papá shook his head. Jaime got his answer.

"I don't want to die. But I don't want to kill people either. What can I do?" he asked the coffee cup in his hands, like a fortune-telling *bruja* might do with tea leaves. Neither the coffee, nor his parents, answered him.

There was nothing he could do. No one escaped the Alphas.

CHAPTER TWO

That evening, family and friends poured into Miguel's home. Still, there were many who couldn't make it—Tío Pedro Manuel and his family didn't have the money to pay for the bus fare; Tía Lourdes and her family didn't know yet, the only phone in their village was out of order.

Everyone brought food—bags of rice, beans of every color, ground corn for tortillas and tamales, whole chickens and sides of pork, plantains to fry, sugar to make desserts, rum to drink away the sorrow. An outdoor patio connected the individual structures of Miguel's house— kitchen, two separate sleeping areas, and the bathroom, but everyone wandered between the patio and kitchen, talking, eating, reminiscing.

Tomorrow, at the burial, there'd be grieving. Tonight,

however, was the time to celebrate Miguel's life.

In the middle of the patio, surrounded by flowers, candles, and incense, stood the wooden coffin. The lid lay on top but could be slid open to reveal the head and chest for those who wanted to say good-bye. Jaime forced himself to, then wished he hadn't. Miguel looked . . . not like Miguel. The beatings he had received had left his face distorted. No amount of makeup could change his shattered nose or the swelling over his left eye. Even with his eyes and mouth closed, no one would say he looked like he was sleeping.

Jaime didn't think anyone should have been allowed to see him like that, but it was a tradition that helped *la familia* accept that he was gone.

The police in the village had called Miguel's death an unfortunate *accidente*. Of course they would say that. Money meant more than morals and justice to the force; whoever paid most had the power, and the Alphas could pay a lot. It also didn't help that the police chief's drug habit funded many of the gang's operations.

Jaime removed his sketchbook from its perpetual nook underneath his arm and pressed it against his head so he couldn't see, wouldn't have to remember Miguel like that. *Why Miguel? Why did being brave have to end so badly? What was the point of being good if it turned out bad?*

With a sigh he turned to a blank page and drafted the

three-dimensional outline of the coffin. He avoided the disfigured face and focused on the other details: Miguel in his best church clothes with his hands clasped over his chest, and his prized possessions—a disassembled clock, minute screwdriver kit, and his horseshoe magnet—laid out beside him.

For Miguel's face he drew the features he remembered, the ones he had seen only this morning: a smile that went up higher on the right than the left; eyes so dark it made the white around them glow; the shaggy black hair in need of a cut. That was the real Miguel, not the beaten-up body left behind. The real Miguel was the one on his way to Heaven.

A hand on his shoulder caused Jaime to jump. It was Ángela, Miguel's fifteen-year-old sister.

Her eyes glanced down at his drawing, and he held the book out for her. She took it, her fingers hovering over the face as if trying to caress her brother's cheek. She nodded slightly before returning the book. Jaime didn't need words to know she was pleased he'd chosen to celebrate the real Miguel.

The next morning's procession was somber. It didn't help that Miguel's mamá, Tía Rosario, was banned from going with the rest of the family to her son's burial.

"I have to go. *Mi hijo*, he needs me. Please, you must!"

she shouted. She pounded her brother's chest as he barred the door. For that very reason, she had to stay behind. It was bad luck to cry or make a scene at a child's funeral. The spirit would then get confused, thinking he needed to stay on earth, instead of making his ascent straight into God's arms, where he belonged. Mamá stayed with her sister at the house, partly to keep Tía company, partly because Miguel had been like her son too.

Jaime's papá and *tíos* carried the coffin on their shoulders toward the cemetery through the unpaved village streets, where houses had once been painted white but now stood dark gray with crud and grime. Ángela clung to Jaime's arm and together they walked after the coffin. Even with all the family around him, Jaime felt alone, as if a part of him were missing. It must have been worse for Ángela. She hadn't said a word since she had heard the news.

It should have been my funeral, Jaime thought. Between the two of them, Miguel should have been the one to live.

Jaime sniffed hard. He couldn't cry. He mustn't. The fate of Miguel's spirit depended on it. Next to Jaime, with her eyes squeezed tight, Ángela let him guide her through the quiet streets. For his cousins, living and not, he had to be strong.

At the cemetery Padre Lorenzo said words Jaime only heard in bits: "chosen by God," "at peace," "loved by all."

None of them even began to describe Miguel—he was so much more.

The coffin was lowered into the grave. Along with the rest of the family, Jaime and Ángela each kissed a handful of dirt before throwing it into the hole. Then holy water was sprinkled on top to keep evil spirits away.

Only it didn't work to keep away the Alphas.

A group of gang members stood on top of the hill overlooking the cemetery. Jaime could just make out Pulguita's scrawny frame in the front line. He wanted to run up there and punch every one of them until they felt the same pain in their hearts he was feeling, and the same pain Miguel endured while they hit him.

Tío Daniel must have felt as Jaime did. When the priest said the last prayer, Tío Daniel's balding head jerked up to the hill, his nose twitching as if he could smell the Alphas' foul scent. He sprinted halfway up before Papá and two other uncles caught and restrained him.

"My son!" Tío Daniel shouted as he fought against the arms holding him back. "Give me back my son!"

The men half lifted, half dragged the resisting Tío Daniel back to the churchyard. The Alphas watched the men's retreat like sinister statues guarding a crypt. Not one of them moved. Except their eyes.

A violent shiver coursed through Jaime's body. They were watching him.

Next to him, Ángela jerked and quivered. Jaime knew she could feel the Alphas' eyes on her, too.

They were right. The Alphas had been watching them.

The next evening, Papá had just come home from work at the chocolate plantation and Mamá was ironing when the front door burst open. Tía Rosario leaned against the cinder-block wall, dark hair covering her face, and gasped to catch her breath.

"Come. Quick. All of you." And then she dashed away.

Mamá unplugged the iron as Papá pulled on his shoes. Panic shot through Jaime as he and his parents ran down to Tía's house. *Why is God punishing us?*

It normally took ten minutes to walk there. Today, because they were running, even Mamá with her limp, it took four. But it felt like forty.

A breath he didn't know he was holding escaped his lips at the sight of Ángela. Nothing had happened to her. Yet. He knew from the hopeless look on her face the "yet" was still to come. She stood in the kitchen, arms crossed over her chest, next to the boxy television with her back slumped against the wall. Jaime inhaled deeply to catch his breath and calm down. He reached for his cousin and held her hand like she had held his at the funeral. Had it really only been yesterday?

Rosita, Miguel and Ángela's older sister, sat at the table

nursing her baby, Quico. Abuela, their grandmother who lived with Jaime's cousins, had been rolling tortillas but now stood tossing a ball of *masa* from one gnarled hand to the other. Tío Daniel sat in another chair looking as empty and hopeless as Ángela. At least everyone was still alive.

A few minutes later Tía Rosario returned with Padre Lorenzo, the same priest who'd facilitated Miguel's burial.

Tía took a deep breath amd tied her hair back. Jaime noticed her hands shaking. "Ángela, the letter."

Ángela pulled a wadded-up piece of graph paper from her jeans pocket. Jaime stopped himself from exclaiming; Miguel always took graph paper with its little boxes to school. He could guess the letter's author.

Tía took it from her daughter, smoothing out the crumpled mess, and read it through the tears streaming down her face. "'*Querida Ángela,* We're sorry for your loss, as your brother's death is our loss too. To make up for it, we'd like to extend our invitation to have you join us instead. We'll give you six days to mourn your brother, then please report to Parque de San José before school. We'd like your help in delivering a gift to a friend. Your cousin can help too. Sincerely yours, The Alphas.'"

The tone of false politeness burned Jaime almost as much as the final line did. In his head the words rang in Pulguita's voice, not that the little flea had the brains to speak so eloquently. *Your cousin can help too.* That was him.

Other than a couple infants and toddlers in the family, he was Ángela's only cousin who lived around here. His life of being in the shadows was officially over. He had been recruited.

Soon he and Ángela would be the ones pushing drugs outside school; he could just imagine what that "gift" was that required delivering. The Alphas would force both of them to take part in beatings, and killings. But with Ángela it would be worse. If the gang members thought she was pretty enough, she'd become one of the gang leaders' girlfriends, whether she wanted to or not. If she wasn't, one of the junior members would get her instead. The thought of Ángela being Pulguita's girlfriend made his stomach turn.

"Forget it." Papá crossed his arms across his chest. "We're not sacrificing our children on a gang's whim. What do they want with us? We've raised good Catholics, not some *malcriado* heathens."

Jaime's and Ángela's eyes met. The Alphas didn't need a reason. They had taken over the whole region because they had the money and power to do what they wanted. Miguel's murder reminded everyone of that.

"Padre." Mamá turned to the priest, her hands outstretched in front of her as if reaching out for God. "Couldn't you talk with them? Make them see the light? Encourage them to repent?"

Padre Lorenzo shook his head. "I have tried, my child.

And while they dare not penetrate the sacred walls of the church, they prey on the weak and insecure of my congregation. I don't see how I can get through to them. Last week they convinced one of my altar boys that they held more opportunities than a life serving God."

Jaime felt ill. There was only one solution, and it was simple. He'd go see Pulguita tomorrow. The little flea lived with his uncle near the dump. They could "talk," for old times' sake. And at the end of the visit Pulguita would see that the Alphas had no use for Ángela; that he, Jaime, would be the better option.

Except, as he thought about it, *it wouldn't work*. They already wanted him. Why would they accept his deal of gaining only one new member when they already had their eyes on both of them? The Alphas didn't work deals like that; they always got what they wanted. He knew it, the whole village knew it, and there was nothing he could do about it. He never felt so helpless. And guilty.

"You'll have to pay them, of course," Abuela said as she whacked a ball of corn *masa* against the counter like she was killing an insect. "Buy the children's safety—"

"*¡No!*" Tío Daniel got to his feet. For a second it looked like he would attack someone, but then he sat back down, the bald patch on his head shiny with sweat. In a low growl he continued, "I refuse to pay the scum who killed my son. It'd be like a reward. No, we'll keep

Ángela and Jaime safe some other way."

Ángela raised her eyes from the floor. Jaime could feel her gaze on him as if she were analyzing the possibilities. He almost let out a sigh of relief. She knew what to do; she would take care of things.

"We could run away." They were the first words she'd spoken in two days. Everyone's eyes turned to Ángela, as if she had said a bad word. Abuela slapped the *masa* on the counter again. Padre Lorenzo opened his mouth to say something and finished it off as a silent prayer instead. Baby Quico, who was draped over Rosita's shoulder, let out a loud burp.

Papá shifted and all eyes turned on him. He licked his lips before taking a deep breath. "That might be the best solution."

Jaime imagined himself living in the rainforest, swinging through the trees like Tarzan, a pet jaguar as his watchdog, surviving off bananas and insects. For a moment he got lost in that world—the hundreds of shades of green, the wildlife camouflaged within those greens—it'd be fun. For a day.

"What do you mean?" Mamá whispered.

Papá cleared his throat. "They can go live with Tomás."

CHAPTER THREE

"*¡No!*" Mamá shouted so loudly the baby started crying. She ran to Jaime and Ángela and hugged them tight. "It's too dangerous. Think of something else."

"We've thought of everything." Papá hid his face in his hands. "It's the only way."

Jaime could barely breathe, and not just because Mamá was squeezing him so hard. The daydream of living in the rainforest suddenly seemed like a vacation. She was right, going to Tomás was too dangerous. Everyone knew the stories. Gangs robbed you at every turn. Immigration officers beat you up before sending you back home—that had happened to a few people in the village. The papá of one of Jaime's classmates had lost an arm boarding a moving train. Jaime could think of two other people from the village who had tried to make the journey and were never heard from again. They were assumed dead. Rosita's best friend, the beautiful Marcela, who Jaime and Miguel used to argue over who would get to marry, had been abducted near the border of los Estados Unidos. Whispers among the grown-ups claimed she had been sold as a slave. She was still missing.

And all of this was just going through México. Then there was crossing the border into los Estados Unidos.

But hardest of all was the idea of leaving home to live with Tomás.

Tomás, his older brother. Memories of him ranged from hazy to facts based on others' stories. The one time his family went to the beach and Tomás pointed out the colors of the stormy sunset reflected on the water, Jaime knew was a real memory. Every time he witnessed a spectacular sunset, with the reds burning into the cool greens and blues, he thought of Tomás and wondered if Tomás could see it too. That sunset would forever stay in Jaime's mind, but Tomás's face had blurred to the poor-quality image the village computer showed during their rare video Skype calls.

"How's my little brother?" Tomás always asked when they talked.

Jaime never knew what to say and would reply with a simple "*Bien.*" Then he'd ask Tomás questions: Did he see the new James Bond movie? Had he met Jennifer Lopez yet? Was it true that the public schools there had art classes?

Jaime had been four when his seventeen-year-old brother had left to work on a cattle ranch in El Norte, in a place no one in Guatemala had ever heard of called Nuevo México. Tomás was lucky, everyone said. Because of Tomás's love for Hollywood movies, he'd learned English perfectly, which had allowed him to move there legally through a sponsorship the rancher offered. Few had that luck. Not that Jaime would call it luck. From what Tomás said, he worked more than sixty hours a week in the scorching sun and the bitter cold. There wasn't much time for enjoying sunsets, or going to movies.

And now his papá was talking about Jaime and Ángela traveling over four thousand kilometers to join Tomás? Jaime didn't blame his mamá for becoming hysterical. He didn't want to go either.

"W-will it just be us two? Can't we all go?" Jaime wished with all his might that someone would give him a different answer than the one he feared.

Glances from the adults shifted from Mamá with her limp to Abuela, who struggled to roll out tortillas, then to Rosita and little Quico. None of them could make the trip, and none of the others would leave them behind.

Tío Daniel shook his head and muttered, "We could never afford that. As it is, two passages . . ."

"It's better this way." Papá articulated his words slowly as if he were trying to convince himself. "And once you're there, you'll be with Tomás, your *familia.*"

"No, no, no," Mamá kept repeating. "You two can't go. Can't."

Ángela escaped Mamá's grasp only to have Tía hug her in the same tight embrace.

Tía looked up to the heavens and wailed, "Two children in one week. Why are you punishing me?"

No one in the kitchen said anything—they just allowed Mamá and Tía to continue crying on their children's shoulders, both of whom were the same height as their diminutive mothers. No one told them to stop; no one told them it was going to be okay.

It was a while before Mamá finally released Jaime. His back was sweaty from where her arms had held him. He wished there were something he could say, something to make her feel better, but this new turn of events had left him numb. If he and Ángela stayed, they could end up dead; if they left, they might end up dead. Either way, life was never again going to be the same.

Their mamás stared at their children a second longer before each tucking a loose strand of wavy black hair behind their right ears and sighing. Without realizing it, Abuela used the back of her wrist to do the same with her silver hair.

"We need to start making plans. I'll contact Tomás. There isn't much time." Papá pressed his hands against his worn pants and stood. He and Tío began conferring in low voices as they headed to the door.

Padre Lorenzo saw his opportunity to leave as well. "I have brothers in México who offer shelter and sanctuary for refugees. I shall contact them."

Abuela said nothing, just grabbed a glass bottle with her arthritic hands and rolled out the tortillas until they were too thin to cook. Rosita shifted the sleeping Quico from her lap and excused herself from the kitchen.

"Do we really have to go?" Jaime whispered to Ángela.

Ángela licked her lips and removed the Alphas' crumpled note from her pocket. She crushed it further in her hands until it couldn't compress any more, then flung it at Jaime's memorial drawing of Miguel, which was taped to the wall. "Would you like to be in the gang responsible for his death?"

"No." He didn't have to think about that.

Ángela nodded as if she'd read his mind. "Then we don't have a choice."

Only those who had been in the kitchen that day knew of the escape plan.

Jaime and Ángela had to pretend nothing was going on and continue as if they were spending the rest of their lives in their Guatemalan village. Jaime volunteered to help paint the backdrop for the Easter pageant, and Ángela told Pulguita she would deliver the mysterious packet in a few days. If people thought they were acting weird, hopefully it was excused as mourning Miguel and not because there was something to hide.

The hardest part for Jaime was saying good-bye to his friends and extended family without them knowing. He gave his two best friends at school the Batman comic books that Tomás had sent him for Christmas, saying he was tired of not understanding the English words. For his little cousins he divided his few art supplies. A gut-wrenching feeling told him there were many people he'd never see again.

Hopefully the Alphas were among them.

A few days after the funeral, Tía Rosario held up jeans that looked a lot like Jaime's favorite pair. Correction: they *were* his favorite pair. The ink stain on the front left pocket proved it.

"You're the one with an eye for detail," she said. "Look at these carefully and see if you notice anything strange about them."

Confused, Jaime took his jeans from his aunt. He searched them up and down. No holes, no new stains. "What's wrong with them?"

"Nothing, but look at them again. Pay special attention to the waistband," she said while grabbing a pair that were probably Ángela's, judging by the stitching on the back pockets.

Jaime squinted at the waistband and ran the material between his fingers. He compared the material with the rest of the pants. He even sniffed it. Nothing. He shook his head. "They seem perfectly normal."

Tía let out a sigh of relief. "Good. Now whatever you do, don't lose them and don't tell anyone about them. We've exchanged fifteen thousand quetzales into a little less than two thousand US dollars and sewed them into the waistband and cuffs. Don't use any of it unless absolutely necessary until you get to the border of El Norte—even then, it might not be enough to pay for the crossing. If someone tries to rob you, hopefully no one will know the money's there."

Jaime collapsed into a chair, gripping his sketchbook tight to his chest.

"Fifteen thousand quetzales for the two of us?" The words came out in a whisper.

Tía shook her head no. She squinted at the seams one more time; glasses were a rich person's accessory. "For each of you."

The world seemed to tilt as he blinked and took several deep breaths. Thirty thousand quetzales. Jaime couldn't imagine that much money. No wonder they were taking days to prepare, just to gather all that money. His insides twisted with guilt; he was going to be sick. The whole family was making sacrifices for him. Doing this because of him. It wasn't worth it. He wasn't worth it.

"You can't do this." The words spilled out of him like marbles from a ripped sack. "It's too much. We'll stay—"

"You won't," Tía interrupted with such determination it sounded like Abuela speaking. "All our work won't be for nothing. You're going so you can be safe. End of discussion."

But thirty thousand quetzales. . . . Of course he and Ángela were the only ones leaving; the family couldn't afford to send anyone else. He doubted his parents together made that in a year.

Just because he hadn't been at the park with Miguel.

All our work won't be for nothing, he repeated Tía's words. But if they really had to take this trip, a lot could happen. Four thousand kilometers was a long way.

If only he and Ángela had passports. And papers that said they could enter los Estados Unidos legally. Like Tomás.

"Are you sure it's well hidden?" Now that he knew what the pants contained, he kept imagining incriminating lumps in the seams or loud crinkles in the fabric.

Tía gave him an odd smile that combined worry with pride. "We can only thank the Lord he gave me a job sewing jeans at the factory. I know how the seams should look."

Jaime took one last glance at the jeans, pretending he didn't know what they held. The neat rows of stitches on the waistband did look exactly like they were supposed to.

. . .

Moonlight was streaming through the empty window when his papá shook him awake. "It's time."

Jaime blinked a few times and rolled out of the hammock strung in the room he shared with his parents. He didn't have to ask what was going on. One day remained before Ángela had to make her delivery. One day before he was expected to join her. Join *them*.

He pulled on a dark green shirt and his favorite jeans, thinking he could feel the weight of the money sewed into the seams. In the backpack Mamá had packed for him days ago, he put his sketchbook, pencil case, and the only family picture he had with Tomás. On the windowsill a lizard watched his every move.

Neither parent had gone to sleep, though Mamá's makeup looked fresh and Papá had shaved. They each put an arm around him as they walked to his aunt and uncle's house. The streets were quiet and still. With an occasional shift the wind brought sounds of cars in the distance and people at the local tavern. The Alphas, if they were awake, were off terrorizing a different neighborhood. Above the walkers making their pilgrimage, the sky was clear, shining every star down on them. If only it were a normal night, and Jaime could curl up in the outside hammock and capture the starry night in his sketchbook.

They walked through the patio into the kitchen, where

anyone who was family or considered family always hung out. But this morning it only held Abuela. A mini-banquet of *desayuno chapín* had been laid out, like those American turkey feasts they showed in movies, "tanks geeveen" or something. Eggs from the chickens out back, Abuela's corn tortillas, black beans, fried plantains, sliced avocados and mangos, pork *salchichas*, and a steaming mug of hot chocolate that had been Miguel's favorite. Such a meal they could only afford on Christmas.

Any other time, Jaime would have dived right in. Any other time, the old television wouldn't be missing from its usual spot.

"*Sentate.*" Abuela commanded him to sit in her regional dialect. Her silver hair seemed pulled into a bun more tightly than usual. She wore a black dress, like she had when Jaime's grandfather had died. "There's not much time and you need your strength." She loaded a huge plate with food and set it in front of him.

A few seconds later Ángela walked in with her parents and sat down wearing jeans and a baggy blue T-shirt, her black hair pulled back in a ponytail. Jaime wasn't used to seeing his cousin dressed so plain. But maybe that was the point. Remembering what happened to the gorgeous Marcela, Jaime didn't want men thinking Ángela was pretty.

They ate in silence. Not because they were hungry. A couple times Jaime was sure he was going to be sick from anxiety or nerves, but one stern look from Abuela and he kept eating what he'd been served. Abuela didn't allow picky eaters—everything placed in front of you had to be eaten, whether you liked it or not.

He was mopping up the remaining bean sauce with a bit of tortilla when he heard the rattle of an old pickup truck. The Alphas. They'd heard about the plan. They were going to get him and his cousin.

Through the window Jaime watched the truck with tall wooden planks attached to the sides sputter to a stop outside Tío's house. A fair-skinned old man with white hair eased himself out of the vehicle, his wrinkled hands braced over the door in the moonlight.

Not the Alphas, just Pancho.

Some days he sold fruit and meats; other days Pancho's truck held furniture. Today it was filled with sacks of used clothes.

"Are you ready? It's over three hours to the Mexican border and it's better to cross it while it's still dark," Pancho rasped.

The remaining bean-drenched tortilla dropped from Jaime's hand onto the plate. Abuela didn't demand he finish it. Part of him wished she would, just so things would feel familiar.

Instead she handed him, Ángela, and Pancho plastic bags of food before walking off into the night. She didn't even say good-bye. It would have been too hard for her.

Tears rolled down his face as he hugged both of his parents.

"*Vamos, patojos.*" Pancho called the youths to go. Jaime and Ángela hugged each other's parents before climbing into the back of the truck. The burlap sacks were scratchy but cushioned, making it easy and somewhat comfortable to be wedged between the goods. They poked their heads through the burlap as the motor turned.

Mamá hobbled, holding on to Jaime's hand as the old truck clunked down the road.

"I love you both. Be safe," she called out louder than she should have. Her hand slipped from Jaime's and she was left panting in the middle of the dirt road.

Jaime watched her until the truck turned a corner and she, his mamá, was gone. Who knew when he'd see her again? If he would . . . no, he wouldn't think like that. Of course he'd see her again. Of course.

They passed the cemetery where they had buried Miguel, the road leading to the school Miguel would have attended in the fall, the park where Miguel . . . Good, he never wanted to see that place ever again.

The village Jaime had known his whole life, gone. His house, his family, gone. From now on, home would only get farther and farther away.

CHAPTER FOUR

Jaime lost track of how long he watched the road they left behind. The sacks of clothes closed in on him like when he and his cousins used to sandwich themselves in couch cushions. His face peered out from the middle of the sacks like a *micoleon*, the slinky, long-tailed, long-tongued mammals that inhabited the forests on the outskirts of his village. For a while he recognized landmarks—a village where distant cousins lived, the tree under which he got carsick, the road that led to the beach where he and Tomás shared that sunset. Then one dark village began to look like another until he was sure he'd never been this far from home before.

It's all your fault, Miguel. If you were still here, we would still be at home. The thought entered his mind before Jaime could stop it. Miguel wasn't to blame. Not when he'd died fighting. *But if Miguel had just given in and joined the Alphas . . .* Jaime shook his head to stop his mind from playing games with him. If Miguel had given in, Jaime would never have forgiven him for that. It would have been a betrayal to him, and the family. Few things were worse. As much as he hated leaving home, he'd have to be brave, like Miguel.

After miles and miles of pothole-filled roads with no streetlights, Pancho pulled onto the highway. The wind rushed against Jaime's ears, and the headlights from the few cars on the road blinded him. Best not advertise to the other drivers that he was back there. He closed his eyes and retreated back between the scratchy sacks.

When he opened his eyes again, the faintest blue crept through the crevices in the sacks. He blinked a few times in bewilderment. Not because he didn't know where he was—sadly, the week's events hadn't been erased from his mind—but because he was surprised he'd managed to sleep at all.

The truck jarred and rattled as it slowed down. That must have been what had woken him up. He shifted, causing the bones in his stiff neck to crack and pop, and started to dig his way out to check where they were.

A hand grabbed his shoulder.

He screamed.

"Shh!" A harsh whisper came from Ángela next to him

and he understood. They were stopping. If they were stopping, there had to be a reason. And until they knew what the reason was, they had to stay hidden. Jaime cursed himself for not thinking. Barely a few hours from home and he could have gotten them caught.

The truck pulled to a complete stop. Jaime kept his breathing shallow to avoid shifting any bags. Pancho didn't get out of the cab or turn off the truck, so that meant he hadn't stopped by choice. Something out there had made him stop.

Through the gaps in the sacks, Jaime could see lights flashing red against the dawn sky. Two sharp and deep barks came from the distance. The bags around Jaime shifted, and he knew Ángela had retreated farther into the sacks of used clothes; dogs scared her to bits.

For a second Jaime wondered if he should be scared too. He liked dogs. But that didn't change the fact that they had teeth he couldn't compete with. And noses that could detect a hidden human. Careful not to shift the burlap in case someone, or some dog, was watching, he tilted his head to listen again. Good, the dogs were far away.

Pancho blared his horn. Three other drivers followed his example. "¡*Oye!* What's going on?"

In the back of the truck Jaime cringed. Why did Pancho have to draw attention to them? Between the distance they'd traveled and the flashing lights, Jaime guessed they must be at the border of México. If they had passports or papers, he and Ángela could sit up front with Pancho, just say they were visiting family for a couple days . . . on a school day . . . with Pancho, who looked more like a weathered gringo with his light eyes and skin than Jaime and Ángela with the black hair and square faces they got from their Mayan grandfather. Hmm, maybe better to enter México this way, sandwiched between bags. As long as they weren't discovered.

It was seconds, or maybe hours, before he heard boots thumping on the pavement toward them. The red flashing lights still cut into the night. By that point, the sky had lightened, bits of green and red mixed with the blue and purple.

"Is that you, Pancho?" came a gruff voice less than a meter away.

"*Claro*, I have things to sell, you know. What's happening?"

"Some kid smuggling. He insists he's been set up, but that's what they all say."

Pancho swore. In his mind Jaime agreed with him. If the border patrol had already caught someone with drugs, they'd definitely search Pancho's truck in case he had some too. Even though Ángela didn't move or make a sound, Jaime knew that, deep among the bags, she must have been thinking the same thing.

A slight weight shifted the truck, like the guard was leaning against Pancho's open window. "So, what you got today?"

"Clothes. Some nice labels—Gap, Calvin Klein. What size is your wife? I got some Levi's she might like." The rustle from a plastic bag up front indicated Pancho was moving things around.

"No, better not," the guard answered, but the truck creaked as if he were leaning farther into the cab. "If they're too big, she'll think I think she's fat. If they're too small, she'll be furious that she's fat."

Still, the sound of jeans being shaken out and held up came from outside the truck. A dog barked again. The chink from the dog's collar implied he was trotting closer. Ángela's nails dug through his thin shirt and into his shoulder. The guard and Pancho kept talking like the dogs didn't exist.

"That one's a good style. She can wear them with sandals or heels," Pancho said.

"Fine, but if she complains they don't fit—"

"Then you give them to your mistress."

The guard laughed and slapped Pancho in the shoulder. "Good man."

A panting breath along with the chiming collar came closer. Jaime couldn't see the canine but guessed he couldn't be more than a car away. Next to him Ángela muttered a prayer to San Francisco, patron saint of animals, and stowaways.

The guard waved Pancho along and the truck jerked forward, creaking over a bridge. In unison Jaime and Ángela let out a huge breath, only to catch it again as they passed a dog that began to bark. The truck, however, chugged along. No shouts called for them to stop, and Pancho didn't. A slight bump in the road and then it suddenly became smoother, as if the pavement had changed textures. If Jaime had to guess, he'd say they'd crossed the border into México. All that fuss and for nothing.

Pancho drove for another half hour before cutting the engine. The truck coughed and seemed to sigh as its worn-out mechanics stopped churning.

"*Fuera, patojos.*" Pancho banged on the side of the truck for them to get out. "*¡Ándale!*"

Jaime grabbed his backpack and the plastic food bag Abuela had packed for him. He tumbled out of the clothes sacks, blinking against the morning sun. His left leg wobbled as blood circulated back into it like millions of scurrying ants. He pushed his chest and belly out as his lungs filled with fresh air and smiled as he looked around.

He should be nervous, he should be scared, but at the moment his sense of adventure had taken over. He was in México! A different country, a new place, a strange town . . .

Which wasn't very different from the towns back home.

Pancho had parked between two concrete buildings, a spot visible only to people who might look down the alley. But no one did—it was early in the morning. Ripped plastic bags wedged in corners and oozing trash littered the alley. The cool of the night was giving way to hot humidity. From where he stood, Jaime could see concrete houses with wrought-iron bars covering the doors and windows along the quiet residential street.

"Where are we?" he asked.

"Tapachula, in Chiapas," Pancho said as he threw a couple of bags back into the truck that had fallen out with Jaime and Ángela's emergence.

Chiapas, of course. The most southern state in México, and the closest to Jaime's home in Guatemala. He could see the map of América del Norte that hung in his classroom. All those hours in the back of the truck and they had barely gone a few centimeters. This was going to be a long trip.

"How are you continuing from here?" Pancho asked, glancing out into the street and trying to act as if he always parked between buildings with two fugitives.

"Bus," Ángela said. "To Arriaga."

Pancho shook his head. "Don't take the bus. Too dangerous."

"Then I guess we can take the train from here," she said slowly.

"Even worse. You won't survive in one piece."

Ángela looked at Jaime. They were running out of options, and they weren't even half a day into their journey.

"What do you suggest we do, Pancho?" Jaime asked. Maybe he would volunteer to drive them a bit farther, another centimeter or so on the map.

Pancho looked at his watch and again up and down the street. His white mustache twitched as if it could detect some hidden danger. "There's no safe way unless you have a lot of money or an invisibility cloak. Most people around here won't pick up hitchhikers, and if they do, the driver might work for a gang or *la migra*. You'll find yourself being held for ransom or deported back to Guatemala."

La migra. Jaime knew about them. Every immigrant did. On paper they were immigration officers hired to keep Central Americans from using México as a passageway to the United States and Canada. In reality they were armed men who made their own rules for the right amount of money.

"And if you walk," Pancho continued, "you risk stumbling into gangs again or bandits, who will rob you and leave you to rot. I can't take you any farther. My work is here."

Ángela inhaled through her mouth and Jaime understood her worry. There was no good choice, but somehow they had to move forward.

"I guess we'll risk the bus." Ángela looked at Jaime for agreement, but he shrugged. *La migra*, trains, bandits, and more gangs. Everything seemed worse than what they had left behind. Except here there seemed to be a greater variety of ways to die.

Pancho grumbled but didn't offer any suggestions. "*Bueno.* The bus station isn't far, just a few streets over. Buses are pretty regular."

A moment of silence overtook them, as no one knew what to say. Good-bye was the obvious response, but it would mean that they were on their own.

"Thanks for driving us here." Ángela kissed him on the cheek like she would a grandfather.

A red flush crept over Pancho's wrinkled face as he glanced at the food bag that Abuela had given him. "Your family has always been good to me."

From Heaven, Jaime could feel Miguel nudging him and grinning. The two had long-standing suspicions of Pancho's crush on their grandmother.

Another awkward moment followed until a car drove past them, bringing them back to the dirty alley. Pancho shifted and his face turned to a hard stare. "I'm late, so listen. If *la migra* stops you, act calm. Only people who shouldn't be here get nervous. Whatever happens, you don't know me, you came here on your own."

"We understand," Ángela said.

"Be careful who you trust. Not everyone out there is your friend."

Jaime hugged his backpack tighter against his chest.

Pancho made his way to the truck but then stopped and turned around. He went to the street and motioned them to follow him. "See that mountain in the distance? That's the Volcán Tacaná."

"On the border of Guatemala and México," Jaime said. They had studied the second-largest Central American volcano in school. Seeing it now reminded him how close they still were to home. And how far away.

He must have read Pancho's mind, or Pancho his.

"There'll be other mountains, other volcanoes," Pancho said. "But if you think of each different one as Tacaná, you'll never be far from home."

This time Pancho made it back to his truck. He waved as he drove out of the alley, not looking to see if cars were coming from either direction. Jaime and Ángela stood there for several minutes in a town that seemed familiar, but the sight of the volcano in the distance reminded them just how far they still had to go.

CHAPTER FIVE

The next bus to Arriaga was leaving in twenty minutes, but if they waited until the afternoon, they could take a bus run by a different travel company for half the price, about a hundred pesos less. For each of them.

"How many quetzales is that?" Jaime whispered as they stood at the ticket counter of the bus terminal. His question was directed to Ángela, but the attendant, an old man with thick glasses, answered without looking up.

"About fifty."

"Two for the afternoon bus, please," Ángela said at the same time as Jaime said, "The cheaper bus is fine." One hundred pesos, fifty quetzales. Enough to buy ten Coca-Colas or twenty bread rolls. Some people in his village didn't earn much more than that in a day. Of course, it was nothing compared to all the money sewed in their jeans, but enough to make them realize just how much money they would still need to get to the Río Bravo, the river dividing the two countries in the north.

With several hours to kill, they walked around Tapachula. People strolled on the shady side of the street. Men called out for them to buy icy juices in big Styrofoam cups cinched with plastic bags for lids. Women sold mangos, guava, papaya, mamey—three for ten pesos. Boys younger than Jaime wandered around with trays strapped to their chests to sell packs of cigarettes.

Unlike at home, where everything was in dire need of fresh paint and repairs, two buildings, the municipal palace and the church, were true works of art. When they entered the yellow and white church, Iglesia de San Agustín, with its tall, impressive pillars, Jaime couldn't stop looking around, feeling like he was within art itself. Never had he experienced something so beautiful and intense. For the first time since Miguel's death, he felt at peace. Why did they need to go all the way to Tomás when here was a place so spectacular that nothing bad could possibly happen? And where they were still close enough to "see" home?

The wood creaked as Ángela slid into a pew near the front. Hands clasped, she bowed her head. Her lips moved in silent prayer while two *gringo* tourists took pictures, their babbling voices echoing across the pews.

Jaime took a second to say his own prayer—for his family, Miguel, Ángela, and himself—before pulling out the sketchbook and lead pencil he'd packed in his bag. Mamá always said his artistic ability was a gift from God. If that was the case, then surely He wouldn't mind if Jaime used His gift to pay tribute in His house.

It took four pages in his sketchbook to do little justice to the beautiful church. He wished he could capture the sensation of being there as well, of being enveloped in the art—a feeling that he couldn't explain in words, or show in his drawing. The architecture, the way the light came in the stained glass windows. Jaime knew there were people who studied art, who knew tricks of shadow and light to accent features and make the flat paper's two-dimensional image jump out like it had three-dimensional life. Jaime, whose school couldn't afford an art teacher, did the best he could. The result, though nowhere near the real-life beauty of the church, wasn't half-bad.

Ángela's hand on his shoulder brought him out of his reverie. From the way the light shifted through the stained glass windows, he guessed it must be midday, hours since they had arrived. What a blessing it was, being in a place where it was so easy to forget everything that had happened.

Across the street from the church, they settled on a

bench at Parque Central Miguel Hidalgo, a stone-paved plaza with a fountain, white-painted tree trunks, and manicured hedges instead of the bare, compressed-dirt park back home where Miguel had . . . No, Jaime wasn't going to think of that park again.

The midnight feast Abuela had made for them back home seemed ages ago. They peered into the plastic food bags Abuela had sent off with them: tamales wrapped in banana leaves, a hunk of queso fresco, chorizo from relatives in the neighboring village, mangos from the tree behind his house, and a pile of her homemade tortillas.

Jaime stopped himself from grabbing half the chorizo and cheese. "How long do we have to make this food last?"

"As long as possible." Ángela grabbed the smallest tamale and began unwrapping the leaves.

Three bluish-gray pigeons strutted back and forth in front of them, just far enough away to keep from being kicked.

"How long do you think this trip is going to take?" Jaime focused on the tamale instead of his cousin. "I forgot to ask Papá."

More like he hadn't wanted to ask. Not then, and not really now. The less he knew, the less responsible he'd have to be. Much better to let the grown-ups make the arrangements, let Ángela make the choices. Then if something went wrong, he wouldn't be blamed.

Ángela shook her head. "I don't know. Tina at school once mentioned her papá made it in four days, but Marisol's took forever. Several months."

"Months?" Jaime choked. How could they possibly survive months? They had left home only twelve hours ago and already he felt lost without his family. What happened when the food was gone, when there was no one to take care of him?

Ángela looked behind her and around the park. Other than the pigeons, there was no one within earshot. She continued talking. "There's a lot we'll need to sort out along the way. Our parents spent more time borrowing money than ironing out the details."

Jaime's hand landed on his waistband. How had his family scraped up so much, so quickly, and without the Alphas finding out? The guilt that had started upon hearing of Miguel's death twisted and burned in his stomach. It was his fault Miguel had died—Ángela must have thought so too; his fault that he was still alive and that his parents sacrificed so much to make sure he remained that way.

"Do you know Tomás's phone number?" Ángela asked.

Jaime shook his head with another pang of guilt. He had never called his brother. Mamá did that, and only after first punching in all the numbers from the phone card into the village pay phone—using Tío's cell phone would have cost too much. "Mamá wrote it down for me. It's in my bag."

Ángela pulled a slip of paper from her pocket. Already it was creased and worn around the edges. "We should memorize it. In case something happens to the paper. Or one of us."

What? He'd been so worried about what happened to Miguel, he hadn't given much thought to what might happen to them. To Ángela. He grasped Ángela's free hand. "I'm not letting anyone, or anything, hurt you."

She avoided his gaze. "Still, we should know his number."

She was right, of course. It'd be stupid not to. Paper could get wet, torn, and easily lost. But by memorizing the number, he would accept the possibility that she might leave him and join Miguel. He didn't want to tempt fate.

Please, Lord, don't make me responsible for another tragedy, he prayed before studying the paper in Ángela's hand. He ran the ten digits around his head, repeating them like a poem and putting emphasis and beats after certain numbers to remember them better. *5, 7,* he chanted like an intro to a song, *5-5-5-5,* he tapped steadily against his leg four times, *21,* like a question, *86,* like the response. *5,7, 5-5-5-5, 21, 86.* He'd have to say it to himself again later.

"Okay, got it." He heard the rhythm of the numbers and visualized them in his head. He'd done his part. He didn't need to know anything else.

Ángela disagreed. She folded the paper and returned it to her pocket. "We get to Arriaga, and stay the night at a refugee shelter Padre Lorenzo arranged, Iglesia de Santo Domingo. From there we have to contact El Gordo, who's already been paid to take us on the train north to Ciudad México—"

"*Sí*, I heard about El Gordo," Jaime interrupted. Maybe if Ángela thought he knew what was going on, they could finally change the subject. "Mamá said Hermán Domingo's cousin used him, but he was expensive."

Ángela nodded her head several times. "In the capital a man named Santos got a deposit to get us on the next train—we'll pay the rest when we meet him, which should get us to Ciudad Juárez."

"And then we cross the Río Bravo," Jaime added, despite his resolution to remain ignorant.

"And then we cross the Río Bravo," she agreed. "Which they call the Río Grande in El Norte."

Crossing the border of México into los Estados Unidos. Tía's words of keeping the money safely sewed into their jeans rang in his ears. But even with the money, how would they manage it? What he knew of that crossing already terrified him. News reports showed immigration patrol officers shooting anything that moved; detention centers packed with people; politicians over there who said all immigrants were rapists and criminals. And before that, there was Ciudad Juárez, the Mexican border city notorious for its violence and human trafficking. It didn't sound like Ángela knew how they would manage either.

His tamale remained on his lap, untouched. He unwrapped it, pretending it was steamed and served warm with Abuela's chia salsa.

Jaime felt as though he already knew too much. Friends at school talked; advertisements on television and on billboards warned of the horrors. In an illegal journey of four thousand kilometers, they were going through places more corrupt than his village, running from gangs more violent than the Alphas, going to a country where no one, except Tomás, wanted them there. Everywhere they'd go on this journey, they'd be unwelcome.

5, 7, 5-5-5-5, 21, 86.

The banana-leaf wrapper from his lap fluttered against a light post, where two pigeons pecked it to death. He and Ángela had to talk about something else.

After a tamale and a mango apiece, they weren't full, but the food, filled with Abuela's love comforted them. They walked around the park some more and settled on a different bench, this time near the statue of Benito Juárez, a Zapotec Indian revolutionary hero in the mid-1800s who became one of México's greatest presidents. Juárez hadn't been influential for Guatemala, but they studied him in school, just like they learned about Abraham Lincoln and Mahatma Gandhi.

Ángela rested with her head on Jaime's lap, her arms folded over her backpack on her chest. When they were younger, Papá used to call them (along with Miguel) Hugo, Paco, and Luis after Donald Duck's nephews—they sometimes fought, they sometimes ganged up on one another, but at the end of the day they'd curl up together like puppies in a litter. They hadn't slept that way in years, but Ángela never went through the phase of being too old to cuddle and comfort her little brother and cousin. Jaime hoped he never did either.

He pulled out his sketchbook from his own bag and balanced it on the armrest of the bench as he sketched with broad strokes the statue of the great hero.

"If there was a *presidente* like Juárez now, do you think gangs like the Alphas would be taking over México and Centro América?" Ángela asked, her eyes shut, but she faced the statue as if contemplating him through closed lids.

"No, he wouldn't allow it." Jaime glanced from the statue to his sketchbook and back to the real statue as his left hand shaded in the eyes. "People even say that if Benito Juárez had come to Guatemala a hundred and fifty years ago, we would have never had the civil war our parents and grandparents lived through. He was that great."

Ángela stayed quiet for such a long time, Jaime thought she had fallen asleep.

"Do you think we'll ever go back?" she asked.

Jaime looked around the picturesque park with its fountain and gazebo; the church that had made Jaime feel like he was living in art; and the statue of the man who changed Mexican history. But the view of Volcán Tacaná, half in Guatemala, half in México, was blocked by the buildings, as if it weren't there.

"*Yo no sé.* I hope so."

"You think it'd be safe?"

If gang members beat someone to death for not joining them, what would they do to two who ran away to avoid joining them? "Maybe in five or ten years, when they've forgotten us. Or if Benito Juárez reincarnates and there's a revolution."

Ángela let out a snort that was half laugh, half disappointment. "I don't believe in that Mayan legend that a great king will return."

"Then, no."

CHAPTER SIX

Spiderwebs of cracks crisscrossed over the windshield of the bus taking Jaime and Ángela from Tapachula north to Arriaga. The engine rattled and groaned like every wheel rotation caused it great pain. Every dark-tinted window was wide open and still the air in the bus was hot, humid, and stuffy—no different from the buses back home.

Outside, the lush jungle foliage seemed to take over the landscape, including an abandoned immigration checkpoint.

After a best-out-of-three battle of rock-paper-scissors, Ángela got the cooler window seat but promised to change places halfway through the five-hour ride. Jaime didn't grumble. From the aisle seat he had better access to unsuspecting subjects. The church visit had inspired him, and he was determined to capture in his sketchbook as much of his journey as possible. It was the only way to make the trip bearable, and to forget why they had to take it.

Jaime turned to a fresh sheet in his fat sketchbook; if he used both sides of the pages, he had about eighty free pages left. Plenty. An anchor to hold his sketchbook steady in the lurching bus would be nice, but every great artist had to learn to draw in less-than-ideal situations.

His first models were obvious—a young white tourist couple sitting up front, their overstuffed camping backpacks wedged between their legs. Jaime couldn't stop staring at the man's hair, orangey-red like the memory of the setting sun he and Tomás had shared. Jaime had never seen hair quite that alarming and was sure it had to be dyed. Except the longer he stared at it, and noticed the freckles on the back of the man's neck and the fine golden-red hair of his arms, the more convinced Jaime was that the color was real. If only he had his paints with him. He would have loved to try and match the exact shade. Instead he settled on switching his colored pencils between pressing lightly with the red and a bit harder with the orange. Not perfect—hitting a pothole in the road gave the man a piercing on his neck—but the color wasn't too far off.

He skipped the teenager playing on his phone (a great artist only chooses subjects of interest) and drew the family with three small children, freezing time with the moment the little girl popped the discovered gum from under her seat into her mouth. He was about to start on the four chickens (two white with black specks, one red, and one with *plumas* so black they looked blue) crammed into a wire cage diagonally from him, when he felt a tap on his shoulder. The small elderly woman behind him in a white embroidered linen dress motioned to herself repeatedly as she babbled in Mayan with an occasional Spanish word thrown in.

"*Claro que sí,*" Jaime agreed with a grin as he turned around in his seat to face her. Although he didn't speak much Mayan and couldn't have translated her words, he understood what the little old lady wanted. He sharpened the brown pencil as the *viejita* smoothed down her silver hair wrapped in a bun.

Friends and family sometimes asked Jaime to draw their portraits—Miguel had begged for one of himself dressed as Superman, and his little cousins especially loved being immortalized as cartoon caricatures—but this was his first time drawing for a stranger. What if she didn't like it? What if he made her look ugly?

Ángela, turning away from the window where she'd been reading the name of every village they passed by, nodded encouragement.

The bus bumped up and down as it trekked north, but Jaime rested the sketchbook steadily on the backrest as he shaded her diminutive features. He smoothed out her wrinkles and captured the brightness in her eyes. The hand-stitched embroidery surrounding the collar of the dress seemed to almost jump off the page. In ten minutes he finished and tilted the book for her approval.

She squealed with delight, placing a wrinkled hand on his cheek, but then pointed to the empty bottom right-hand corner, waving her fingers as if she were holding a pen.

Jaime remembered what his fourth-grade teacher had said when they had studied Leonardo da Vinci's *Mona Lisa*: "The famous painting is unsigned, but at least we know Leonardo painted it. If not, it would be virtually worthless." Not that his art was worth anything, but it was fun to pretend it would be. He switched from the colored pencils to the lead one, and wrote his full name in a lavish scribble: *Jaime Antonio Rivera Muñoz*.

Slowly, carefully, he tore out the page from his book. He picked at the raw edge to remove the scraggly bits of paper. It was worth it to see the *viejita's* skin crinkle into a smile and to hear her utter words of gratitude he didn't specifically understand as her spotted hands clutched the portrait to her heart.

At the next village she once again nudged his shoulder. She stood, barely a meter and a half tall, with her fist outstretched. Jaime shook his head. "*No es necesario.*"

"*¡Sí!*" she said with such insistence it would have been

rude for Jaime to disobey. He held out his hand, and three coins tumbled into it.

"*Gracias*." He beamed at her as she waved her hands over him in a blessing and shuffled off the bus, one hand laden with her shopping bags and a cane, the other cradling his drawing as if it were a treasure.

Ángela, who had alternated between looking out the window and watching the transaction, nudged him in the ribs. "How much did you get?"

Jaime turned over the heavier gold-and-silver coin and then the two bronze ones to read their value. "Twelve pesos."

"Look at you, Diego Rivera," Ángela teased. "You keep this up and you can fly us to Tomás on an airplane."

Jaime rolled his eyes but was secretly pleased. It wasn't too hard imagining he was related to the famous Mexican painter—after all, they shared a last name. But to someday be known around the world for his paintings like Diego Rivera? He couldn't imagine how great that would be.

He did the peso/quetzal conversion quickly in his head. If he was right, twelve pesos would only buy him a drink and, if he was lucky, a cookie. Didn't matter how little twelve pesos translated to. He was now officially a "professional" artist. Nothing could take that away from him.

There were no villages around when two men appeared from the bushes and flagged down the bus. Their clothes were dirty and torn, as were their faces. One had crusted blood from a gash on his forehead, while the other's bottom lip hung like a wet sock on the washing line. They each gave the driver a coin and hovered near the front instead of going the length of the bus and sitting down.

About ten kilometers later the bus driver pulled over again to the side of the road. A truck zoomed by with a whoosh that made it feel like the bus would tip over. The battered men thanked the driver and disappeared back into the bushes.

A few minutes after that, the brakes squeaked and protested as the bus slowed down again. Through the open window Jaime saw no village, no buildings anywhere in sight, just lush trees, overgrown bushes, and long grasses all squeezed together, fighting against one another for their right to live on a bit of earth. Everyone on the bus shifted to look out the cracked windshield, where lights flashed their warning.

Something was wrong.

A hushed whisper vibrated through the bus. "*La migra.*"

Orange cones blocking the road forced the bus to come to a complete stop. Only one guard was on duty, but a rifle hung from his shoulder, ready to be snapped into his hands the second he needed it.

Jaime clenched his pencil tightly.

The guard leaned into the bus, hands on the open

doorjamb, to peer inside. Jaime jerked away before they could make eye contact and felt his face burn with self-indignation. So obvious. So guilty. The guard was sure to know he didn't belong in México. But the guard just turned back to the driver. "Anyone new gotten on? Anyone I need to know about?"

The driver shook his head. "No."

It was mostly true. After all, the men they'd picked up in the middle of nowhere weren't on the bus anymore. They must have known about the stop, and how to avoid it. Clever. And at the same time risky. The bus driver could have easily mentioned where he dropped them off; drivers back home would have if they thought they'd get paid for the information. Instead this driver seemed content in minding his own business and doing only his bus-driver job. The guard returned his gaze outside, taking in the six cars waiting behind the bus, then moved a few cones out of the way and waved them by without asking any further questions.

No one was on duty at the next checkpoint, a tiny wooden structure on the side of the road, and it was only because Ángela read the sign announcing it that Jaime even realized what it was.

He let out a deep breath. Maybe there was nothing to worry about. Maybe the stories he'd heard—stories of how *la migra* beat you up, sent you to prison, and then returned you to your country in pieces, if you were lucky—were just stories, tales told to prevent people from attempting the journey.

Except he didn't really believe they were made up. Especially when they arrived at the next checkpoint.

A large building stood alone in the middle of the jungle. Concrete and steel with spotless white paint, just its presence radiated a sense of foreboding against the lush green.

Ten cars waited in front of them, and many more beeped their horns behind them. Loads of guards milled around, their rifles ready in their hands.

On the window seat next to him, Jaime felt more than heard Ángela utter a prayer. He could feel her fear. Jaime sent a prayer of his own, this one to Miguel. *Please help keep us safe.* As far as they had traveled, they were still only in Chiapas, the most southern state in México. They were going to need a lot of help.

Sweat dripped down their faces as they waited in the sweltering bus for permission to continue. The driver opened the door, but no breeze entered, and no one dared exit. It felt like hours before a guard stomped on with thundering steps. He didn't have a rifle, but his hand was wrapped tight around the leash of a dog. Ángela tried to wedge herself between the seat and the window. Jaime seized her hand, both for comfort and to keep her from doing something stupid. With her pathological fear of dogs, he wouldn't be surprised if she was tempted to jump out the window and risk her chances against the armed guards.

The dog, though, was small and looked like Snoopy with floppy ears framing its cute face. His black nose twitched as he investigated the front crevices of the bus.

"Don't worry," Jaime whispered so low he hoped Ángela heard. "He's just a sniffer. He won't hurt us." Except dogs smelled fear, and Ángela was practically oozing in it. A sudden dread overcame Jaime. Maybe this was a new thing—training dogs to smell fear in people so the guards could weed out the foreigners.

No, he thought, taking a deep breath and letting it out slowly. There was nothing to worry about. Unlike Ángela, who still had the teeth marks on her leg from where she'd been bitten as a little girl, he liked dogs and this one wasn't intimidating. Especially if he imagined the dog sitting on top of his doghouse wearing an old-fashioned fighter pilot cap.

After giving the driver a quick sniff, the dog started whining at the tourist couple up front.

"*Abran las bolsas*," the guard said, pointing to their backpacks. The orange-haired guy said something in an unfamiliar language but then opened his backpack.

The guard riffled through and quickly came up with a little plastic bag holding what looked like dried herbs. Orange-haired guy tried to explain in his foreign language, but the guard didn't care. He looked out the window, checked the location of the other guards, and pocketed the bag before moving the dog on.

The dog trotted down the aisle, panting in the stuffy bus, wagging his tail, and poking his nose in everyone's luggage. Through his brown, black, and white coat, Jaime could count his ribs.

When the dog got to them, Ángela squeezed Jaime's hand extra tight. She kept shifting her gaze between the dog's open mouth and the open window. Jaime squeezed her hand back.

Maybe it was Jaime's imagination, but the dog seemed to take an extra-long time checking out their food bag. They'd spent the day in Tapachula and while they'd kept their things with them the whole time, was there any chance someone might have slipped something incriminating into their bags? Were he and Ángela mules, transporting illegal drugs without knowing it? That had happened to Marcela's brother and he had spent months in a Mexican prison.

Or maybe the dog liked sniffing good food. Whether due to bravery or poor judgment, Jaime offered the dog a sniff of his free hand.

"*¡No lo toques!*" The guard jerked the dog away to the next people but not before Jaime felt the softest lick on his palm.

In the back of the bus the dog began barking like crazy. Ángela cowered and held Jaime's hand to her chest, but

Jaime, along with everyone else on the bus, glanced quickly to see what was happening.

Two men were sitting on the bench in the back of the bus, their hands resting on two black duffel bags. Jaime couldn't remember if they had been on the bus at Tapachula or had gotten on elsewhere. He couldn't remember them at all. They weren't loud, their faces could have blended into any other face on the bus (except the tourists up front), and their jeans and T-shirts were what everyone wore. If Jaime had to remember all the people on the bus, those two would have been left out. Maybe that was their job, to be forgettable.

Except now, with the dog barking like crazy, no one would forget about them.

The men, however, didn't even flinch. The one on the left, whose dark eyebrows joined above his nose, reached into his pocket and then held out his hand. The dog handler shifted to shake the man's hand and in an instant put his hand into his own pocket. It was impossible to see what happened unless you knew. And everyone on the bus knew. These two unrecognizable men had just bribed the guard to keep his mouth, and the dog's, shut.

"¡Cállate!" The officer ordered the dog to shut up and gave him a sharp jerk on the lead. The dog obeyed but kept staring at the men's bags. The guard turned to leave and had to yank the reluctant dog several times; the dog didn't seem to understand why he was being punished for doing *his* job right.

"*Pobrecito*," Jaime said once the dog, and his corrupt handler, had left.

"What do you mean, 'poor thing'? He almost attacked us." Ángela let go of her cousin's hand and wiped her palms on her jeans.

Outside, the dog was being yanked to the next vehicle, his *café*-colored eyes fixated on the bus like the bone that got away.

"He just wanted a friend. Someone to give him chorizo and believe him when—"

"Shh." Ángela pretended to stretch so she could glance at the non-memorable men in the back of the bus. When she straightened back up in the hard seat, she glared at him. "Nothing happened in here. The dog came in and left. That's it."

Jaime's lips pressed and scrunched. "*Pero*—"

"No but." Ángela grabbed his shirt to bring his ear close to her mouth. "Think about it. Remember the Alphas, what people with that kind of money, that kind of power, can do if they think you'll give them trouble. Nothing happened."

Jaime grumbled as he pulled his shirt out of her grasp, but then nodded.

He turned to a new page in his sketchbook. In a corner

a brown, black, and white Snoopy dog appeared, his teeth gleaming in a smile as his tongue retrieved a bit of chorizo clinging to the strap of his fighter pilot cap.

Involved in his drawing, Jaime barely noticed that the bus still hadn't moved until Ángela nudged him.

"Change places with me, *rápido*," Ángela muttered, already climbing over him. Jaime paused in mid-doghouse sketch and slid over to the window seat without questioning her.

Moments later another immigration officer stomped up the steps into the bus, a rifle slung over his broad shoulders. He ignored the tourist couple as if they weren't even there and asked the teen who had been playing on his phone where he came from.

"Acaxman, just outside of Tapachula," the teen said.

"Poor you." The guard snickered as if there were few things worse than being from Acaxman. The teen shrugged, but the guard had already moved on to speak to the family with three young children.

"*Niños*, tell me where you're going."

But the children, the oldest no more than five years old, stared at him with wide eyes; the girl, the middle child, still chewed the gum she'd found under the seat. The guard waited, and nothing. Finally he turned to their parents. "*¿Son mexicanos?*"

"*Sí.*" The *papá* pulled out some documents from his

back pocket and smoothed them out for the guard. *La migra* looked through them and grunted before handing them back and moving on.

He chatted a bit with the lady with the caged chickens, asking what she was cooking and teasing, or threatening, that he'd stop by for dinner. Two seats from Jaime and Ángela, a young woman was also asked where she came from.

"*Por favor,*" she pleaded. "I come from Chiapas."

Jaime sneaked a glance at Ángela, and she confirmed his suspicion with the slightest shake of her head. Judging by the woman's accent, Jaime would have guessed she came from El Salvador. The fact that she twitched almost uncontrollably, shifting her head as if she were looking for a hiding place, didn't make her lie more convincing.

The guard seemed to guess the same thing. He crossed his arms over his chest and stood with his feet shoulder width apart. "Chiapas? Do you have proof? You sound Central American to me."

From his seat Jaime noticed the back of her brown neck reddening as she cleared her throat. "No, no, I have allergies, my throat, it always happens in the spring."

His patience gone, the guard pointed his rifle at her and barked, "Get off the bus. We're sending you back to Guatemala."

"But I'm not Guatemalan," the woman insisted, no longer lying.

"Who cares, you can return to your country from there."

"Please, you don't understand," the woman cried and pleaded. "I must get to Texas. My husband, he beats me. My children, they have nothing to eat. Please, in God's name." The woman clutched a lumpy plastic bag to her chest, as if it would shield and protect her.

It didn't. The guard grabbed her and dragged her off the bus, pushing her toward a guard waiting outside. That man whacked her across the head with his arm. She crumpled to the dirt, blood oozing from the side of her head where the guard's watch had caught her. Not that he noticed or cared. A sharp nudge in her stomach from his rifle and the Salvadoran woman was back on her feet. For a second she looked like she would bolt, but the outside guard took hold of her arm and twisted it behind her back until she had no choice but to follow. Her screams echoed across the jungle until she was flung into one of several windowless white vans waiting a few meters away.

The bus driver did nothing. His job was only to drive the bus and collect the fare. If this was his regular route, he probably saw this happen every day.

It took every clenching muscle in Jaime's body to keep from wetting himself. In a few minutes that could be him and Ángela too.

"Keep drawing, keep drawing," Ángela muttered as

the *gringa* tourist gasped and seized hold of her partner's freckled arm.

Jaime stared at his sketchbook as if he'd never seen it before. Draw? How could he draw at a time like this, when he'd just seen a woman literally thrown out of the bus? But Ángela was right. He had to pretend he had nothing to be scared of. As if he belonged. As if he were *mexicano*.

Hand shaking a second time within the bus ride, he began doodling next to Snoopy. Before he realized what he'd drawn, the Bat-Signal appeared at the top of the page—the sign that someone in Gotham City needed Batman's help.

Great, no hidden symbolism there. Could his sketch be more obvious? Still, he didn't erase it, just continued with the next doodle.

By the time their guard was back on the bus and at their side, Jaime's page not only had Snoopy and the Bat-Signal, but the Teenage Mutant Ninja Turtles and Mickey Mouse scattered around. Half the kids at school had similar doodles in their notebooks. Hopefully the guard had kids.

"Are you two together?" the guard asked. His breath reeked of coffee and too many cigarettes. Jaime glanced at him briefly before returning to shaping Yoda's ears just right. Keep calm and blend in.

"Yup," Ángela said with more assurance than Jaime felt. As she continued, he couldn't help but notice her accent had changed. She was putting less emphasis on the last vowels of her words, making her tone more neutral. "Abuela needs help for a few days. It's getting hard for her to roll out the tortillas."

The beauty about that lie was that it really wasn't a lie. Their grandmother was struggling with the tortillas and always welcomed any help. Jaime doubted those lie detectors they showed in movies could have picked out the deception. After all, it wasn't as if the guard had actually asked where they were going.

"You're not from Chiapas, are you?"

"Veracruz," Ángela named a different Mexican state without hesitating. But a state not exactly where the bus was heading, nor where it came from. The lie detector in Jaime's head flashed warnings like the lights on the guards' cars outside. If Ángela realized her mistake, she didn't show it. "*¿Ha estado allí?* Have you been there? It's beautiful."

Again Jaime noticed the difference in her accent, particularly her verb choice. In Guatemala they would have said, *habés estado allí. Good call, Ángela. And thank you, Mexican TV shows.*

The guard caught the verb use, and at the sound of it gave them a slight nod of approval. Just as Jaime was about to relax, the guard reached over Ángela and poked him in the shoulder, causing the pencil to slip and streak, giving Yoda a double-ended lightsaber.

"What about you, boy, do you like helping your *abuela* make tortillas?"

"Sometimes," Jaime said with a shrug, even though his brain had gone into panic mode. He didn't know if he could imitate a Mexican accent and remember to use the verb forms they did. He stuck with what he did know—sketching and doodling.

"What you got there?" The guard grabbed the notebook out of his hands and began thumbing through it.

Jaime swallowed a gasp. His book. How dare this guy take it, his grubby hands leaving prints on the fresh sheets. It took all the restraint he had to keep from grabbing it back. On the floor, blocked from view by their bags, his cousin dug her heel into his foot. Her message couldn't have been clearer: don't you dare do anything stupid.

The anger turned to fear as he tried to remember what he'd drawn, and whether there was anything that would obviously link them to Guatemala. He mentally flipped through the pages in reverse order. The people on the bus, the statue of Benito Juárez, the church. Then recollections of his last week at home—Rosita playing with Quico; Tío and Tía outside in the patio; Abuela struggling with her tortillas; Mamá taking a *siesta*; Papá sticking his tongue out at him; Laura, the pretty girl at school he never got the nerve to talk to, and now it was too late; Miguel's funeral . . .

The sound of ripping paper returned him to the

stopped bus. Bits of paper clung to the rings from where *la migra* officer had torn a page. Ángela's foot pressed against his, a reminder not to freak out. A page. Only one. Jaime allowed himself the smallest breath.

"My son likes lizards. He always saves them from the cat." The officer waved the drawing Jaime had done when he had gotten the news about Miguel. The book thumped back onto his lap.

One hand flapping the lizard portrait to fan himself from the stuffy bus air, the other resting on his rifle, the guard moved down the aisle to question the next people.

Too soon to breathe properly, Jaime held the sketch-book tight in his lap. It felt like a different book, worn and more pliable, the cover not as crisp as it had been. He could live with this different, violated feeling, he supposed, just as long as he never lost the book completely. It was his life, or what remained of it.

Five minutes later the guard left the bus. No cars blocked their way anymore, and a different guard waved them off. Heavy sighs of relief escaped everyone, from the bus driver to the youngest in the family of children. As they passed the windowless white van, everyone turned to stare at it, and then at the empty seat that a few minutes before had held a woman searching for a better life.

CHAPTER SEVEN

The bus jarred to a stalling stop in Arriaga. Jaime
blinked a few times as his sleepy brain tried to make sense
of what was going on. Right, time to get off. Ángela
looked like he felt—tired, disoriented, and grumpy—
except her black hair was matted into a huge knot from
where the wind had tangled it. They made sure to grab
their backpacks and the food bags before following the
rest of the passengers off the bus.

"Stay close to me," Ángela said, not that Jaime had any
intention of doing otherwise.

The bus ride had taken close to six hours with all the
checkpoints. A clock inside the station said it was 9:53 p.m.
The people who got off the bus took off in various directions and disappeared into the night. Jaime and Ángela

stayed within the lights of the bus station, looking around.

The bus station seemed to be in a mostly abandoned part of town. If it was a town.

The wind shifted, bringing scents of salt water and rotten fish from the Pacific Ocean ten kilometers away. An old man staggered by, muttering to himself. He stopped in front of a burned-out light post and began swearing at it for ruining his life. Next to the station two cars sped down the main *carretera* that the bus had come in on, engines roaring as they zipped by going a million kilometers an hour. A handful of rundown storefronts stood in front of the station, locked up tight for the night. Cigarette butts, candy wrappers, and dog poop littered the area between the station and the gravel street.

Other than that, there wasn't much beyond trees and electrical posts. Unless you counted the graffiti painted on the locked partition of one of the storefronts: "¡*Váyanse centro americanos!*" followed by rude words. The graffiti gleamed with fresh spray paint.

"They don't want us here," Jaime said under his breath.

Ángela stood on her toes as if the extra height would help her see their destination. "No one knows we're here."

"Not us, you and me. Us, Central Americans." Jaime pointed to the tag that seemed to bleed from the store.

Ángela pressed her lips and then turned away quickly. "We need to find this refugee shelter."

"What's it called again?"

"Iglesia de Santo Domingo."

"Which way is it?"

"I don't know, I don't know!" she cried, and hid her face in her hands. Jaime tried to place a hand on her shoulder, but she shook him away. "Stop with all the questions!"

Ángela crumbled onto the concrete. Jaime crouched next to her and put his arm around her. This time she didn't resist. In his head he heard what Tía, Ángela's mother, always said when one of the children cried: *He's just tired. Poor thing needs to sleep.*

Tired. So much had happened in the last twenty-four hours. *He* had fallen asleep in Pancho's truck; *he* had dozed off in the bus. He never thought whether Ángela had as well. He didn't even know if she had slept the night before.

He licked his lips. He wasn't used to worrying about other people. That was Mamá's job. And Ángela's. And Miguel's. What would Miguel do?

The answer came as if Miguel were right there whispering in his ear: break things down and look at everything logically. *Un paso a la vez.* One step at a time.

Jaime gave Ángela's shoulder an extra squeeze. "We'll figure it out. First thing we have to do is find this church. We'll have to ask someone." Preferably not the old man who was now shouting random words at the light post.

Ángela took a deep breath as she tried to regain control. "We have to be careful. The security checkpoints we went through, they weren't just for drug traffic. Remember the Salvadoran woman. *Los mexicanos* really don't like us. They think we're all criminals and not as worthy in the eyes of God."

He knew all this, of course. He knew their lives were at stake. Just as he knew what would happen if they were sent home. "We have to find this church. We can't sleep here."

"Right." Ángela stood up, wiping her eyes with her sleeve. "We'll have to find a pay phone and use our last pesos to call Papá. Hopefully he can get ahold of Padre Lorenzo, who can—"

Jaime waved her to stop. His attention returned to the graffiti like a magnet pull. Something was written under the hateful words. He edged closer to the grass median that divided the bus station parking lot from the street, to be sure he read correctly. "God welcomes all at Santo Domingo, 17A. Norte."

"Ángela, look!" He pointed at the writing. "Could it be a trick?" The address could lead them straight into whatever gang ran Arriaga or into *la migra* headquarters. But he had a feeling they could trust it. Late as it was, with no one around to ask, it was their best option. There were no pay phones in sight.

"We don't have another option," Ángela said. "We have to try it."

The street corner in front of the bus station told them what number avenue they were on and the cross street in front. Assuming Arriaga worked on a grid of some kind (as Tapachula had, as well as the villages back home) with number streets going up or down, they should eventually find the church. If they had the right address.

They followed the dark paved highway until it crossed the railroad tracks and the streets changed from *sur* to *norte*, but then encountered a series of wrong turns.

In the dark, in a strange town, every place seemed dangerous. Down one gravelly dirt street, rowdy voices screamed behind closed doors until something like a gunshot demanded silence. Ángela and Jaime grabbed each other's hand and ran the other way. Another wrong turn led them down a dark street where two men outside a bar leered and beckoned to Ángela.

"*Ven, muñeca*, I want to show you something."

Jaime did what Miguel would have done: he told them off for being disrespectful pigs whose mamás had not raised them properly and that they should rot in hell. Except while Miguel would have said it out loud, Jaime said it inside his head. Outside his head they both ignored the men and hurried to find a safer street.

After some other streets that dead-ended at someone's house or by the river, they finally found a street that crossed 17A Norte. A wooden cross with the faded words

"Santo Domingo" written on it was nailed to a post. An arrow pointed down the street.

Smoke rose into the night sky from what smelled like a bonfire, and laughter echoed from the nearby river. The residential street of crumbling houses ended in front of a rundown church. Its stone and concrete structure was barely standing, requiring the aid of rope and string in a few places. A few men sat outside on the steps smoking hand-rolled cigarettes and speaking in low voices. When Jaime and Ángela approached, the overweight man in the middle stood up.

"Are you looking for shelter? I'm Padre Kevin, *bienvenidos*."

Padre Kevin looked nothing like any priest Jaime had ever seen before, with his sandals, flowery Bermuda shorts, blue tank top, and the cigarette stuck to his bottom lip. But he wore a silver crucifix around his neck, and the faded words painted on the wall behind him did say "Iglesia de Santo Domingo." *At least,* Jaime told himself, *he didn't look like an officer or a gang member either.*

"*Gracias,*" Ángela said. "Do you have space for us?"

The priest inhaled from his cigarette and laughed. "There's always space for God's children, just as long as you don't mind squeezing a bit. You, kid, do you want to sleep with the men or stay with your sister and the women and children?"

Too tired to think, he shrugged. Of course he didn't

want to stay with the little kids, but he'd never slept anywhere without a family member in the same room, or a cousin in the hammock next to him.

"We'll stay together," Ángela answered for him.

Padre Kevin took a deep drag from his cigarette before handing it to one of his *compañeros*. He led the way into the church, which was little more than a large room with pews pushed to one side. Through the moonlight seeping from the open windows, Jaime saw mounds and shapes huddled across the floor.

"If you need the bathroom, the river's less than two hundred meters away. The church's plumbing is clogged, but there's a water basin through that door over there." Padre Kevin kept his voice low as he pointed out the features of their first night's accommodation.

He gave them two tattered blankets and waved to a spot near a wall that was free. Ángela laid one blanket over the dirt floor. They took off their shoes and lay down, using their backpacks for pillows, and covering themselves with the second blanket.

It had been twenty-four hours and five hundred kilometers since Jaime's parents had woken him up in the middle of the night. Now, as he lay next to his cousin on the hard, dirt floor in a rundown church run by a weird priest, he took a deep breath. Before he'd finished exhaling, he fell fast asleep.

CHAPTER EIGHT

The sun coming through the open church windows woke them up earlier than they would have liked. But even without the sun, the people shuffling around and babies crying would have gotten them up anyway. It took a few blinks for Jaime's eyes to focus, and a few more for his brain to register what the church looked like.

To say it didn't compare to the church in Tapachula would be like saying a rock wasn't like a rainbow. The two had absolutely nothing in common. This one had a "natural" skylight where the roof had caved in, no paintings, and a crucifix that was little more than two branches tied together into a cross. Patches of the stone walls were missing; dust crumbs from the wall next to Jaime and Ángela clung to the tattered blanket. Bits of cloth were sewed together to make a curtain in the middle of the room, separating them from the men. In the thick humidity, body odor mingled with dirty diapers and whiffs from the polluted river occasionally joined forces. When Jaime grabbed his shoes, a black cockroach scurried from the laces to find a new hiding place.

And then there were the people. About fifty women and children crammed into their half of the church, making it hot and stuffy despite the draft. On the other side of the curtain there were probably just as many men. Or more.

"Is everyone here going to El Norte?" Jaime asked Ángela as he gave his shoes a good thump before putting them on.

"*Me imagino.*" Ángela looked around at the women and children waking up. "Gangs like the Alphas are all over Centro América."

Jaime stopped to think about it. If there were about one hundred people here, in this one little church, in a little town, how many other immigrants were there in other refugee centers throughout México? There must be thousands, maybe even tens of thousands, heading to El Norte every day. That couldn't be right. He must be adding it up wrong; Miguel had been the one good at math. On the other hand, Jaime's logic made perfect sense. "Even if only half of them make it across the border, which we know is very hard, how can one country fit so many extra people?"

Ángela licked her lips as if she didn't want to think about that. "That's why they're building a wall. I saw a picture of a fence going into the ocean. They say it's to keep their country safe. But really, it's to keep us out."

Jaime recalled a couple of photos that Tomás had sent of the ranchland where he worked—pastures and mountains with no buildings as far as the eye could see, so different from home, where houses clustered together with banana trees growing between them like weeds. True, El Norte was huge, and there were some empty parts. But how long would the land stay empty, especially if there were thousands sneaking in each day? He knew they were unwanted, unwelcome. He could only hope that there'd be some room left in the world for him and his family.

He followed his cousin through the thick tropical growth to the river, where they kept watch for each other, before returning to the church hall.

"Mangos or tamales?" Ángela looked through their food bags. "Or there's still some tortillas and a tiny bit of cheese."

If only Abuela had packed the breakfast she had made yesterday. They'd definitely enjoy it more today. Jaime's stomach groaned and ached as he remembered home. "Tortilla with mango and we might as well finish the cheese, too, I guess."

A girl close to Ángela's age with a baby slung around

her chest and a handmade bag hanging from her shoulder looked up as she folded her tattered blanket.

"The church provides us with food." She spoke with an accent that implied Spanish hadn't been her first language. She didn't look Mayan; Jaime wondered if she was Xinca or Pipil Indian instead.

Ángela smiled and waved hello at the baby. "Thank you, but we're already grateful for the shelter. We shouldn't take when we already have."

The baby reached out to Ángela with thin arms. The mother hesitated for a second before passing the baby over. "Save what you have and go to the table anyway. Tomorrow we could all be starving."

Jaime and Ángela looked at each other. The girl had a point. They only had food for another day or so and then what? Even if they boarded the train today, it could easily be a week before they got to Tomás. Or more.

"*Tenés razón.*" Ángela colloquially agreed with the woman as if she were talking to a girl friend, not the formal way she had spoken with the guard on the bus. "We'll eat what God provides."

Jaime remembered Quico's plump belly and chubby cheeks that broke into a smile when tickled. In comparison this baby seemed frail and small. Ángela rocked her for a few more seconds before handing her back.

The girl pulled her baby close. They both giggled as the

girl burrowed her face into the tiny tummy. She adjusted the infant into some rags that worked as a carrier against her chest. "Better take your food with you, and your other belongings. Things grow legs when you're not watching."

"*Gracias.*" Jaime hugged the backpack to his chest. If anything happened to his sketchbook . . .

The girl turned in a circle to give her sleeping spot one last check. The blanket she had used lay perfectly folded in a corner.

"Are you leaving now?" Ángela frowned.

"Her father"—the young woman looked down at her baby with a sad smile—"tried to take her away from me. I can't let him find us."

It was then that Jaime noticed the bruises on the girl's arm, the cut almost hidden under her hair, her feet wrapped in scraps of cloth instead of shoes. Although she looked nothing like them, it wasn't too hard imagining her as Ángela. If only they could help her.

From their plastic food bag Ángela took out one of Abuela's tamales wrapped in banana leaves and a mango that had grown behind Jaime's house and handed them to the young woman with the baby. "For tomorrow."

The cousins folded up the bed blankets and returned them to a *viejita* who placed them on a stack before they were allowed outside.

A grumpy woman with dark, thick braids served breakfast on a long table under some trees near the river. Her gruff glare deterred anyone from asking for second helpings. Not that anyone would. Breakfast consisted of lumpy cornmeal cereal and soupy pinto beans, both of which tasted like nothing.

"I miss Abuela's cooking," Jaime said under his breath, though the snicker of agreement from Ángela meant she had heard and agreed.

If they were home, they'd have fried plantains, sweet bread, and sausages. Even when money was tight, there were always eggs from their chickens, fruit from the trees, and an endless supply of savory black beans.

Jaime took more bites, imagining the food had salt, sugar, or lard. Something to make it less bland. When the plastic plate lay empty on the ground in front of him, he knew Abuela would be proud. He had a feeling that picky eaters wouldn't survive this trip.

About a hundred people ate their breakfasts on the ground under the shade of avocado trees picked bare of any fruit. Grown men in various shades of tiredness. Women clumped together, keeping their heads down and avoiding attention. Quite a few children and teens, mostly without their parents. Some people were barefoot; some sported raw bruises on their faces; some looked like their soul had left their body and all that was left was a corpse operated by memory.

Jaime closed his eyes for a second and said a prayer of thanks. He had (he rapped his knuckles against the avocado tree he was leaning against) Ángela, they had food and money, and they had their health. Compared to the others huddled around this ruined church, they could be in much worse conditions.

Bright and perky for so early in the morning, Padre Kevin walked among the travelers, asking how they had slept and if they needed anything. When one teen in a cap said he needed *café con leche*, eggs, and a side of bacon, Padre Kevin pressed his hands together in prayer and then reminded him that stranger miracles had happened.

The padre came up to Jaime and Ángela with a huge smile. He must have gotten less sleep than they had, but there he was, fully alert, freshly shaved, and in hot pink shorts and a T-shirt with a picture of Jesús and the English words "Who's your daddy?"

"Ah, if it isn't my midnight *chapines*," he said, using the colloquial word for Guatemalans, and welcomed them each with the traditional greeting cheek kiss. "How did you sleep in my luxurious house of God?" He raised his arms with pride to embrace his rundown church.

"Very well, thank you," Ángela said as she set down her finished plate. "We appreciate you letting us stay here."

Padre Kevin looked up at the hazy grayish-blue sky with a sense of tranquility as if Ángela were thanking the wrong person. "Of course. And how long do we have the pleasure of your company? You can stay as long as you like."

Jaime and Ángela exchanged looks. That part of the plan was still vague. Last night Padre Kevin had said there was always room, but maybe he wasn't good at math and didn't realize how full the church already was.

"We need to get in contact with a man called El Gordo," Ángela said. "Do you know where we can find him?"

Padre Kevin's perky grin changed to a frown as his eyes shifted among the crowd. "You won't find him, he'll find you."

"He knows we're here?" Jaime asked. The feeling of being watched made him shiver. He glanced at the bushes behind him, just to be sure.

"He'll be around the day before the train comes in." Padre Kevin suddenly seemed tired. "Have you already paid him?"

Ángela nodded. "Our parents have."

Jaime slipped his thumbs into his jeans waistband without realizing what he was doing. When he did, guilt overtook him. The money, the sacrifice his and Ángela's parents must have gone through to get everything ready in a few days. Just for their safety. *They gave us everything they had. And more.* Jaime sent another prayer to his family, sending his love and thanks. He just hoped their sacrifice was worth it.

He hoped he didn't end up like Miguel.

"Hmm, well, that's that." Padre Kevin looked like he wanted to say more about El Gordo but instead turned to greet the next group of people.

"Wait." Ángela got to her feet. "When is the next train? When will El Gordo come?"

Padre Kevin's face twitched as if his brain were fighting for control against his mouth. "Next train's in two days, so he'll be here tomorrow afternoon. Make sure you are too or you'll lose your money." When he welcomed the people sitting next to them, his previous perkiness was missing from his tone.

"What should we do today?" Jaime asked as he and Ángela walked back to the table to return their plastic colored plates.

Ángela looked around as if she, too, wondered whether they were being watched from the dense bushes. "I don't know. We don't know how safe it is here. Remember the graffiti? But I don't like staying still, either."

Good, he didn't want to wander around the town. After all, Miguel had been killed in broad daylight in the village they'd lived in their whole life. Who knew what could happen in this unfamiliar place.

Before Jaime could make some suggestions—guess the drawing, quiz each other on movie trivia, or walk through the thick bushes lining the river in search of smooth stones for a game of marbles—the grumpy woman at the food table yanked the plates out of their hands. "You can help around here, that's what you can do. This isn't a hotel, you know. Things don't just magically get done."

"Of course not," Ángela said, sounding surprised and offended. Back home, everyone always helped out however they could. It was what families did.

"Yeah, well." The woman's voice softened a bit when they didn't complain or argue. Jaime wondered if most people tried to get out of helping, or never thought of volunteering. "Padre always forgets to mention it when he makes the rounds. He seems to think that help should be given willingly, and not because one feels obligated. But then I'm left doing it all myself."

Jaime nodded. "What can we help you do?"

"Dishes, for one thing. And you three!" she shouted at the boys behind them, who were also returning their empty plates. "You're helping with the dishes as well, and don't let me catch you stealing anything from the kitchen."

Just like Jaime and Ángela, the boys didn't challenge the idea of helping out in exchange for food and shelter. Or maybe they were too scared; the youngest boy definitely flinched a bit. The woman's gruff "don't mess with me" tone had returned.

The tallest boy looked vaguely familiar with his ruffled black hair and dark skin, but Jaime didn't know from where.

The boy picked up a stack of the dirty plastic dishes from the ground next to the table and carried them into a separate decaying wooden building that operated as a kitchen. They all followed him without another word. The kitchen held two large steel washbasins with tubs underneath the drain and a stove with six burners, but no refrigerator. Bags of rice, beans, and ground corn sat under rickety shelves that held plates and pans. In a corner a swarm of flies buzzed around a huge banana bunch. Jaime got the feeling he was looking at the lunch menu.

Once in the kitchen and away from the grumpy woman, Ángela and Jaime set their bags in a corner. The older boy placed the dishes in a washbasin and turned to Ángela.

"*Hola*, Veracruz," he said.

Ángela looked surprised. It took Jaime a second to understand what the boy was talking about, and suddenly it hit him. He had been on the bus with them yesterday, sitting up front and playing with his phone. Unlike the guard, it seemed he wasn't fooled into thinking they had come from the southern Mexican state.

"*Hola*, Tapachula," Ángela replied. She didn't seem to believe he was from where he had claimed either. With the few words the boy had spoken, Jaime couldn't figure out where he came from but was willing to bet it wasn't anywhere in México.

"Acaxman." He corrected with a wink of his green eyes, which stood out against his dark features.

Of course. Jaime had forgotten that this boy had been the first one the guard interrogated. The one who had had the easiest time convincing the guard he was local. Looking at him, Jaime understood why. The boy was wearing a white collared uniform shirt from a school in Tapachula, the school's emblem bright over the left breast with the name encircling it. Good disguise. Jaime wondered how much he had paid for that shirt.

The teen smiled perfectly white and even teeth as he continued, "Have you been to Veracruz? I hear it's beautiful."

Jaime raised his eyebrows. This guy was repeating what Ángela had told the guard. What else did this guy know about them? And should they be worried?

Ángela stood her ground, though her cheeks flushed. "Well, I feel sorry for anyone who comes from Acaxman."

The guy grinned as if he and Ángela had been communicating in a secret language only the two of them understood. "Xavi."

"Ángela."

They kissed on the right cheek in greeting.

The second boy, small and scrawny but with a few dark, wispy chin hairs, adjusted his ball cap before kissing her too. "I'm Rafa."

The third boy was Jaime's age, maybe a bit younger.

His shirt hung like a tarp to mid-thigh, and his hair looked like he'd cut it himself. This boy kept his distance. Jaime would have done the same. While it was fine to accept greeting or farewell kisses, often forced upon by his mamá's friends, it was weird to think of kissing girls his age.

The youngest boy shuffled his feet but barely raised his eyes to say his name. "Joaquín."

Jaime introduced himself and the five set to work. Washing dishes for one hundred people was no easy task. Washing dishes for one hundred people with no running water and clogged plumbing: eternal. Water was hauled up from the river, sterilized with lime juice (which first had to be squeezed), and dumped back outside once it got too dirty.

Jaime and Joaquín were in charge of drying and putting away the plates. Jaime had offered to wash the dishes, but Ángela volunteered instead, saying she could do them faster—which was true. The other two were on water-hauling duty. Between buckets they started to get to know each other. The other three boys had just met that morning at breakfast.

"*Mi madre* in Honduras, she drinks a lot." Rafa spilled his life story without being asked, almost as if he were bragging. "We never have enough food. She's pretty, too, so she has lots of boyfriends. I have ten brothers and sisters; most of them don't know who their real papi is. Not me. I know mine's in Texas. I'm going to find him. We're going to get fat, discover oil, and become rich together."

Jaime and Ángela looked at each other with raised eyebrows but said nothing to Rafa about his plan. It wasn't their place to ruin someone's dreams.

"What about you, Xavi?" Ángela asked when he came in with a bucket of water. "Are you getting fat and rich too?"

Xavi laughed. "I don't need to be fat and rich to be happy. Just . . ." He averted his eyes as if the idea of what he needed to be happy was painful. He took a deep breath before continuing. "I just want the freedom to make my own choices and be in control of my future. I didn't have that in El Salvador."

"Us too," Ángela said, and Jaime agreed. Had they joined the Alphas back home, their lives would never again be their own. There would have been no future to call their own. Like Xavi, they kept their story vague. No mentioning Miguel. It felt safer to keep personal details minimal. At least the details that could come back and hurt them.

Joaquín said nothing except that he came from Honduras too.

They were almost done when Xavi hauled out the dirty water, his arm muscles cut against his dark skin, and Ángela pulled Jaime close.

"I need a favor," Ángela muttered as she looked out the

kitchen into the thick vegetation surrounding the shelter. On the flattened undergrowth that marked a path to the river, Rafa was returning with the not-as-dirty river water. Ángela rushed her words. "When Xavi comes back, ask him how old he is."

Jaime frowned. "Why don't you ask him?"

"I don't want to." Ángela rolled her eyes as if she expected him to get it.

"Why?"

Ángela let go of his arm but then turned back to him and whispered even lower just as Rafa returned, sloshing water on the floor. "Just do it. *Por fa.*"

Jaime rolled his eyes back and glanced at Joaquín to see if the boy knew what Ángela was talking about. But Joaquín kept his head down and dried the plates. Jaime thought he knew his cousin, but every once in a while she went all weird. Girls.

Xavi returned with the empty dishpan a few minutes later and stretched his arms over his head, his back cracking.

"You creak like an old man, Xavi," Jaime teased. "How old are you?"

"Sometimes I feel like a *viejo*, but I'm just seventeen. You?"

"I'm twelve. Too young to feel like an old man." He grinned and got a few chuckles from Xavi and Rafa.

"Seventeen too," Rafa volunteered. He turned to look

at Ángela with a grin. "What about you, *mamacita*?"

Ángela shook her head at Rafa in annoyance, then turned to Xavi. "*Dieciséis*."

Jaime had to bite his lip and focus on the dish he was drying. Sure she was sixteen. In five months.

They all turned to Joaquín, waiting for his response. Maybe it was the heat of the day, already making sweat pour down their foreheads, but Jaime was sure Joaquín reddened just a bit before saying, "*Once*."

"Eleven? And you're by yourself?" Rafa asked. "What kind of trouble are you running away from?"

Joaquín left the kitchen and when he came back, he had three forgotten plates in his hands, which he immediately began washing himself. Xavi picked up one of the damp rags they were using to dry the dishes and finished the task. Once that was done, the older boy placed a hand on Joaquín's shoulder.

"Hey, you can travel with me." The words were quiet, but the other three still heard. "We'll look after each other."

Joaquín looked up, his dark eyes wide with . . . surprise? Fear? He seemed like he wanted to say no, then changed his mind. He nodded in agreement and quickly grabbed the remaining plates from Xavi's hands to place on the shelf before leaving the kitchen.

"C'mon, man," Rafa said in a low voice. "Why'd you

say that? You don't even know the kid. He's only going to slow you down or get you into trouble."

Xavi didn't answer right away. He draped the dishtowels over the faucet that didn't work and grabbed the broom to sweep water out of the puddle they had made on the floor.

"You remember that woman on the bus yesterday?" he asked. "The one they hauled off?"

Rafa hadn't been on the bus, but Jaime and Ángela nodded. How could they forget? The way they dragged her off and whacked her to the ground as if she had no right to seek a better life.

"I recognized her," Xavi said, his arms leaning against the broom handle. "She was from the next village over. I lived with my grandmother, who is *la curandera*. The bus woman came over one night with a horrible black eye and fat lip. But more than something for her injuries, she asked my grandmother how to break the evil curse that caused her husband to beat her so much. It was my grandmother who said the curse was strong and the best way to break it would be for the woman to leave her husband.

"I didn't recognize her until she got dragged off the bus. I don't know if it was good or not that she didn't recognize me." Xavi put the broom back where it belonged and fiddled with the stacked clean dishes, straightening them in the rows Jaime had color coordinated.

"You couldn't have saved her," Ángela said softly. She reached out a hand but then dropped it before it touched his shoulder. "If you'd have tried to stop them, they would have taken you, too."

Xavi spun around, his green eyes narrowed and dark. "Would you have sat by while they deported Jaime?"

"Of course not." Her response was quick and hostile, as if he dared suggest such a thing. "But we're family."

"And the woman left hers because of mine. Those guards will probably treat her worse than her husband did."

Jaime wished he could have helped her too, but not if it would have gotten him, or Ángela, into trouble. But at what point do you stop helping people? He and Ángela had grown up together; his mamá had taken care of her and Miguel while Tía worked; they were practically brother and sister. He'd like to think he'd help anyone in his family if he could, but what about family members he didn't know, or friends? Where would he draw the line between those he'd help, and those he'd let get abused and deported?

"But they said they were only going to take her back to Guatemala. She can come back to México and try her journey again," Jaime said, grabbing the only optimism he could from the grim situation.

"If she has the strength. Or the money," Xavi reminded them. "Would you?"

Ángela shook her head sadly. "Home's not safe for us anymore."

"But neither is this trip." Xavi turned back to Rafa, daring him to question his motives again. "That's why Joaquín is coming with me."

CHAPTER NINE

They spent the day with Xavi, Rafa, Joaquín, and
other kids hanging out and playing *fútbol* in front of the
church with a semi-deflated ball. The street dead-ended
at the church, and the people who lived farther up never
glanced in their direction. Padre Kevin assured them the
church was safe from *la migra* or any gangs. César, a Nicaraguan boy who joined their game, said it was safe because
El Gordo controlled the area and it was in El Gordo's best
interest to keep the immigrants safe.

The more Jaime heard of this El Gordo, the more he
didn't like him.

Jaime wasn't sure if he liked Rafa, either, who talked
too much and seemed to have unrealistic ideas about the
future. They still knew nothing about quiet Joaquín except

that he didn't know how to swim and had no interest in cooling off in the river with the other boys when it got too hot and humid. But Xavi? Xavi was what he imagined, and hoped, Tomás would be like.

Xavi hadn't mentioned where in El Norte he was heading, but Jaime hoped he'd travel with them for a bit. Ángela, Jaime knew, would agree. If anything, there would be safety in numbers.

When night fell, Rafa tried to convince them to go with him to a dogfight a few kilometers up the river. "I have a hundred pesos I'm putting on this one dog that honestly can't lose. Just think, if we put our money together, we can make enough to hire our own private smuggler. Whatcha think, *mamacita*?"

Ángela shook her head with her nose scrunched up. "Absolutely not. I loathe dogs."

"Besides," Jaime said, "those fights are really cruel." Not that he'd ever been to one, but he didn't need to in order to know how bloody and heart-wrenching it would be.

Rafa laughed. "Nah, it's fun."

"If I wanted to watch animals rip each other apart, I would have stayed home," Xavi said. He didn't elaborate, but Jaime got the feeling he wasn't talking about four-legged animals.

Joaquín didn't say anything, but he huddled closer to Ángela as if just the thought of a dogfight scared him, too.

"Fine. Look me up if you make it across the border. *Hasta.*" Rafa waved and headed off with some other men hoping for the same fortune at the mercy of dogs with sharp teeth.

The four stayed at the church, where some of the older men built a bonfire next to the river. Xavi's phone, freshly charged by a neighbor's outdoor electrical socket, didn't have any minutes to use as a phone, but contained some great music on it—hip-hop, pop, salsa, rock, and even some songs in English. Xavi and a couple of other boys began showing off their street dance moves. At least two insects flew into Jaime's mouth as he stared in awe at Xavi's break dancing and acrobatic talent. By the bonfire light, Jaime sketched the older boy holding all his weight on one arm while his body was parallel to the ground like a sideways star.

In a moment of bravery, Joaquín slipped out of the shadows and performed a series of cartwheels without stopping. Jaime outlined a sketch of that, too, but decided he needed proper light to execute the drawing he had in mind, a graceful circle of human blur.

Even Ángela jumped in with some invented hip-hop moves. For a few minutes she and Xavi seemed to be having a conversation with their dancing where one would dance and the other would respond. Jaime drew that, too—Xavi staring intently at Ángela with his hands on the ground like he was doing a push-up, but with his legs curled into the air like a scorpion's tail, while Ángela shook her finger "no" at him but with a huge grin on her face.

It was late when the kids made their way the few meters back to the church; the older men had gotten drunk and rowdy, especially after Padre Kevin put his flip-flop foot down, saying they couldn't sleep in the sanctuary in that condition.

"Are you staying here, Joaquín?" Jaime pointed to the women and children's section of the church. "You can set your blanket next to us."

"I'm not a girl," Joaquín answered sharp and quick, the most words he had said all day in one mouthful.

Jaime yawned, barely able to keep his eyes open any longer. "Me neither. But we're still kids, so it's fine."

Joaquín looked from Ángela to Xavi as if to get their permission.

"You're welcome with us, *cariño*." Ángela used the word of endearment she often reserved for younger kids, or kids she needed to mother. Something she picked up from their mothers. "But if you feel more comfortable staying with the men, Xavi will look after you."

A roar of laughter came from the bonfire through the trees. Joaquín took hold of Ángela's hand. "*Pues, con vos.*"

Jaime collected three tattered blankets from the same old woman who had taken them in the morning, while

Ángela and Xavi exchanged kisses on the cheek in the traditional farewell gesture.

"See you in the morning." Xavi waved before heading to the men's side of the church.

It seemed Jaime had barely closed his eyes, when an arm reached over him to wake his cousin.

"*Chapina*," Padre Kevin whispered to Ángela. "*El chico salvadoreño*. He needs you."

Jaime, Ángela, and Joaquín sat up, almost whacking Padre Kevin in the mouth. The sun was just coming up, but they gathered their things in seconds, the advantage of sleeping in their clothes and never unpacking their bags. They folded the blankets quickly and returned them to Padre Kevin, who once again was the epitome of cheery. If Jaime hadn't been so worried about Xavi, he would have been annoyed at the priest.

Xavi stood waiting for them in the trees by the embers of last night's bonfire. The drunken men were nowhere in sight.

In Xavi's arms he cradled a wet, bloody blob.

"What is that?" Jaime asked as he rushed over. It was impossible to tell where the blood was coming from—Xavi or the thing he held.

"A dog."

Ángela backed away.

Xavi continued, "I think they used her as bait for the dogfight last night and threw her in the river when they were done. I found her in the bushes. Poor thing. She's barely breathing."

Ángela's mouth twitched as if she wanted to say something but wasn't sure what. Jaime saved her from having to make a decision. "What do you want us to do?"

"Water." Xavi took a deep breath. "And some limes to disinfect the wounds."

Without a word, Joaquín sprinted off through the thick undergrowth to get the supplies. When he returned, Xavi sat on a rock near the fire pit with the dog in his lap and began gently dowsing it with water. The lump twitched but didn't, or couldn't, try to escape. Xavi's white uniform shirt soon became soaked through and pink with blood.

Jaime could see it was a miracle the dog was still alive. One ear had been completely ripped off. Bite marks oozed blood all over the body. But the worst was the gaping wound on its side.

How could Rafa have thought that dogfights were fun? For a second Jaime thought about Miguel and how he'd been beaten to death, how the Alphas may have even thought that was fun. Sometimes Jaime really didn't understand humans.

"*Mira*, Jaime, can you hold her? I want to look her over better."

Jaime reached over to accept the bundle, but Ángela stopped him.

"Wait, take off your shirt first."

Good thinking—he only had one other as a spare. He handed Ángela the T-shirt, which she promptly folded, and took the wet, white-and-brown, bloody mess from Xavi. The dog was about the length of his forearm and weighed next to nothing. Not only had her previous owners subjected her to being ripped open, but they had barely fed her.

The dog shivered but didn't move beyond that. Against his chest Jaime could feel her intense body heat, as if she were running a fever. But that was good, right? Didn't that mean she was still fighting?

Their two heartbeats raced a thousand kilometers a minute to the point that Jaime couldn't tell whose was whose.

Xavi gently poked and prodded the dog all over. When he touched the skin around the open wound, she let out a loud whimper.

"Can you save her?" Joaquín asked, his voice high-pitched and matching the dog's whimper. "Please?"

Xavi looked up at Ángela, who was still standing at a distance from them as if her job was only to keep guard. "Any chance you have a needle and thread?" he asked.

Ángela put her hands on her hips. "What, you think

just because I'm a woman I go around carrying a sewing kit?" But then she dug around the front pocket of her backpack. Of course she would, Jaime thought. Tía was a seamstress, after all, and had taught the whole family, including the men, how to sew. Jaime wished he'd thought of bringing something as practical as a sewing kit. Or that his mamá had.

"I don't know what I'm doing," Xavi said, half to himself, holding the swath of cardboard with three needles of various sizes, a spool of blue thread, and a miniature pair of folding scissors. "People didn't often come to my grandmother for stitches and I don't know how to sew. I've butchered pigs, but this is the opposite, isn't it?"

"I can sew," Jaime said.

"*Yo también*," Joaquín whispered.

Xavi nodded and handed Joaquín the needles and thread. It took three attempts for him to thread the largest needle. He crouched beside Jaime, Xavi, and the dog. Jaime held the dog secure against his chest while Xavi pushed together the pieces of open skin. The dog whimpered again. Joaquín's hand shook as he approached the flesh with the needle. He had barely poked the skin when the dog yelped, causing Joaquín to jump away.

"I can't do it," he cried. "I don't want to hurt her."

Jaime bit his lip. He agreed with Joaquín. He wouldn't want to hurt her either. But they couldn't leave her like this—they *had* to save her. Or at least try.

Xavi opened his mouth to say something—that the dog would die if they didn't or maybe to suggest that Jaime try instead—but Ángela beat him to it.

"Give the needle here." She bit into a lime to break the peel and squeezed a few drops of juice onto the needle before crouching down. "Whatever you do, don't let it bite me, or I swear I'm drowning it in the river."

Jaime shifted his arm so that the snout was clamped between his bicep and ribs but still able to breathe. He held her still with his other arm before giving his cousin a nod.

The dog wiggled and whined as soon as Ángela made the first stitch. Jaime held her tighter against his bare chest and Xavi, with his hands holding her belly together, helped stabilize her. A prayer to San Francisco, patron saint of animals and children, came from Joaquín.

Ángela didn't bat an eye. She pulled the needle in and out as if she were mending socks. Jaime was sure if he had tried sewing up the dog, he would have panicked like Joaquín. Ángela secured each neat stitch individually with a knot until the dog's side was nothing more than wet fur with a ten-centimeter line of blue thread.

With a gentleness that surprised him—it was a dog, after all—Ángela dabbed the wound with a wet rag before squeezing the lime juice onto the blue seam to prevent infection. The dog squirmed, but Jaime kept her tight in his arms, telling her it would be all right, and wishing he could believe it as he said it. What Ángela had done was truly a miracle. The other boys saw it too.

"Thank you," Xavi said softly. "You saved her. You saved her life."

"It's fine." Ángela shrugged away the praise. She stood up, wiping her hands with the rag and more lime juice. She shifted from one foot to the other as if she didn't know what to do with herself. "Have they served breakfast already? I'm starving."

She took two steps and then stopped when she noticed the boys were still huddled around the dog.

"What are we going to call her?" Jaime eased his tight hold but kept the dog against his chest as he got back on his feet. She no longer whimpered from the citrus sting, but her breathing remained heavy. Her white-and-brown–patched fur would look pretty once she dried. "How about Pinta?"

The worry lines on Xavi's forehead lifted as he took deep breaths of relief. "I was thinking of calling her Vida."

"Sí," Joaquín said before Xavi had finished the words. "Vida."

Against Jaime's bare chest the canine's heart thumped with life-giving approval. A smile crossed Jaime's face as he gave her a gentle cuddle. Ángela looked down, her face twisting with sadness and maybe regret. Jaime knew she was thinking about Miguel; he was. Then she blinked in agreement too. The other two seemed to be lost in the world of deceased loved ones as well; little Joaquín looked ready to burst into tears. But then he, too, relaxed when he looked at the recovered dog with promise and hope. Vida, life. That was a good name.

Jaime stood next to Ángela as Xavi and Joaquín gathered the rags and bucket. Before Jaime could stop the patient, a pink tongue escaped the lips of the wounded mutt as she gave her seamstress a kiss of thanks on the palm.

Ángela's hand snapped back. For a second Jaime was sure she was going to swat the dog on the nose. Instead Ángela smoothed down the brown-and-white fur sticking up in the spot between the dog's one ear and where the other should have been.

CHAPTER TEN

On Jaime and Ángela's second day at Padre Kevin's refuge, just as the sun was losing its battle with nighttime, a white Mercedes with black-tinted windows roared down the street and braked in front of the church with a huge cloud of dust.

The *fútbol* players abandoned their game quickly to avoid getting hit. Jaime hugged his bag tight to his chest; the other kids who had possessions did the same. Ángela grabbed Joaquín's hand, or maybe it was the other way around. Xavi scooped up Vida, who had been snoozing away her injuries while they played in the street. Rafa, who not only lost all his money at the dogfight but was also beaten up for trying to win it back, pulled his cap low over his face. Still, everyone, including Vida, watched the doors of the Mercedes open.

From the driver's seat, huge hands pressed against the open door and the roof to extract a body too large for the sleek sports car, like an oozing snail escaping a confining shell. The stench of expensive cologne wafted from the large man, reminding Jaime of rotten eggs preserved in alcohol. He almost didn't notice a second man slip out of the passenger side inconspicuously.

The giant slug was completely bald but made up for it with such a thick black mustache, it looked like an animal had stuck itself to his lip. He wore a white linen shirt and slacks with a polished black belt and shoes. The day's remaining sunshine reflected off his clothes and shiny head.

El Gordo had arrived.

"Kevin!" he yelled, even though the padre had exited the church as soon as he heard the engine's roar.

Padre Kevin walked toward the giant. The men were similar, both large and bald, but the contrast between them was stark. Today the padre donned rainbow-striped shorts and a lime-green shirt that in six pictures showed the evolution from ape to saint. On closer inspection, El Gordo did look a bit like the first, Neanderthal-type image on the padre's shirt.

Padre Kevin nodded to the men as if to imply that *he* at least hadn't forgotten courtesy. "*Don* Gordo."

El Gordo surveyed the crowd that had leaked out of the church and come from the growth along the river at the sound of his arrival. While yesterday there had been a hundred refugees sheltering at the church and some had already left, like the girl with the baby, now there were closer to a hundred and fifty, and most of them were present.

"They breed like rabbits and infest us like parasites, don't they?" El Gordo said to Padre Kevin, and laughed. Padre Kevin didn't find the joke funny, nor did any of the people watching and listening.

"So." He clapped his hands. It was hard to tell with his mustache covering most of his mouth, but Jaime was pretty sure El Gordo was giving the crowd his widest grin as if he were about to devour them. "Which of you little pissants is getting on the train early tomorrow morning?"

Jaime and Ángela looked at each other out of the corners of their eyes. Neither wanted to draw attention to themselves, let alone speak with this man. Maybe there was some way to get on the train without having to deal with El Gordo.

Everyone else seemed to feel the same way. No one said a word, even after a minute of being stared down. Padre Kevin did nothing to encourage anyone to speak up. He kept his eyes averted from El Gordo as he muttered words that might have been prayers but could have been insults.

Jaime shivered as El Gordo laughed again and surveyed the crowd. "I'm kidding! I love you guys. Twelve of you have already paid to ride the train. If you don't tell me who you are, there are no refunds."

One man in a blue bandanna lifted his arm slowly, followed by a woman with two children, a girl about five years old and a boy about seven. A few others hesitated before raising their hands. Jaime had to force his arm up. Worse was when they had to give their names to confirm against the list that El Gordo kept somewhere in his thick skull. Jaime was sure something would go wrong. It did, but for someone else.

El Gordo nodded as if he were bored when Jaime and Ángela told him who they were. It was the next man who wasn't so lucky.

"I don't have a Gonzales," the smuggler said. He tried to cross his arms over his chest. Except his arms were too large to complete the crossed X.

The man bobbed his head uncontrollably. "*Sí*, Octavio Gonzales Peña."

"No Gonzales, no Peña." El Gordo scratched his mustache. Jaime imagined fleas colonizing his monstrous mustache and knew how he'd draw El Gordo later.

The man kept bobbing his head, an action that made him sweat profusely. "But my wife paid. We sold everything we own. Paid a man named Chuy, who was going to give it to you."

El Gordo shrugged. "I don't know this Chuy and I

didn't get it. Maybe you need to get yourself a new wife." He winked at Padre Kevin, but the padre made no response.

"She did pay, she did!" The man's face crumbled and he flung himself to the ground, crying on El Gordo's shiny shoes. Huge mistake. El Gordo swung his leg and caught the man right on the ear.

"I need four thousand pesos before I get you safe passage." El Gordo turned away from the hysterical man and addressed everyone else. "That's right, only four thousand pesos. That's not very much for a guaranteed safe ride on the train, let me tell you. If you don't go through me, half of you won't make the train ride in one piece. Not with the immigration checkpoints, or the gangs that control the rail lines, ready to beat you up or throw you off the moving train."

A man with buzzed hair swallowed and limped forward. Two men who looked like brothers with matching round bellies kept their eyes down as they shuffled toward El Gordo as well. They extracted money from their pockets, socks, and underwear. El Gordo snapped his fingers at his minion. Until that moment, Jaime had forgotten about the second man, who now counted the crumbled and dirty notes before nodding to his boss that the right amount was there.

When it looked like no one else had any money for a safe passage aboard the train, El Gordo turned back to his immaculate car. "We'll come back for those of you who've paid or changed your mind at one o'clock in the morning. The rest of you who are going to face the Beast, thanks for feeding the vultures."

He laughed again and motioned to his minion, who popped open the trunk with the push of a button. From there the minion extracted a leg of raw meat. Jaime hoped it was pork or beef and not something more sinister. The minion went through the trees by the river and slapped the meat on the table outside the kitchen that held their meals.

"For your troubles, Kevin." El Gordo waved a fat hand at the food. "Always a pleasure doing business with you." And once more his laughter rang across the street.

"Of course, God thanks you," Padre Kevin said through tight lips.

It took a couple of minutes for El Gordo to squeeze himself back into the cramped driver's seat, and then he and his minion were gone. A collective sigh, almost as loud as El Gordo's satanic laughter, vibrated in the now-quiet street. No one's sigh was louder than Padre Kevin's.

People shuffled back into the church or returned to their previous activities. Yesterday's grumpy woman got César and some other boys to haul the meat into the kitchen and ordered some women to help her cook it. Jaime and his friends looked at the semi-deflated ball and seemed to agree the *fútbol* game was over.

Three Honduran boys who had been playing *fútbol* with them shoved their hands in their pockets.

"Four thousand pesos? Who does that fat cat think he is?" said Gusti, one of the best strikers Jaime had ever played with.

Sebastián, who preferred refereeing to playing, grumbled, "I bet he just takes the money and feeds people to *la migra*."

"Any chance we can come up with four thousand pesos in six hours?" asked Omar, who had been their goalkeeper.

"Sure." Gusti smirked. "If a purse of money falls from the heavens."

The other two boys stared at the overcast sky for a few seconds, as if wondering whether there was any chance of that happening. As they headed up the street, Omar picked up an empty beer bottle lying in the bushes; they could get a couple of copper coins for the glass. At that rate they would need thousands of bottles to earn enough to pay El Gordo.

"Our parents paid double that," Ángela muttered under her breath. She took Jaime's hand and they turned to walk back into the church with their other friends. Jaime worked the math in his head to figure out how much that translated into Guatemalan quetzales—about his father's three-month salary. He hated thinking of the trouble he'd caused everyone. Their whole family must have chipped in; the women Mamá worked for must have given her loans; Tomás probably sent his wages too. All to be overcharged. But there was nothing they could do. They certainly couldn't ask El Gordo for a refund.

"Maybe they'll give us nice seats with air-conditioning on the train," he joked. He didn't know what to expect—he'd never been on a train before—but he doubted El Gordo's way was even legal. *We're lucky*, he kept reminding himself. His family could pay for El Gordo's train, and maybe, just maybe, they were better protected as a result.

"I'm not surprised your parents paid more," Xavi said. "There are middlemen to pay off and others who just take advantage. The ignorant are always the ones who pay more."

"Our parents aren't ignorant," Jaime defended quickly.

"I meant ignorant in terms of smuggling costs. Someone told them a price and they didn't negotiate it."

Xavi did have a point. Neither his parents nor Ángela's had ever made this journey, nor anyone in the immediate family. Tomás had papers and sponsorship that allowed him to travel through México the whole way by bus without any complications. His parents could only go by what someone said or another recommended.

If only his parents hadn't had to pay so much. If only he and Ángela hadn't had to leave Guatemala. He should have been nicer to Pulguita back when they were friends. He should have let the boy continue stealing from him. He should have stopped Miguel from telling Pulguita they didn't want to be friends anymore.

It all came down to Jaime, and the ways he could have stopped any of this from happening.

CHAPTER ELEVEN

No one slept that night. And there was no bonfire.

Only about fifteen of the hundred and fifty staying at the church were using El Gordo's services. Inside the church the sheet that divided the men's quarters from the women and children was pulled aside as more than half of the people gathered their things and made plans to face the Beast, or *la bestia* as it was nicknamed. Also known as the train. Advice bounced around from the veteran train riders, and everyone else who liked to give an opinion.

"Don't travel by yourself," said a man who had been deported twice back to Nicaragua.

"Don't trust anyone," said a pregnant Honduran woman, wrapping a shawl tight around her shoulders.

The grumpy woman who served them food grumbled,

"You're better off just going home. You'll never make it."

A few others, particularly the old people, murmured in agreement. One man added, "If the train slows down, it could be an immigration stop. Or a trap."

"If you jump off, don't be scared of the ground. It'll hurt you less than the train wheels, or the gangsters' gunshots," the Nicaraguan chimed in again.

César, who played *fútbol* with them and had been on the train a few times, told everyone they weren't that bad. "Just give the gangs what they want. No big deal."

Of course it was a big deal, especially when the gang wanted your life.

But warnings and opinions weren't enough to change minds. Most people were determined to board *la bestia* anyway. They didn't have a choice.

"I'm still getting on the train," Xavi announced as their group sat by the river, with Vida licking a bone from the meat El Gordo had brought. "Rafa, Joaquín, you're coming too, right?"

"Obviously." Rafa looked at him with mock disbelief, as if there could be another answer.

Joaquín stared at Xavi with scared eyes as he shifted from one foot to another. Then he blinked in agreement.

"Do you have any money?" Jaime asked. It'd be much better if they went with him and Ángela. If only El Gordo would strike a deal with them, take whatever the three could afford, and call it even. But Jaime knew El Gordo would never go for that kind of deal. Not after he'd kicked that man who had insisted he had paid.

Xavi ran a hand through his hair, which made it stand up as if his thoughts had electrified it. "I left El Salvador in a hurry, with only enough money for the bus ticket here. I stole this uniform shirt from a washing line just over the Guatemala-México border. I have nothing left except my phone and charger."

From Joaquín's pockets came two Honduran lempira coins. The boy turned them over as if he were studying the engravings. Jaime had no idea of their value, but he guessed it was next to nothing. Rafa, Jaime knew, had gambled away the little money he had. Inside Ángela's backpack they had the remains of the food from home, and a few pesos for another couple of meals. It was better than nothing but still not fair. These boys didn't even have a change of clothes.

"How are you going to stay in the train without any money?" Ángela put her hands on her hips in a way that gave her an uncanny resemblance to Abuela, and no one messed with their grandmother.

Xavi couldn't look her in the eye. "Not in. On."

Jaime remembered playing trains with Miguel when they were younger. Miguel always liked to balance the passenger toy people on top of the train cars and see how fast he could roll the train before the plastic people fell off. Xavi was talking about doing the same, except as a real-life person.

Ángela shook her head. "Don't. It's too dangerous."

"But what's the alternative?" Xavi folded his arms over his chest and paced back and forth. "If we walk or hitchhike, sooner or later we're going to get caught. This whole journey is dangerous. Most people have to attempt it several times. César's on his sixth try. None of us can return home, either. We're not staying here to wash dishes for Padre Kevin for the rest of our lives."

"But you can wash dishes for someone else until you've earned enough money to get properly on the train," Ángela pointed out.

Rafa laughed as he put a casual forearm on Ángela's shoulder. "It would take ages to save up that much. I don't want to work that hard. Besides, who's going to hire us when we saw half our *fútbol* team also looking for jobs to pay their way north?"

Ángela pushed his arm off her and gave him a reproachful look before turning back to Xavi. "What if something happens to you?"

He didn't look at her. "Things happen all the time."

"Sure, if you go looking for trouble," she snapped back.

"You're not their mother," Jaime told his cousin in a low whisper. He didn't want anything bad to happen to these boys either, but he understood that what they did was their choice.

"Don't worry about us, it'll be fun," Rafa said. *Fun, right*, Jaime thought. That boy sure had a twisted idea of what "fun" meant. But, Jaime imagined, if their lives weren't at stake, riding a train cross-country would be fun—going through big cities and one-horse towns, getting the conductor in his striped hat to toot the horn, borrowing a piece of coal to draw it all. Yes, that would be fun. If it were realistic. Maybe not thinking of the reality was what kept Rafa optimistic.

"What will you do if *la migra* catches you?" Ángela demanded, as if she knew they didn't have real answers.

"Drop it," Jaime said, this time loud enough for them all to hear, though no one listened.

Xavi pointed to the uniform shirt that claimed him as a "student" at a Mexican school. *La migra* officer on the bus had bought the disguise. Except now the shirt was stained with dirt and Vida's blood. "It's worked for me so far."

Rafa pulled a letter from his jeans pocket and showed it to Xavi and Ángela. As usual, he volunteered information without being asked. "I sent this to myself, using an address here in Arriaga. The letter contains a long plea from my *'abuelita'* up north to come for a visit before Grandfather dies. See, this way, if *la migra* tries to deport me, I have the letter with 'my' Mexican address, dated a couple weeks ago. They'll think that I'm southern Mexican, which explains my accent."

Jaime and Joaquín looked at each other and then at the older kids, not knowing what to say. It was Xavi, after glancing through the letter, who finally said, "Except this letter supposedly came from the northeastern state of Coahuila, where your 'grandparents' live. But it has the Arriaga postmark." Xavi folded the letter back into the envelope and returned it to its owner. Rafa's mouth dropped open in disappointment as he realized his plan wasn't as clever as he thought.

"Do you have a way to avoid getting deported?" Jaime asked Joaquín. The boy seemed so helpless and innocent, Jaime wondered how he could possibly have made it this far on his own.

"I can sing the Mexican national anthem," Joaquín said to his shoes, and didn't notice the others looking at him in surprise. Partly because it was a much better ruse than the fake letter, partly because he knew the words. But mostly because he'd dare sing it when he barely spoke.

Ángela wrapped the young boy in a tight hug before grabbing Xavi's hand and giving it a squeeze. "Fine. I'll help you get ready. You need a plan, and a few backup ones in case things go wrong, 'cause they will."

She led the way back into the church to the wall where route maps and safe-house locations were displayed. Jaime lagged behind with Xavi while the older boy dragged his toes along the dirt floor.

"I'm sorry she's acting like this," Jaime muttered. "She's not usually so bossy."

The corners of Xavi's mouth went up, but the smile seemed sad, distracted. "It's her way of showing she cares."

Jaime supposed. He knew Ángela liked being in charge and taking care of people—she was a lot like Abuela and his mamá that way. But he'd never seen her like this before. Before Miguel, she never . . . Maybe that was it. Maybe she also thought there was more she could have done to save Miguel. Maybe by helping these boys, they could make it up to Miguel. If that was the case, he was all in.

There wasn't much to do to help prepare the boys for their journey—they had no money, no supplies, and not much time left. The best they could do was memorize the locations of the safe-houses throughout México (Jaime drew replicas of the maps in his sketchbook and gave a copy to everyone) and come up with ideas to keep them from harm. Other than "do not get caught," there weren't too many options.

Still, Ángela fussed with their clothing, tried to rid Xavi's uniform shirt of bloodstains, and offered to tailor Joaquín's clothes to fit him better. The little boy tugged the sides of his extra-large shirt and bunched the excess fabric to his chest like a blankie. He fiercely shook his head.

She didn't pressure the boy but turned to Xavi, her eyes moist. "Please take care of Joaquín."

"Of course," Xavi said. He took a deep breath and then nodded to the trees along the river. "Walk with me for a second."

The two walked toward the river. Jaime placed a hand on Vida to keep her from following. With a little food, and a lot of attention, life had returned to Vida. She still whimpered every time she tried to walk, but a doggie smile when she sat next to her humans showed she was glad to be alive. Jaime was going to miss her. He'd never had a pet. Animals back home weren't companions. They either produced food like eggs or milk, or they were food. But because he'd helped save Vida, she had become a friend, too.

Ángela and Xavi came back a couple of minutes later. The nighttime made it hard to tell, but Jaime was pretty sure both of their faces seemed redder than before. Had they kissed or something?

"We better go." Xavi snuck a glance at Ángela, who was definitely blushing.

Jaime hugged each of the boys while Ángela gave them the traditional farewell cheek kiss. Joaquín, however, wrapped his arms around Ángela's neck and planted an actual kiss on her cheek, like a little kid to his mamá.

Xavi picked up Vida and placed her between the two hammock slings that Ángela had sewed from rag scraps Padre Kevin gave them. Because of Vida's belly injuries,

Ángela thought it would be better for Xavi to wear two slings, one on each shoulder that crossed over Xavi's chest and back. This allowed the dog to be supported by her front end and hindquarters instead of her middle. Vida struggled at first but then settled down when Ángela placed a reassuring hand on her head and rubbed her one ear.

"We change trains in Medias Aguas. If there's a long wait, we'll see you there," she said, repeating the plan even through they had already gone over it. "Otherwise, at the safe house in Lechería."

"*Sí.*" But it was impossible to tell by the sound whether Xavi had said "sí" meaning "yes," or "si"—"if."

"Keep on the lookout for any trouble. Don't get caught. Be safe," she called out.

The three boys walked briskly up the road. At the top they turned around and waved before disappearing into the dark night.

For several minutes, the cousins watched the top of the road, the last place they saw their friends.

"You like him, don't you." Jaime didn't have to clarify which "him" he meant.

"I barely know him." Ángela scuffed her sneaker back and forth on the dirt road. "But, yes."

Jaime took a deep breath to distract himself from thinking what he didn't want to think—that meeting up with their friends when the train stopped, either in Medias

Aguas or farther north in Lechería, probably wouldn't happen. "Well, as the man of the house at the moment, I permit you to see him."

"Man?" Ángela shoved him playfully in the shoulder. "You can't even grow a mustache yet."

Jaime shrugged. "I'll paint one on."

They teased back and forth until a dog barking in the distance reminded them of their friends. Ángela instinctively grabbed Jaime's arm. Jaime held her close, holding her arm that was holding his. Even with Vida's rescue, Ángela hadn't gotten over her dog phobia. Jaime didn't mind. It was a nice feeling knowing that he could comfort Ángela from some of the scary things the world had in store for them.

CHAPTER TWELVE

Padre Kevin handed out water bottles and encouraged everyone getting on the train with El Gordo to use the bathroom (and by that he meant the river) before boarding. When the mamá with two children asked what the train ride would be like, Padre glanced at the two youngsters before answering, "There are no toilets."

A mixture of worry and adrenaline coursed through Jaime. He understood what Padre hadn't said, what he would have said if the children hadn't been present: the train ride was not going to be fun.

Nerves made Jaime need to pee twice in the time he and Ángela stood outside the church in the middle of the night waiting for El Gordo. Not only had he never been on a train before, but he'd never had his life in the hands of a stranger either. Pancho, who had driven them across the Guatemala-México border, had been selling his wares in their village for years before Jaime was born. As far as Jaime was concerned, the old man was like a trustworthy distant relative. But Jaime definitely didn't trust El Gordo.

For one thing, how would the gangs who patrol the trains or *la migra* know who had paid for protection? Would El Gordo hang cardboard signs from their necks that read DON'T BEAT THIS GUY UP, HE PAID? Jaime shifted from one foot to another and wiped his sweaty hands on his jeans. Anything could happen.

A dozen people, mostly men but also a few women and two children, waited with Jaime and Ángela on the dirt street outside the church for El Gordo, where earlier that day Jaime and his friends had played with a semi-deflated ball. The mamá clung tight to her children. The water bottles Padre Kevin had handed out seemed to be their only possessions, except the little girl also held a scrap of pink cloth that might have come from a blanket. The man in the bandanna, who'd been the first one brave enough to go up to El Gordo, paced back and forth. The two brothers crouched with their knees to their chests, trying to get a bit of sleep. At least half of them looked as scared and nervous as Jaime felt. The others seemed more lost and empty, as if they had nothing left to lose in this world.

If Jaime ignored the murky-brown river, the shreds of

plastic bags tangled in the undergrowth, and piles of garbage, the area surrounding Padre Kevin's sanctuary would be pretty. He would miss it.

"*Chapín, ven aquí un momento.*" The grumpy woman in charge of the food motioned to Jaime to come over to her by the outdoor kitchen.

Jaime looked from Ángela to the empty street. He was wondering whether to use the river one more time but supposed he could go to the woman quickly. Any engine that came down the road would be heard immediately. He trotted over to her, keeping his eyes on the street, and on Ángela.

"*¿Sí?*"

The grumpy woman pointed at a weather-worn box nestled next to a bag of dried beans.

"A missionary donated five hundred lead pencils. We'll never go through them in a million years. I saw you drawing the map of the shelters. You got talent. Would you like to take some pencils with you?"

"Sure!" The pencils weren't good quality. Jaime could tell by the way they felt that the wood would chip when sharpened, the lead would be prone to breaking, and the eraser would smudge the page with a dark streak instead of wiping the markings clean. Still, they were free and the pencils he had brought with him were wearing down. It wouldn't hurt to take a couple. And besides, it was the nicest thing he'd seen the grumpy woman do or say.

"Thanks!" He gave her a quick kiss and then ran back to the crowd as he heard a car coming down the road.

It was a van, not a car. Of course, they wouldn't have all fit into El Gordo's Mercedes, not that Jaime thought El Gordo would let them near his fancy car. The windowless van reminded him of the one that woman on the bus had been thrown into by *la migra* officers. Except this one was black, with dents along the sides as if it had been rammed into several times. Could this all have been a trap? Had they paid El Gordo to send them back home? Jaime wanted to believe that Padre Kevin wouldn't allow that, but on the other hand, he had seen how the padre disliked the smuggler and yet still felt compelled to work with him. Maybe Padre Kevin didn't feel he had a choice, like Jaime.

El Gordo's minion got out of the driver's seat this time and opened the rear door. Ángela took a deep breath before she seized Jaime's hand. They followed the others into the back of the van. It smelled of dirt and sweat, at least better than El Gordo's offensive cologne. Blessings and prayers came from those staying at the church to brave the train another day, or maybe not at all. Their faces more anxious than envious.

"*Que Dios los bendiga.*"

"God bless you."

"Safe travels."

"Don't give up."

And, of course, Padre Kevin's own untraditional words: "Jesús loves you—it's everyone else you have to convince."

Jaime hugged Ángela's hand to his chest as the van's door shut and another chapter of their journey ended.

A narrow bench had been fitted to either side of the van. The people were crammed so tight, heads and knees were the only things capable of rocking and bumping into each other as the van pulled away. No one spoke, including the driver upfront. For the first few minutes Jaime tried to draw a mental map of where they were going—left, right, right—but he soon lost track. Not that it mattered. Not that he knew where they were going. Or that he would need to get back.

He lost all sense of time. It might have been a few minutes or a few hours. Lights came through the windshield, but the large man sitting next to Jaime blocked the view. At some point the driver turned off a paved road, and the van began to bounce as it hit craters and rocks. Jaime gripped the underside of his seat to hold himself steady; Ángela banged against the side of the van with a yelp. The woman with two children cut her hand on a bit of metal sticking out on one side but ignored it to calm her crying kids. The driver slammed on his brakes, and one of the men on the opposite bench popped out of the wedged bunch. Nearly everyone on that side fell off their seats into a mosh pit on the floor or on top of the people in front of them.

"Shh!" El Gordo's minion uttered his first sound, sharp and full of urgency, as he ducked in his seat. Jaime bit his lip to keep from crying out. His left foot was trapped and twisted at an odd angle between two people on the floor. The mamá clamped her bleeding hand over her daughter's mouth and glared at her son to stop crying. As if someone had pushed the mute button on a television, the whole black van fell quiet in an instant.

They remained in the tangle of sprawled bodies for several minutes, not daring to move lest they make some noise. Just when Jaime was sure his ankle couldn't bear the pain of being smashed any longer, the back of the van opened slowly without its usual metal clamor.

The dim glow from a distant light post illuminated a pockmarked face with eyes set so deep they couldn't be seen. The guy's arms, black with tattoos, held open the back door to keep it from squeaking.

"If you value your life, you'll come quickly, quietly, and keep out of sight," he said in a low voice.

The passengers untangled themselves and tumbled out of the van. Jaime and Ángela crouched in the vehicle's shadow, Jaime's sore ankle aching from the weight. The guy couldn't have been too much older than Ángela, but the scars on his face made him look like he'd been beaten up a few times. In the dim light Jaime noticed the tattoo covering his arm was tightly wound vines with thorny roses. A gang tattoo, for sure. The guy held out his tattooed arm low to the ground to signal that everyone should stay put.

Jaime took the time to look around. They were in a rail yard with lines of cargo train cars on different tracks, but no passenger cars. Under the far-off lights, workers loaded boxcars with goods. By the way the sacks hung over their shoulders, Jaime guessed some were filled with something soft like cornmeal. Others retained their shape and looked like they held cement. Uniformed men strutted along the train cars and peered into shadows and underneath the cars while clinging to their automatic weapons.

As his eyes adjusted to the dim light, Jaime picked up other details. Or, more specifically, other people. Figures darted from behind one car to another. Stealth shadows flickered over the top of some of the cargo cars. Jaime gulped. The cars were much taller than he imagined, and the train could go faster than an automobile. Falling from the cars would not be a small bump like the plastic men endured when he and Miguel used to play with trains. New worry filled his head. With every shadow he saw, he wondered if it was Xavi, Joaquín, or even Rafa. Would Jaime ever see them again?

He pulled the straps of his backpack tighter around his shoulders. The edge of his sketchbook dug into his spine as if to reassure him it was still there. He rotated his banged ankle. It still felt tender but not enough to keep him from walking—or running if he had to.

From the corner of his eye he caught Ángela taking a deep breath. Then she nodded, as if trying to reassure him that everything was fine. He knew her better than that. She was just as scared as he was, but pretended otherwise for his sake. In turn, he pretended he believed that everything was fine.

An insect made a soft chirp and with that, the man pointed to Jaime, Ángela, and two others, waved his tattooed arm, and took off close to the ground like a coyote. The chosen four ran after him to the shadow of an abandoned hopper car. From there, their tattooed guide motioned for the second four to scurry over. Jaime squeezed Ángela's hand and they dashed to the open-topped hopper, keeping close to the ground with their heads scrunched between their shoulders like turtles.

Between the train wheels they saw the legs of a uni-formed man pass in front of the hopper. His boots shuffled on the ground as if he were bored and looking forward to the end of his shift. Any second he would check behind and underneath the train car and see them all.

Ángela linked her elbow through Jaime's and kept him tight to her side. If Miguel had been there, he would have thought of some way to distract the guard because Miguel always knew what to do, how to solve problems.

The sound of a match being lit hit their ears, followed by the unmistakable smell of a cigarette. The armed man seemed to forget he hadn't surveyed the shadows in the hopper behind him as he should have. Jaime couldn't help but wonder if Miguel was somehow responsible for the distraction. Just thinking of his cousin made him feel braver. *Querido Miguel*, he prayed like he had on the bus. *Please help us stay safe.*

Their leader wasted no time and had them sprinting across an open stretch to the next shadow-concealing car. With Jaime still linked to his cousin, this run was awkward, like they were newborn calves. Jaime kept his eyes on the ground and repeated inside his head, *If I can't see them, they can't see me. If I can't see them, they can't see me.* Miguel, the scientist, would have teased Jaime for his superstitious belief. Another warming thought.

Men shouted and a gun fired. Jaime and Ángela sprinted with all their might, their steps falling in sync. It wasn't until they were once again crouched in the shadows of a train car, shaking like a bowl of *gelatina*, that Jaime realized the gunshot had been fired somewhere else in the train yard.

"*Adentro.*" Their guide ordered them inside a boxcar attached to many other cargo cars.

The opening was only about half a meter wide—a couple of men had to turn sideways to get in. Ángela pushed Jaime forward to go before her. The separation from his cousin almost made him cry out for her. Adrenaline from the gunshot still made his heart beat faster than ever. What if they took her away, didn't let her get on the train? He looked around the train car. In the darkness he couldn't see anything. He didn't know what kind of train ride he expected, but it hadn't been this. He choked down another cry.

Jaime crawled on his hands and knees until he felt another person and the corner of the metal enclosure. With his backpack against the metal wall, he hugged his knees as he stared at the opening. A figure that looked more like shadow came next. That couldn't be Ángela. Unless the shadow had already devoured her. *Where was she?* A high-pitched whine escaped his body. It had happened. What he feared more than dying. He was all alone and would never see his cousin again.

"Jaime," came a whisper.

"*Aquí,*" he replied. A second later the monstrous shadow crashed into him. He grabbed the hand, bringing it to his face. A faint smell of mangos and dog came from it. "Is that you?"

"*Claro*," said the voice he'd recognize anywhere. He expected her to tease him for freaking out and not being able to be alone for fifteen seconds, but she wrapped him in her arms and kissed the top of his head.

Outside, the streetlights had been scarce. Inside, the car was almost pitch-black except for the opening, which let in minimal light. People kept entering, more than the others who had been in the van with them. Sometimes seconds apart, other times at several-minute intervals. No one said anything other than the occasional hushed "*¡ay!*" when stepped on.

A couple of people began to snore. As tired as he was, Jaime kept his eyes on the opening. If one of the armed men poked his gun through, there'd be no hope for anyone.

With an eerie metallic shriek the door thundered closed. The clanging sound of a bar sliding across metal jerked the sleepers awake. Panic and adrenaline rose in Jaime. Some people screamed. He clung tighter to Ángela. They were locked in a pitch-black train car with no way of getting out, prisoners in their escape for freedom.

CHAPTER THIRTEEN

The train lurched and rattled as it pulled out of the rail yard. There were no seats to fall off, but everyone still bumped into one another as the train was set in motion.

"Help, help!"

"Get us out of here!"

Two people screamed and banged on the locked sliding door. The children who had been in the van with their mamá started crying again.

"Shut up, fools. Do you want to get us all deported?" warned a voice low and deep in the car. Jaime recognized the voice as the man with the bandanna. The children and one of the other voices quieted down.

The other man continued his hysteria. "I don't care. Anything is better than dying here."

The sound of a body being knocked into the metal wall shook the whole car. There was a whimper, and the deep bandanna voice once again cautioned, "The more you scream, the more oxygen you're using, and the quicker we all die. Everyone shut up."

No one said anything, but a murmur passed through the car. This was it. This would be how they ended their journey. So much for the first-class cabin with comfy seats and AC. They were no better off than cattle going off to be slaughtered. Except maybe cattle cars had more ventilation. Jaime wondered how long they had, how much oxygen was left in the car. If only Miguel were here. He was the one good at math and science. He would know how much time they had left.

Not that it mattered, Jaime supposed, as he shifted his backpack to a more comfortable position and leaned into Ángela. The lurching of the train was surprisingly soothing. If they had ten minutes, or ten hours, dead was dead.

Jaime woke up slowly. Information entered his brain in incoherent bursts. Math. His sketchbook. The smell of dog. Gunshots. A rocking motion. Dead.

For a few moments he wondered if this was what it was like to find himself in Heaven. He tried to look around but couldn't see anything. Then he opened his eyes.

The freight car was dark, but it wasn't pitch-black

anymore. He could just make out shapes and mounds of people, but nothing that would identify one from the other. He knew Ángela was still next to him only because he would have felt her move if she had. A few pinpricked holes where rust had eaten away the metal sprinkled the car with sunlight like a disco ball. A thin gap between the floor and the sliding metal door also provided faint light from under the train. The ventilation these holes provided was minimal, and with all the people crammed inside, it was stuffy. The rising heat in the car didn't help.

Jaime shifted and rotated his stiff neck. Just above his head was one of the pinprick ventilation holes. He raised himself to kneeling to peer out. Between the tiny hole and the speed of the train, he could see nothing but rushing shades of green with an occasional bit of gray. Squinting through such a tiny hole gave him a headache, and he raised his nose to the opening instead. A tiny stream of fresh air tickled him, and he had to turn away to keep from sneezing. Next to him the bundle that was Ángela moved her head from one side to the other but didn't wake up.

His stomach grumbled, but he ignored it. Better wait until Ángela awoke and they could eat together. Thank goodness they still had a couple tamales and mangos that Abuela had packed for them.

He settled back down against the metal frame and pulled out his sketchbook and one of his remaining good pencils. He opened the book toward the back, where he knew there were blank pages. He couldn't see the paper, much less the lead lines, but it was an experiment, a new stretch of his artistic abilities. Besides, there was nothing else to do aboard the train.

In his mind he imagined what each gesture of the pencil created on the page and a couple times turned the pencil over to erase what he'd drawn, or thought he'd drawn. He could only go by feel and sense, and more than anything, guess. Still, he enjoyed the challenge of this new drawing style. It made him pay attention to his sketch in new ways. If he ever saw sunlight again, he'd be interested to see how it all turned out, how abstract it would be: the drawing of people huddled and trapped in a dark train car with nothing but minuscule disco lights to ventilate and show the way.

He was just adding texture to what he hoped were the ridges of the metal walls above the huddled bundles when someone made the first comment of the morning.

"Mamá, I need to go pee-pee," said one of the children, the girl.

Everyone began shuffling, waking those who were asleep. People stood and ran their hands along the walls as if searching for some compartment no one had found yet. Of course, there was nothing. Padre Kevin had said there were no toilets, had insisted, several times, that they use the bathroom before boarding the train. Other than the strip where the door didn't quite reach the floor, there were no holes by their feet.

"Can you hold it?" the mamá said.

"No."

"Then go along that crack by the door. We could be here for a while."

People shifted again, and those who had been strategically placed near the opening grumbled at having to give up their prime airy real estate.

"Great, now any fresh air we get will reek of urine," vibrated the deep bandanna voice from last night.

It didn't. At least not right away. Jaime and Ángela got through a shared tamale and mango, eating the peel and sucking the juice from the large center stone, which kept the stuffy air pleasant instead of foul. Someone on the train ate an orange, another some kind of cured meat like chorizo.

"Excuse me, *señor*." The little girl tapped Jaime on the leg. "Can we have the mango once you're done?"

It felt like a stone the size of the mango's center lodged in Jaime's throat. There was no juice left on their mango. He and Miguel used to compete to see who could leave a mango stone drier; Jaime usually won. Except now. This *niñita* obviously needed that extra juice more than he did.

"This banana leaf has some *masa* stuck to it. You can

have that, *mamita*." Ángela offered their tamale wrapper and then, as an afterthought, one of Abuela's tortillas.

"You might as well take the rest of this orange, too," grumbled the bandanna man. "It's too sour for my taste."

A few other people offered to share what little food they had with the children. Their mamá kept thanking and blessing everyone. It was hard to tell with the minimal light, but Jaime was pretty sure she didn't take any food for herself.

"*Oye.*" Jaime spoke in a more optimistic, cheery voice than he felt as an attempt to distract them from their hunger. "Do you know this tongue twister? I bet you can't say it really fast, *un tigre, dos tigres, tres tigres.* Try it."

The two children, and then soon the whole train, joined in with the tongue twisters. The little girl, Eva, was particularly good while her older brother, Ivan, kept laughing trying to say, *Pancha plancha con cuatro planchas.*

The tongue twisters lightened the mood until the train abrubtly stopped. Everyone turned to stare at the door, waiting to see if it would open. It didn't, and after a while the train lunged back into motion, making its way north and west. Everyone in their car let out a massive sigh, of disappointment the door hadn't opened, of relief that they hadn't been caught. This happened again the next time the train stopped, and again, and again, until Jaime lost count of how many stops they'd made.

A couple times Jaime thought of Xavi, Rafa, and Joaquín, as well as some of the other boys who'd played *fútbol* with them, wondering where they were and if they were okay. Back in the train yard he'd prayed for Miguel's protection. He didn't know if he was allowed to ask Miguel to look out for their friends as well. It couldn't hurt.

"Do you remember the time Mamá was cooling a hot iron on the bed?" The tongue twister of *Pancha plancha* beat like a mantra in Jaime's already pounding head. The train car seemed to be getting hotter by the second. "She warned us to be careful."

Ángela let out a breath that might have been a giggle. "But Miguel jumped on the bed a second later, and landed smack on the hot iron."

"He said later that the bed looked so soft, he forgot all about the warning and didn't see the iron." Jaime smiled at the thought of his cousin. Oh, Miguel.

"He had the burn mark for months," Ángela remembered.

"But he still kept jumping on the bed whenever he came over." Jaime struggled to take a few deep breaths. The train car was getting stuffier. "I really miss him."

"Me too." Ángela sighed before wrapping an arm around Jaime's shoulders and planting a kiss on the back of his head, not knowing where his face was in the dark.

The smell really got bad when one of the older men

followed the little girl's example and used the space between the floor and door as a bathroom as well. It didn't help that the temperature was getting hotter, and soon everyone was sweating.

The side walls became too hot to lean against, and everyone was forced to huddle in the middle of the car, touching the people next to them, which in turn created more body heat. The man next to Jaime smelled particularly ripe. Jaime drank some water, aware that the more he drank, the less he'd have for later and the more likely he'd need to use the designated pee spot. Still, he drained half the bottle without realizing it. He'd never been so hot. He took off his shirt and wanted to remove his jeans, which stuck to his legs, but he didn't dare. Not when there was so much money sewed into them, not in such a dark car where he'd never be able to find them again.

"Keep your shoes on as well," Ángela whispered in his ear so softly, the people next to him wouldn't have heard.

"*¿Por qué?*"

Ángela hesitated, as if she were looking around to see if anyone was watching and listening. Impossible to tell in the speckled darkness. "It's something César said at the church. If anything happens, and you need to run, it's the people without shoes who are more likely to get caught."

Others on the train hadn't heard César's advice; foot

stench added to the bouquet of odors. Not that Jaime wanted to add to the bad smell, but it sure would feel nice to air out his feet. "We don't need to worry about that in here. No one's going anywhere."

"Still doesn't mean we can trust them. We don't even know what most of them look like."

Jaime glanced at the closed door. If . . . *when* someone finally opened it, there'd be no place to run, no way to escape. But he supposed Ángela had a point. It would take a few seconds to put his shoes back on and a few seconds could make all the difference. He couldn't risk losing his shoes anymore than he could risk losing his jeans.

He wished he could trust these people. They were all on the same journey—they should help each other, especially seeing as they were locked in the train car together. Sure, there was a moment of bonding with the tongue twisters and giving the kids scraps of food. But when it came down to it, they were only going to look after themselves. And anything that could help them get ahead could be used. Even shoes.

He used his shirt to mop the sweat from his face and then flapped it in front of him to shift the air. It didn't do any good. The temperature in the car kept rising.

"It's like an oven in here. We're being cooked alive!" The same voice that had complained last night started yelling and banging on the door. Once again the train had made a stop, but there was no telling where they were.

Rattles and clanks came from outside. The boxcar shifted and bumped, making the screaming people yell louder. Jaime wondered whether anyone outside could even hear them.

Others joined in the banging, desperate to get anyone's attention. A few even put their mouths near the gap under the door that had become the urinal to shout. This time, the deep-voiced man didn't try to stop them. Jaime thought about joining the shouting party—more voices would make it louder—but he didn't have the energy to get up, and forget about shouting. Much easier to stay in the center of the car with his shirt pressed against his face. There was still the faintest smell of home from the soap his mamá used.

I wonder, Jaime thought, though even that required more concentration than normal, *if we're in Medias Aguas.* That would explain the clangs and shrieks of metal against metal if their car was being detached and reattached. Or it could be monsters, he supposed. Monsters taking over the train. *I wonder what they look like . . .*

With a lunge the train was back on its way and the yellers settled down, crying and whimpering that they couldn't stand it anymore and hoped death would come quickly.

"Mamá, are we going to die?" asked Eva.

Jaime expected her to say, "Of course not." Instead the mamá took a deep breath.

"That's up to God to decide. He chooses who joins Him. But whatever happens, you're going to be in good hands, either mine or God's." She began singing some hymns. Others joined her in jagged breaths—no one seemed to have enough oxygen to carry a proper melody.

Jaime reached for Ángela's hand, though both his and hers were hot and sticky. He wanted to ask her the same question the little girl had asked but didn't want to hear the answer. The heat was so intense, like being in a car left in the hot sun and not being able to open a window. His brain was growing fuzzy and pounding with a headache. The dark shapes shifted side to side like they were on a boat instead of a train.

"I feel sick," he muttered to himself, but his cousin heard.

"Drink, eat." Ángela handed him the water bottle and the last mango. "You're dehydrated."

He did as he was told, finishing the water and biting into the skin of the mango to suck some of the juice. The world began to make sense again. It was still stifling hot, but at least now he didn't seem so loopy and out of it. He handed the remaining mango half to his cousin.

"No, you eat it," she said.

Jaime shook his head before realizing she couldn't see him. "No, we both need it."

She took it and finished it off but left the stone with the little juice that remained for Eva and Ivan. The hymns had stopped, the effort too much in the hot, poorly ventilated air. Maybe he should pull out the sketchbook again and have another blind attempt at drawing. Except with the heat, the pages would get moist and be prone to tearing. Besides, he didn't think he could focus well enough on the page without being able to see to make the drawing even remotely good. He would have to distract himself from the heat by thinking of other things.

"Are you scared to die?" he asked in a whisper. He didn't have the strength to be angry or upset that their parents' sacrifice to get them out of Guatemala had been for nothing.

"No." Ángela spoke with the same tiredness. "More like disappointed. There's a lot I'd still like to do."

"Like what?"

"Little things. Play the role of Julieta in front of an audience. Get old. Have children. See and eat snow. What about you?"

Jaime thought about that for a while. He knew he had future plans, something about art and museums and maybe university, but in the heat couldn't think of what they were. "I want to see and eat snow too, but I am scared to die."

"You shouldn't be. Miguel wasn't. He can take care of you."

Part of Jaime wanted to say he didn't need anyone to take care of him, but, oh, how great it would be to see Miguel again. "I wish Miguel were here. I wish we could have left before he was killed."

"Me too."

But then Miguel would be in the oven train, cooking along with them, and Jaime didn't want that. Not for his cousin who'd suffered enough anyway. He wondered how long it had taken for life to leave Miguel's body. How much pain he was in before he couldn't take it anymore. Jaime supposed if he had to choose between being beaten to death and being cooked alive, he'd rather go like this. At least on the train he wouldn't have to go through so much pain. He hoped.

"If I die," Ángela rasped, but Jaime cut her off before she could continue.

"You won't." If she died, they both died—he wouldn't be able to continue without her.

Ángela hugged him. Even though the body heat made the temperature more unbearable, breaking away from her grasp was the last thing on his mind. It was several minutes before she seemed to gain enough strength, or breath, to continue.

"If I die, at least I'm with family and not alone."

Neither said anything else, but they both thought it. Miguel had died alone.

CHAPTER FOURTEEN

There were no more disco lights dancing in the train car when Jaime opened his eyes again. *It must be nighttime.* He wasn't sure if he had fallen asleep or fainted from the heat. Had no way of knowing how long they'd been in this cage. The last thing he remembered was finding it hard to focus and wondering if he would ever stop sweating.

He wasn't sweating now. In fact, he felt a bit chilly, even in the boxcar's stuffy air. He found a shirt he hoped was his and put it on. The faint smell of Mamá's soap embraced him.

"Jaime?" Ángela got up next to him.

"*Sí, soy yo.*"

"Good." She made stretching moans and scooted back to lean against the metal side, which had cooled down to the point it no longer burned to touch it. "Hungry?"

"How much longer are we in here for?"

"No clue, but the food won't last another day, if it hasn't rotted already."

They didn't have much left. One tamale and a couple of Abuela's tortillas, which tasted a bit off. If he could see them, he wouldn't be surprised if they had green spots. But since he couldn't see the spots, he pretended he couldn't taste them. In terms of food, they had nothing else. If they got off the train, alive, how easy would it be to get? The safe-house in Lechería would probably provide them with something while they were there, but what about after?

Others in the boxcar began shuffling around, waking up from the heat-induced slumber. Plastic bags rumpled, zippers unzipped, and water bottles crackled as people dug into their limited food stores. But the noises didn't last long. Most people, it seemed, had little food left, if any.

"Mamá, I think this man is dead," the little girl said.

A hush swept through the train, as if someone had turned off the sound to everyone's voices.

"Where is he?" the deep-voiced bandanna man grumbled.

"*Aquí*," Eva said, her voice high and squeaky in comparison.

Everyone kept quiet as the man went to the fallen body's side.

A slap across the face rang in the train car, and a few

seconds later the bandanna man grumbled again. "I can feel a pulse, but only barely. I think he got heat stroke. Anyone have some water left?"

Jaime shook his plastic water bottle. Nothing. Next to him he heard Ángela going through the same motions; hers was empty as well. Other people shuffled through their belongings and said no, but some said nothing. Jaime knew they were saving it for themselves.

When no one volunteered any water, the unconscious man was moved and everyone kept their distance. If the intense heat hadn't drained everyone's energy, Jaime might have worried about a fight breaking out, or at least someone stealing any remaining water. But just breathing seemed to be all everyone could manage. Every so often the deep-voiced man went over to the body and responded each time with the same phrase, "Still with us."

Jaime opened his eyes again when the train rocked side to side as it switched tracks and slowed down.

Just another stop in this endless journey, he told himself. He tried to shift himself into a more comfortable position—after all, there wasn't much else to do but sleep, and it did pass the time quicker. Instead he woke up completely. It was night again, or maybe still, and he found himself staring at the flickering exterior lights on the metal walls.

The sound of metal clanking against metal woke everyone up. Cars were being removed or added to the train. Faint voices yelled indistinguishable orders. Jaime refused to get his hopes up. Were they? Could they—

They had stopped for hours, it seemed, before the metal bar screeched and clanged as it slid across the train car door. A second later the bright light almost blinded them, and the freshest, sweetest air filled the dark and suffocating boxcar as the door opened several meters wide.

"*¡Sálganse!*" A voice ordered them to get out.

Everyone bumped into one another as they stood on weak legs, still blind from the sudden light.

Jaime blinked several times. With each bat of his eyes his vision cleared. Then he wished he were still blind.

The light came from a streetlamp, and it shined on an immigration officer standing outside the train. Ammunition crossed his chest like an X, and he pointed his automatic rifle into the car.

It was the first time Jaime got a look at the people who shared the car with him. Those who had ridden in the van with him from Padre Kevin's were all there, as well as twenty others he didn't recognize. The looks of surprise and confusion quickly changed to fear as they realized the nightmare of being captured was real. Ivan stared at the officer in awe, while Eva clung tightly to her mamá's hand and her pink blankie scrap. At least they weren't crying.

"I said, get out," he repeated with a wave of his gun.

Backpacks in place and hands clasped, Jaime and Ángela slipped past the officer and out of the train car along with everyone else. The ankle he had banged in the van gave only the slightest complaint. More pressing things were on his mind. Like how badly the officers would beat them up before returning them to Guatemala. Whether he and Ángela would try to make the journey again and how many times they'd have to attempt it before reaching Tomás, or whether they would give up, return to their families, and accept the punishment the Alphas would give them for fleeing the gang.

The officer leaned into the empty train car to poke the fainted man with his gun. "What's with him? Is he dead?"

As if it were planned, all the passengers broke into a mad run and split in every different direction. Ángela and Jaime took off through the train yard, dodging cars and going over the hitches. Shouts and gunshots rang out. Two men unloading cargo stopped to stare at them, but they neither helped nor hindered the escape. A flash of pink caught Jaime's eye. An officer had caught Eva and Ivan's mamá, the scrap that remained of Eva's blankie flapped in the dim light. In the split second it took for Jaime to wonder how he could help them, the officer let them go and jogged with his gun outstretched in a completely different direction. The pink scrap disappeared into the night.

Jaime smiled for a second—*So there were some merciful*

migra *officers*. The cousins jumped over tracks laden with trash and junk before running out into the dark streets. After a few turns they looked over their shoulders. No one was following them. Their ribs heaved with exhaustion as they crouched in the shadow of a stoop and caught their breath.

Once calm, they met each other's eyes. All their adrenaline and nerves exploded and they clung to each other, crying and laughing—even though there was nothing funny about what had happened.

Ángela rested her hand against her chest. "It's great feeling my heart pumping."

"Like being alive," Jaime agreed. Between the scorching train and the armed officer, it was a miracle they were.

"But let's not do it again anytime soon."

"If Rafa were here, he'd say that was fun," Jaime said as he straightened up.

"Crazy," she said with a shake of her head. "We are in Lechería, not Medias Aguas, right?"

"Lechería," he confirmed. They were in a bourough of Mexico City, the capital, halfway through México. Halfway. He smiled and pointed in the direction they had come from. "I saw some signs at the rail yard while we were running from the officer."

"Let's find this safe-house and meet up with the others." Thanks to Ángela making them memorize the safe-houses back at Padre Kevin's, and the maps in Jaime's sketchbook, they found the low-roofed, cinderblock house much easier than they had found Padre Kevin's Iglesia de Santo Domingo. Except this safe-house was closed. Boards covered the windows and garbage wedged between a wrought-iron gate and the locked front door. They tried the gate and the windows: there was no secret entrance. No notice saying where a different safe house could be found. Nothing except a lot of graffiti on the walls, most of it bad words, and all of it directed to *centro americano* scum.

The dryness of Jaime's throat scratched as he swallowed hard. No point in whining about how much he had been counting on some water and food; Ángela must have felt the same. Jaime wondered if now would justify using some of the money in their jeans that Tía had said to keep for absolute emergencies. He supposed not. It didn't matter anyway—no store was open.

They waited a bit in hopes that their friends would appear. This was where, after all their careful do-not-get-caught planning, they had agreed to meet. But they saw no one.

"I don't think they're coming tonight." Jaime bit his lip, trying to remain optimistic. "Maybe they were left behind in Medias Aguas."

Ángela's face pinched with worry, but her tone forced optimism. "You're right, and we shouldn't stay here much longer. We're too exposed."

Jaime agreed with a kick at some garbage on the street. He wanted to wait longer, just in case their friends showed up. But whatever, or whoever, caused the safe house to close could come back. What should they do? Where should they go? The plan B they had arranged was to wait a couple days at the safe house if the others were delayed. They hadn't thought of an alternate plan for a closed safe house.

Where were their friends now? Still in Arriaga, not having been able to get on the train? Waiting for them in Medias Aguas? In a white van driving them back to the Guatemalan border? Images of plastic men toppling off toy trains filled Jaime's head. Except the plastic men had faces of real boys. He'd been stupid to hope he'd ever see them again.

From one street over came the roar of drunken men yelling into the night. The hairs on the back of Jaime's neck rose. He grabbed Ángela's hand. Neither one needed any further encouragement to get out of there, and fast.

"Should we go back to the train yard? Don't we have another train to take us to Ciudad Juárez?" He hated the idea of going back where the armed officers were and hated even more the idea of getting locked in another sweltering train car, but anything was better than standing outside a safe-house that was no longer safe. Right?

"Maybe we should skirt around the station. Ask where

we can find Santos," Ángela said, and continued hurrying back the way they came, away from the roar of drunken men.

Jaime looked at the sky. Light pollution and cloud cover prevented him from seeing the stars. The sun hadn't even started to come up. "It's probably safer to do that during the day, don't you think? To scope out the area and find the smuggler?"

The shatter of breaking glass and a few seconds later police sirens made them walk faster.

"But where are we going to spend the night?" Ángela asked.

That was the ultimate question. The neighborhood they were in was definitely poor. Tiny houses needed more than paint to make them look nice. The windows that didn't have bars were too small to fit even a small kid. The few cars parked on the side of the streets were old. Jaime doubted anyone would let them stay in their house, or even patio. Especially after being woken up in the middle of the night. There were trees, but none of them were big enough to climb for shelter. Lechería wasn't one of the safest places to be.

Still, there had to be someplace, somewhere, that would be safe for the night. His eyes landed on a small white car with more rust than paint parked along the side of the road. Usually it was Miguel who paid attention to cars, but this one made Jaime give it a second look. He grabbed Ángela's elbow to stop her. "Do you think you can fit under this car?"

Ángela crouched down to peer at it. The distance between the street and the frame wasn't much more than mid-leg. "Barely. But what if the owners start it up?"

Jaime pointed at the dirt and trash wedged between the wheels and the curb. "It hasn't been driven in a while. A few weeks at least, probably more."

"I guess it'll have to do." Ángela removed her bag from her back and pushed it under the old car. She got on her stomach and scooted herself under. Jaime did the same behind her. His empty stomach moaned as he lay on top of it. The street underneath the car was covered in dirt and debris with a few wrappers and cigarette butts mixed in. The tangy smell of some kind of engine fluid rose from the spot under the hood. A bang on the backside of his skull reminded him he couldn't raise his head more than a few centimeters.

One hand on his bag, and the other curled around Ángela's, he felt strangely secure and relaxed in this dirty little car cave.

CHAPTER FIFTEEN

A scuffling whine caused Jaime to open his eyes. A black nose followed by a white-and-brown, one-eared head poked through the debris to sniff under the car.

"Vida!" Jaime cried as he grabbed his bag and wormed his way out. A bump and a moan came from Ángela as she banged her head, having forgotten the low clearance. The rescued dog wiggled in delight as she gave first Jaime, then Ángela, a thorough facial bath.

There they were, their friends, alive, but looking different from how they had at Padre Kevin's. All three of them were a darker brown than they had been. Scratches, bites, and burns covered their arms, and their clothes were dirty and ripped. But on each of their faces, including the dog's, was a smile wide enough to make it all seem worth it.

"You're here, you made it! How did you find us?" Ángela threw herself into Xavi's arms and cried into his shoulder. Xavi held out an arm and Jaime joined the group hug. When they let go, some of the dirt from underneath the car stuck to Xavi's no-longer-white uniform shirt.

Not that the dirt stopped Joaquín. The younger boy jumped into Ángela's arms and clung to her like a baby. Rafa patted Jaime on the back and ruffled his hair.

Down by their feet Vida let out a happy yip. Jaime crouched down to her level. He was no veterinarian, but the stitches sewing up her belly seemed to be working. The flesh wasn't as red as it had been, and the skin looked like it was healing.

"Vida was the one that found you," Xavi said, still grinning.

"*¿Cómo?*" Ángela gently removed Joaquín's arms from around her neck and let him grip her hand instead. She glared at the dog as if she still had mixed feelings about her, especially after the cleaning the mutt had given Ángela's face. Vida ignored the glare and thumped her tail.

"We went to the safe house," Xavi started, and everyone else continued talking at once too.

"Even though we heard it had been closed," Rafa butted in.

"We had to meet you," Joaquín whispered.

"But you weren't there," Xavi continued.

"We were, for a bit," Jaime said.

Xavi nodded. "We know, we—"

"We had to get off the train a few kilometers from Lechería. This place is swarming with *migra* officers," Rafa bragged, as if proud of their clever escape.

"We know." Ángela smiled.

Joaquín nodded to the dog. "Vida warned us."

"By the time we got to the safe house, you must have left," Xavi said. "We climbed onto the roof and slept there just in case you'd come back."

"We should have thought of that," Jaime told his cousin.

"I missed you." Joaquín clung tighter to Ángela.

"This morning Vida started sniffing around the sidewalk," Xavi went on.

"I thought she had to take a dump," Rafa joked.

Xavi shook his head. "She must have remembered your scent and followed it. When we got to this street, she dashed to the car. Seconds later you guys crawled out."

The wide grins returned to all their faces.

Jaime bent down to scratch Vida's one ear. He knew dogs were smart, but she had only known them for a day and still remembered them, her pack, after that long train ride. Her family.

Ángela leaned over to pet her too. "*Gracias, mamita.*"

They started walking through the streets of Lechería, where children in white uniform shirts headed to school and old women pushed shopping trolleys filled with groceries. The boys had heard from others on the train that there was a bridge where they could get information for the next stretch of their journey. Vida trotted between their legs, eating scraps she found along the street littered with trash and leaves, never straying more than a few meters away even though they didn't have a rope to keep her close. If it weren't for the blue thread peeking out from her coat, no one would guess she had undergone "surgery" just a few days ago.

Joaquín, who had not let go of Ángela since he dived into her arms, swung the hand that held hers. "Are you hungry?" he asked.

Ángela smiled down at the young boy. "A bit."

A bit? They were starving. At least Jaime was, now that Joaquín had reminded him. Yesterday's food on the train hadn't been enough for one meal, let alone the whole day. His throat was parched from the train, not to mention all the dust under the car.

The three boys grinned at one another like they had a secret. That's when Jaime noticed a plastic bag swinging from Rafa's hand.

"Where'd you get that?" Jaime asked.

"You were right, Ángela," Xavi said with a teasing smile. "It is beautiful in Veracruz."

"The people that live there are poor but so nice. They

kept throwing us food. Like that cartoon where food comes from the sky," Rafa said.

Jaime's nose scrunched up as anger built up inside. The boys had ridden on top of the freight train illegally and had gotten free food thrown at them while he and Ángela had paid a lot of money to almost get cooked alive? How could that be?

But his jealousy quickly faded when Rafa placed a fat doughnut filled with sweet potato into his grimy hand. He downed it in two bites before swigging the water Xavi held out. Never had he tasted anything so wonderful in his life. A banana and a small piece of meat later and it was like a black cloud lifted from his body. If only he could wash his face and hands, he'd be back to feeling human again.

The bridge wasn't far and they got there around mid-morning. Cars roared above them while slower traffic crossed underneath the bridge. The stench of urine mixed with car exhaust dominated the area. At first it looked like no one was there. Then Jaime noticed a cloud of cigarette smoke coming from the gap between the bridge and the sloping support beam. He peered closer and saw a figure propped against the concrete.

"What do you *patojos* want?" a man demanded. His voice wheezed, but the accent still sounded Guatemalan.

"Excuse us, *señor*," Xavi said. "We were hoping for some information on the next train north."

The man took a last drag from his cigarette and flicked the butt in their direction. "What will you give me?"

They all looked at one another. Jaime didn't want to give up the twelve pesos he had earned on the bus. This man didn't seem like the kind who would take a drawing as payment.

"We have two sugar doughnuts," Xavi said, ignoring the scolding look that Rafa sent him.

"Bring them here."

Xavi took the plastic bag with the doughnuts and walked up the steep underside of the concrete bridge to give them to the smoker while the rest waited below near the road. The man gobbled one up and set the bag with the other by his legs.

That's when Jaime realized both of the man's legs ended at the knees in dark stumps. Joaquín took a sharp breath and Rafa looked like he was about to ask what happened, but Ángela nudged him to be quiet.

"A bit stale," the man complained as he brushed the sugar from his mustache and beard, but then reached for the second doughnut. "So, first thing you need to know is that it's almost impossible to get on the train here in Lechería; security is very tight. You're better off boarding near Huehuetoca, twenty-four kilometers away. The train won't stop, but it slows down enough to jump on board."

Jaime blinked. Twenty-four kilometers? He'd never

walked that far. That would easily take all day, maybe part of the night, too.

"Can you tell us how to find Santos?" Ángela said.

The man pressed against the concrete underneath him to change into a better position. He grabbed one thigh and then the other to shift them a bit. "Do you have any more doughnuts?"

Xavi shook his head. "Those were our last ones."

"*Que pena.*" He acted like he wouldn't say anything else without another bribe, but he lit a new cigarette and blew the smoke in their direction. "There is no more Santos. They killed him two days ago."

Sadness for a man he'd never met filled Jaime. Or maybe it was selfishness, disappointment. How much money had his parents lost in that transaction? But at least they hadn't paid him for the whole journey. Maybe they could use the money that had been meant for Santos to pay someone else. The possibility of being cooked alive in another boxcar did not appeal to him, but neither did riding on top of the train.

Xavi sent a sympathetic nod in his direction. "We're sorry to hear that. Thank you for letting us know."

"How shocking. A *guanaco* with manners."

Jaime shifted uneasily. While Guatemalans didn't mind being called *chapín*, to call a Salvadoran a *guanaco* was insulting. Especially after they had given him two perfectly good doughnuts.

Xavi, however, didn't let the insult bother him. "You still haven't answered my first question. When's the next train?"

"Where are you going?"

Xavi stepped back as he lost some of his composure. "Excuse me? We're all heading north. To los Estados Unidos."

"I know that, *guanaco imbécil*," he snapped, flicking ash at Xavi. "But from here the trains go in four different directions."

"Ciudad Juárez," Ángela said quickly to keep peace.

"Mexicalli," Joaquín whispered.

"Whichever is shorter," Rafa said.

Xavi, Jaime noticed, didn't mention a destination.

The man swore and took another drag from his cigarette. "*Típico*. Nuevo Laredo is the next train and the shortest journey. That train comes tomorrow night. Mexicalli the following morning, Ciudad Juárez that afternoon. Sure you have nothing else to eat?"

Xavi dug into his pocket and tossed a hardened *caramelo* his way. The man caught it with one swift gesture.

"Follow this road up toward Huehuetoca until you get to the third bridge. If you get there before sunset, volunteers drive by with a food wagon. The food tastes like sewage, but it's edible. Tell Olga she better bring me a plate."

"Thanks again." Xavi ran down the steep concrete to the road, where the others were waiting.

They hadn't gone far when the legless man shouted out his last piece of advice. "If you don't want to end up like me, you'll watch out for the train wheels!"

CHAPTER SIXTEEN

It didn't take long to get to the third bridge. Instead of waiting around doing nothing until the food van came, Xavi decided to try to find some work at the nearby *mercado*. His phone, the only thing he had owned, had been picked from his pocket on the train.

"I'm selling the charger, and it might be smart to get some food and water for the train as well. We can't count on people throwing us supplies again."

Jaime remembered the hunger and thirst from his train ride. Working to pick up some extra supplies was a good idea. The money to pay Santos remained sewed in their jeans; Tía's instructions to save it echoed in Jaime's mind.

Hundreds of stalls crammed into a warehouse building that made up the *mercado*. With no straight aisles, the place was like a labyrinth of tables and displays. Fruits and vegetables of every color and degree of ripeness crowded tables. Handmade shirts waved next to a cobbler measuring an old man's foot. Pirated DVDs turned on wobbly stands.

Most of the vendors in the *mercado*, however, didn't have enough money, let alone work, to spare. Others swore and told them to go back home.

A man held his shoe up in the air as if he were going to hit them with it. "Get lost, *desgraciados*, before I call *la migra* to kick your scrawny butts."

Rafa turned to tell the man off, but Xavi grabbed him by the shirt and they scurried away. As hard as it might be for *la migra* to catch them with all the people milling about, there was no point in looking for trouble. They were a bit more cautious, and polite, when asking the next vendors for work.

"*Ven chico*," one man with a gray ponytail called out to Jaime. "You can help us unload the fruit from the truck."

Jaime agreed by lifting one of the boxes the man indicated, staggering under the weight. Still, it was a job, and this man was the nicest anyone at the *mercado* had been. Two stalls away, Ángela hacked away at pineapples to sell in chunks for a woman who looked about a hundred years old. Around the corner Joaquín scrubbed clean the cages holding live chickens. The other two had disappeared with Vida into the crowded marketplace, still looking for work; the merchants seemed more willing to trust girls and younger boys than teenagers.

After an hour carrying heavy boxes, the gray-ponytail man gave Jaime two overripe, squashed papayas and a pat on the back. Better than nothing, he supposed.

On the table at the other side of Ángela, a woman with more gums than teeth sold *turrón* made with almonds, sugar, and egg whites. Jaime spent ten minutes haggling the price of a broken piece and a water bottle with the twelve pesos he'd earned on the bus.

Xavi, Ángela, and Joaquín didn't fare much better. As they got ready to leave the *mercado* an hour before sunset, they collectively had four cracked raw eggs, some broken tortillas, a slab of lard, and a handful of overripe fruit, all of which they put in Ángela's backpack. Vida had dodged kick threats but made out with a pretty full belly. Jaime didn't want to know what she'd found along the market floor, but at least she seemed happy.

They waited for Rafa at a busy street corner near one of the entrances to the *mercado*, where the smell of pork rotating on a spit had their mouths watering.

"Every year for my birthday," Jaime said with eyes closed to savor the moment, "Mamá makes the best pineapple pork."

"Last year's was amazing," Ángela agreed. "Tía Lourdes brought up the pig and Miguel gave up, after two weeks of trying, to become a vegetarian. It was around that time Mamá tried to show me how to make her *flan de coco*, the best dessert on earth. I still can't make it like she does."

Ooh, what Jaime wouldn't give for some coconut custard right now. "I can't tell the difference."

Ángela nudged him with a smile before turning to Joaquín. "What about you, *papi*? What food do you miss?"

"Black beans with *tostones*," he said, referring to fried green plantains that Jaime liked as well. "But I'll never eat them again."

"Of course you will. We're all going to make it. You'll see." Ángela wrapped Joaquín in a hug and didn't see the young boy's dark eyes moistening. He said so little of his life, but Jaime wondered if maybe someone close to him used to make the beans and *tostones*, someone who might have died, or been killed.

"Well, my abuela," Xavi said to lighten the mood, "makes the absolute best *pupusas*. You know what they are?"

Joaquín nodded, but both Ángela and Jaime shook their heads.

"Fried corn *masa*, stuffed with meat, beans, and oozing with cheese—"

Jaime waved his arms in the air. "Okay, stop. You have even Vida drooling."

The mutt yipped at the sound of her name and sure enough, a wet drop marked the pavement below her open mouth. They had agreed to wait for Rafa before breaking into any of the food they'd been given, but if that boy didn't show up soon, they might as well forget about him.

A yell came from the market, and they all turned to see none other than Rafa zooming toward them.

"Go, go, *¡ándale!*" he screamed.

Jaime grabbed Ángela's hand and they took off with Xavi and Joaquín at their sides, Vida at their feet.

"Grab him!" an old man shouted after them. People stopped their shopping to look around, but Jaime couldn't hear anybody chasing them. After a few blocks he glanced over his shoulder. There was no one there. Hands on their knees, they caught their breath as they looked around. No one came after them.

"Well, that was fun." Rafa grinned while readjusting his ball cap. The others stared back at him, not grinning.

"What happened?" Xavi took a deep breath as if he didn't want to know the answer.

Rafa shrugged like it wasn't a big deal. "Old geezer didn't want to pay me after all the work I did, so I took these." He held out two packs of cigarettes.

Jaime and Joaquín jumped to Ángela's side as Xavi grabbed Rafa by the shirt and looked like he was about to beat him up.

"You almost got us caught for a couple stupid packs of cigarettes?"

"*Y chicle.*" Rafa showed them the fruity bubble gum he'd also stolen. "Want some?"

"*¡Idiota!*" Xavi let go of him and threw his arms in the air as he paced back and forth. "This is exactly why Mexicans hate us here. For stupid acts like that."

"He was trying to stiff me after I cleaned his display," Rafa insisted, but Xavi wasn't listening.

"I have not come all this way to get arrested over cigarettes." Xavi marched back to Rafa and pointed a finger in his face. "If you ever pull something like that again, you're going to wish you were back in Honduras."

"Fine, man. I'm sorry." For a moment Rafa looked scared, but then he smiled and waved his hand again. "Here, have some gum anyway."

Xavi swore, paced a bit more, and then sighed as he took a piece. Rafa then offered some to everyone else. Jaime didn't chew gum often and didn't realize how much he missed it. Sweet and fruity, it was like a *fiesta* in his mouth. He and Joaquín competed to see who could blow bigger bubbles. He didn't like that Rafa had stolen it, but since he had, there was no reason not to enjoy it.

"I didn't know you smoked," Jaime said as he tried to retract the bubble that had burst over his chin. They walked slowly back to the bridge, where they hoped the legless man was right about the food truck.

Rafa blew his own bubble and slipped it back in his

mouth so it'd pop inside. "I do sometimes, but that's not why I took them. They'll be good for bartering. For some people, cigarettes are more important than food."

Jaime didn't know what to say. For once, Rafa seemed to have a very practical idea.

There were about forty people huddled under the third bridge in small groups when they got back. Old, young, in between. Some were missing teeth or limbs. Some had gashes so deep or beatings so bad Jaime wondered if there was a doctor they could go see. One man had had all his clothes stolen hours before and sat naked, asking everyone who came if they had a spare pair of pants. It was like being surrounded by the homeless, which Jaime supposed they all were. From the sound of their accents there were a few southern Mexicans, but most were Central American from Guatemala, El Salvador, and Honduras; at least half of them had given up hope on ever getting to El Norte and had resolved to stay in Ciudad México or return home. The Promised Land, they decided, was a dream for other fools.

The food wagon was run by a local charity. It fed them mushy chicken-flavored rice with some beans mixed in, which was better than the legless man suggested, and powdered lemonade. After a few days of barely eating anything, Jaime liked the feeling of finally having a full stomach.

The five of them were tucked away where the

underside of the bridge met the concrete hill at the top of the bridge. Dirt had been hollowed out, giving them more cave than exposure. A good thing because many of the others under the bridge were getting drunk on cheap liquor or high on glue. So far, they were leaving Jaime and his friends alone. Jaime hoped Rafa wouldn't provoke anyone with his big mouth.

Light from a streetlamp shone enough for Jaime to sketch out their little group—Joaquín fast asleep with his head on Ángela's lap and his arm around Vida, who also had her head on Ángela; Ángela leaning against the concrete, her hand stroking Joaquín's hair; Rafa looking through a dirty magazine he found; Xavi lying down with his knees bent and arms behind his head. Jaime could hear him as he told Ángela about their experience on the train.

"We were lucky. The train kept stopping to load and unload cargo, or sometimes for security checkpoints. A lot of people would jump off when the train slowed down, not knowing what kind of danger was up ahead. Then after we passed the town or the checkpoint, new people would get on."

"But you didn't get off. Were people scared and jumping off for no reason?" Ángela asked.

Xavi took a while to answer. Jaime put down his sketchbook to stare at the older boy.

"No, there was a reason," he said to the concrete road

above his head. "Gangs run the tracks. *Migra* officers sometimes work with them. It was dark and we were either still in Chiapas or just into Oaxaca when twenty gang members got on board. They demanded money and threatened anyone who didn't pay up. One boy about Jaime's age insulted them. They caught him, threw him off the train, and shot him in the air like a pigeon. I don't even think they killed him. I imagine him lying helpless by the tracks, bleeding to death."

Ángela removed the hand that had been petting Joaquín's hair to place it on Xavi's shoulder. "You couldn't have done anything for him."

"I know, but he wasn't the only one. Another boy tried to get on board, slipped, and was gobbled up by the train in an instant. Didn't even derail the car." Xavi turned away from the underside of the bridge to roll over on his side, one hand holding up his head as the other took Ángela's hand. "I'm glad you weren't there. The gang was horrible to one girl. We kept hearing her screams. If we had tried to help her, they would have done the same to us. Joaquín didn't stop shaking for hours afterward. I don't think he's slept in days."

The young boy didn't even shift at the sound of his name. His breathing remained deep and steady as if he were on a feather mattress in a grand hotel instead of under a concrete bridge with a leg for a pillow.

"How did you three avoid the gangs?" Jaime asked softly, not sure if he wanted to know. He couldn't think of any explanation that didn't involve bribery or agreeing to join the gang themselves.

Again Xavi took a few seconds to respond, as if he wasn't sure he wanted to relive what happened. "I helped out César. Remember him from the *fútbol* games? He tripped trying to board the train, but somehow I caught him and got him on safely. He'd been on the trains six times already, but kept getting deported back to the Guatemalan border once he got farther north. One of those times he must have gotten friendly with the train gang; I didn't notice until we were riding with him that he had their tattoo of a bleeding heart on the underside of his wrist. The gang left him alone and because we were next to him, they left us alone too. With *la migra*, he pointed out where immigrants were hiding and gave them other information in exchange for our safety. I almost wish we had jumped off at each stop along with the rest of the people."

Ángela lifted Xavi's hand and shook it to show him she wasn't letting go. "But then we wouldn't have seen you again."

Xavi tried to smile but then shook his head no. He didn't release Ángela's hand either. "Back home I never would have associated with a bottom-feeder like that. Here

I hate feeling so helpless, like I have no choice. Is it worth going against your morals just to stay alive? I don't know."

While Ángela consoled Xavi, Jaime opened up his sketchbook and glanced through the pages. There were drawings of Miguel's funeral and the people on the bus. Of Ángela and Xavi dancing in front of the bonfire, and the blind sketches he'd done in the dark train car, slightly distorted and creepy with elongated skulls and askew mouths half on the face, half floating in the air beside the person. He went back to the beginning and found the drawings of his family—Papá, Mamá, Abuela, Miguel, Tíos Daniel and Rosario, Rosita with her baby, Quico. He missed them. Maybe he should have let the Alphas recruit him, just to see his family every day.

But then they would have made him someone he wasn't. And what would have happened if the Alphas had made him hurt someone he loved? Ángela, or another cousin. He wouldn't have been able to do it. Like Xavi, he could only hope that this whole journey would be worth it. He owed his family that much.

Whether it was the low growl from Vida or the click of a gun being cocked, the five woke up with a start from their puppy-pile sleeping arrangements.

Dawn wasn't too far off and the streetlight that shone into their bridge cave was still on. Jaime didn't need to blink for his eyes to register a teen with a shaved head holding a pistol at them.

"Good morning." He grinned as if he were holding out a cup of *café* instead of a pistol. He glared at them with red eyes that didn't seem to focus. "Which of you wants to do us a favor?"

No one said anything. Jaime held his breath, unable to move. It was like he was a clay model, waiting for a sculptor to mold him into shape. Even Miguel wouldn't know what to do.

The bald teen laughed and pointed the gun directly at Joaquín's head. "What about you, little boy. Don't you want to reach El Norte? We'll help you, if you help us."

Joaquín cowered but kept his wide eyes on the gun. Everyone did. The word "help" stabbed Jaime like a bad memory.

"What kind of favor are we talking about?" Rafa asked slowly. The gun shifted to him in an instant.

Jaime cringed. Couldn't Rafa for once just keep his mouth shut?

"Ah, a volunteer," the guy said with a cackle like an evil witch.

Rafa paled slightly but pretended to keep his cool. "No, just want more information."

The pistol waved up and down in Rafa's direction as if to remind him of what it could do. "Information is costly."

"Yeah, but if you kill me, who's going to do your favor?" Rafa crossed his arms over his chest.

Santa María, Madre de Dios. The prayer ran through Jaime's head. He wished he had the courage to cross himself before Rafa got them all killed.

Either the thug thought Rafa had made a valid point or he figured by holding the gun he had nothing to lose, but he went ahead and answered the question. "We have something we want you to carry over the border. You do that, and we get you across."

Rafa stroked the few hairs he had growing out of his chin as if he were mocking the gangster by pondering the proposal. *"Bueno,* I can be your mule."

"¡Rafa, no!" Ángela exclaimed through closed mouth. The gun shifted to her.

Jaime kept reciting Hail Mary in his head even though he was sure his heart had stopped. *Not Ángela, please not Ángela.* He hated to pick someone, but if he had to, better Rafa than any of the others. He was the one who had gotten them into this anyway. Or rather, he was the one who had volunteered to get them out of it.

"It'll be fun," Rafa said as he stood up. But behind his forced overconfidence, Jaime saw a scared boy who had left home because his mamá preferred to get drunk rather than feed her children.

"Yeah, fun." The thug smirked. He grabbed Rafa's arm

with one hand while still pointing the gun with the other. "Anyone else want to have some fun?"

They said nothing, and he shrugged. He pulled Rafa down the bridge, where they were met with another armed boy who had recruited a few other "volunteers."

Jaime sent another prayer, this one to San Francisco and Miguel. *Please take care of this crazy boy.*

"Send me a message on Facebook when you get there." Rafa waved his ball cap with one last attempt of his carefree tone. No one answered aloud, but said their good-byes and well wishes through thoughts and prayers.

Within seconds he was gone, and Jaime got the feeling they would never see or hear from him again. Instead he left behind a great act of chivalry and two packs of cigarettes.

CHAPTER SEVENTEEN

It took the whole day to walk to Huehuetoca. They left Lechería behind and followed the train tracks littered with plastic bags and scraps of clothes through boroughs and empty grasslands, then villages and a couple farms.

What started out as a nice warm day turned to light rain in the afternoon. Still they kept walking. Tired, Jaime dragged his feet, not paying attention to where he was going except that it was north. Always north. A few times a plastic bottle lined the tracks and he or Joaquín would kick it out of the way for something to break up the endless walking. A single tennis shoe lay on its side near the steel rail. Jaime swung his leg and gave the shoe a forceful punt.

The shoe was a lot heavier than he expected, and not just because it was waterlogged. It only traveled over the rail before rolling down the slope. When it stopped, it exposed a brown-and-red mass with a pale rod protruding from inside the shoe.

Jaime's stomach wrenched and Xavi's arm flew out to stop the others from getting closer. Too late. Everyone saw the mangled foot inside the shoe.

Vida crept forward to give it a sniff before Xavi uttered a reprimanding hiss and she returned to his side.

Not far from where the shoe had landed, two police officers with their backs toward them huddled around something in the tall grass near the tracks.

Xavi motioned them off the tracks, skirting through the undergrowth and mud to avoid attention. The officers' voices carried.

"Dead. *El tren se lo comió.*"

Jaime's stomach lurched some more. They were talking as if the train were alive, gobbling people up . . .

"Do you want me to look for the rest of the pieces?"

. . . and spitting them back out.

"No need. Stray dogs or birds will take care of him. But take a picture of the head to put up at the station, in case anyone comes looking for him. They never do, though."

Ángela seized Jaime and Joaquín's arms and hauled them away before any of them caught sight of something else they didn't want to see. Xavi paused to make the sign of the cross before catching up with them.

Jaime forced himself to take deep breaths.

Ever since the news of Miguel, Jaime had thought death was the worst thing that could happen to a person, whether it was being beaten to death by people who had once been friends or suffocating in a soulless train. Jaime hated remembering how Miguel had looked in his coffin, his face distorted and grotesque. At least Jaime had been there, had known his cousin's fate. But this unidentified person chopped to bits by the train, that was worse. He'd died by himself, in a strange country, and his family would never know.

As the day progressed, others joined them: a young couple, then a man whose face looked like it had been burned. A sign on a rundown building said they were in the small town of Huehuetoca, but rumor had it that the ideal place to get on the train was a few kilometers farther north.

"Right here the tracks form a straight line and the train just zips by," said the man with the burned face. "Once clear of the town, the tracks curve and that's where it slows down."

Too tired to care, Jaime dragged his feet behind the others and let them figure things out. At least it had stopped raining. The "waiting spot" was obvious: there were a few others scattered around the tall grasses and shrubs where the tracks bent. Ten, maybe twelve, people in total. Jaime nodded and greeted each traveler politely, but didn't feel like making conversation. Not when he knew how easy it was for any of them to die. Not after having said good-bye to Rafa. Soon he would have to do the same with Joaquín. And maybe Xavi. The older boy still hadn't mentioned where he was going.

They slept in some bushes near the tracks and woke up early. The legless man had said the train heading to Mexicalli would go through in the morning but hadn't said when, not that anyone had a wristwatch. They had left the populated city behind during their long trek the day before and were now in grasslands with scattered trees and occasional buildings.

Jaime joined Xavi to use the bathroom in the bushes, but Joaquín, like always, chose to go alone. After ten minutes the young boy hadn't returned. Ángela sent the other two to go look for him while she stayed with Vida for protection.

Joaquín wasn't far away, crouched under a shrub and hugging his knees to his chest. By his feet was some scuffed-up dirt as if he'd buried his business.

"Are you okay?" Jaime bent down next to him while Xavi, a few meters away, tried to identify edible plants.

Joaquín didn't answer, just stared into the bushes, half-shocked, half-scared.

"Is it your stomach?" Jaime wondered if the boy had soiled his pants. It wasn't unreasonable, and it'd explain the embarrassment. Parasites were hard to avoid, especially when they were eating and drinking whatever they could find.

Joaquín shook his head no.

"Do you want me to get Ángela?"

With this, Joaquín nodded vigorously.

"¡Ángela!" Jaime called out.

Ángela was there in a second with Vida at her heels. She dropped to her knees and put a hand on Joaquín's shoulder. "What is it, *papi*?"

Joaquín stared at Jaime and then at Xavi, who had stopped his gathering to glance at the boy. Jaime got the hint, though he wasn't happy about it. He walked away with Xavi, leaving the other two to a private moment. He thought he and Joaquín were friends, even though the younger boy still didn't talk much. They laughed together, rolled their eyes when Xavi and Ángela gave each other sappy looks, had bubblegum-blowing contests. It wasn't fair that he trusted Ángela more than him.

Ángela came back a few minutes later with the most deliberately blank expression she could muster.

"What's up with him?" Jaime asked quickly. If Joaquín was sick, would it be worth taking him to a hospital? Would they even treat him if he couldn't pay? Jaime had imagined all the worst things that could happen on the trip, but had never once thought about what to do if someone got sick.

She set down her backpack at her feet and shook her head, still pretending like it wasn't a big deal. "I can't say."

"But I'm your cousin, you can tell me anything."

This time her expression did change as she glared at him like he was a misbehaving little kid. "Except someone else's secret."

Fine. He kicked a bit of dirt under his shoe. He supposed he would have to respect that. "But is he at least okay?"

"There's nothing to worry about," she said, but didn't meet his eyes.

Joaquín emerged from the bushes a few minutes later, not looking at anyone. In his hands were some long grasses he was weaving together with extreme concentration. In other words, he didn't want to be bothered. Jaime sighed and told himself at least Joaquín didn't look any different.

They breakfasted in silence on the cracked raw eggs they'd gotten from the *mercado*, a few leaves Xavi promised weren't poisonous, and an overripe papaya that they divided. Their food stores had dwindled to a couple of fruits and a few broken bits of tortilla they'd slathered with lard. In his backpack Jaime saved the water bottle and *turrón* he'd bought.

"Why don't you come to Ciudad Juárez with us?" Ángela suggested to Joaquín as they waited for his train. The look of motherly concern etched across her face made her look older than fifteen. "Then you can travel through El Norte to get to your aunt in San Diego. That has to be safer than going by yourself on the train. *Por fa.*"

Joaquín stared at his shoes. The sole of the right one curled as if it were opening its mouth. It took him forever to speak. "This is the way I know. The way I promised to go. To keep going."

"*Claro.*" Ángela understood. "But staying together will make it easier to keep going."

"You can trust us. We'll help you no matter what." Xavi looked at the boy in concern. He didn't seem to know Joaquín's secret either.

Joaquín started crying. "Yes, but that way there's a river and I can't swim! Besides, I understand things here, I speak the language. I don't know the national anthem in El Norte." Joaquín looked around the bushes, where litter had been thrown, and then at the train tracks. "I know how to survive here."

Ángela took him into her arms and rocked him until he stopped crying. "You'll learn to survive there, too. Don't you worry, *cariño.*" She used her term of endearment before kissing him on top of the head.

Xavi came over and put a hand on the boy. "Why don't I go with you, Joaquín. One place is the same for me as the next."

"Where's your family?" Jaime asked. Xavi was the

only one of them who hadn't shared any of his plans. His decisions had always been more for the moment than the future.

Xavi pointed up toward Heaven. Then, as if making a joke, pointed down to Hell as well. No one laughed.

"My parents"—Xavi didn't look at them as he watched Vida, who was tracking an insect that buzzed around her head—"were taken by government officials five years ago. Most likely they were executed for political disagreement. That's when I went to live with my *abuela*. But even her *brujería* wasn't enough to keep me safe."

Ángela reached out to touch him, but Xavi turned away with his head still hung low.

"When my aunt, two uncles, and cousins were killed, I only just got away." Xavi sniffed. "My abuela in El Salvador is the only family I have left. One day I'd like to send for her, but I have no idea when or where that will be."

Jaime shook his head in disbelief. He had a great big family back home who loved him.. He had his brother, his own flesh and blood, waiting for him in Nuevo México. Most of all, he had his cousin at his side all the time. Xavi did not have any of that.

"*Pues*, you should go with them. They can be your family," Joaquín said in his soft voice, looking up from Ángela's arms with red but determined eyes. "Someone needs to take care of Ángela."

"Hey!" Jaime exclaimed. He might not have been big and muscular like Xavi, but he could take care of his cousin. Except maybe not. Not if they were attacked by gangs. Not if some thugs forced her to be their girlfriend. Maybe Joaquín was right—he couldn't take care of her, just like he couldn't take care of Miguel. But at least he'd die trying. "I think you need Xavi yourself. You shouldn't be alone."

"Trains aren't safe for girls." Joaquín choked when he said this.

"They're just as dangerous for you." Ángela gave him a stern look. Joaquín turned away. What was this secret they weren't sharing?

"Do you want to take Vida?" Xavi asked. The dog tilted her head and looked between them as if trying to understand why they were talking about her.

Joaquín just shook his head no. "She's your dog. Yours and Ángela's. I don't want anything to happen to her. I made it to Arriaga on my own. I can do this."

Something other than stubbornness lined Joaquín's face. Fear? Worry?

"*We* can do this," Xavi corrected.

"Xavi, please." Joaquín's eyes shifted to Ángela. "I don't want this trip to take another mamá."

His mamá. The realization hit Jaime like a coconut landing on his head. No wonder the boy clung to Ángela, why he was so worried about her. *Had he witnessed his mamá's death? Witnessed and not been able to do anything about it?* Imagining Miguel's death was hard enough; actually seeing it probably would have killed Jaime. A new admiration filled Jaime for the boy with the extra-large shirt and bad haircut.

Xavi looked between Joaquín and Ángela, as if debating what he wanted to do, and what he should do. Finally he nodded. "Fine, if that's what you want."

Joaquín jerked his chin down in confirmation, but he looked like he was going to cry again.

"I really wish you'd come with us instead." Ángela placed her hands on his shoulders and stared at Joaquín intently again, as if she were trying to tell him something secret and important.

"Me too," he whispered.

The rumble of an approaching train began in the distance. They all got up and quickly hugged the young boy good-bye. Xavi gave him a few of the tortilla scraps and one of Rafa's cigarette packs for bartering. Ángela slipped him something small but indistinguishable. Jaime handed him two sharpened pencils he'd taken from Padre Kevin's. "For self-defense. Just in case."

Joaquín kissed everyone as if they were family and straightened up.

The train came toward them, black and smoking. As promised, it slowed down as it turned around the bend. Jaime crouched down and wrapped an arm around Vida's neck so she couldn't chase it, as Joaquín and Xavi ran out to meet it. Other people who had been hiding among the grass and bushes popped out as well. Xavi lifted Joaquín onto the ladder coming down from a boxcar and then stopped running to watch him. For a second Jaime worried the train would tear Joaquín apart, but Joaquín seemed to know what he was doing. The boy grabbed hold with an elbow locked in place and then scrambled onto the top of the car like a monkey. He stood there waving from the top. The other people who got on board waved too. Jaime didn't want to think that soon it'd be his turn to do the same.

He watched the small boy in the too-large shirt, and something else clicked into place. Something that had been bothering Jaime, without realizing it had bothered him.

Jaime kept his eyes on the never-ending train even though he could no longer see his friend. "Joaquín's not really a boy, is he?"

Ángela wiped the tears with her shoulder and shook her head. "No, she's not."

CHAPTER EIGHTEEN

The train heading to Ciudad Juárez came later that afternoon. Jaime shifted his weight from one foot to another as he crouched near the tracks. He'd never gotten on a moving train before. He'd never gotten on any moving vehicle. Scenarios filled his head. The worst, of course: he could trip and get swallowed by the train. He could trip and have the train bite off his arms or legs. He could trip and get left behind. They weren't just horror stories. They were events that happened to real people he'd met—the legless man under the bridge in Lechería, the papá of a classmate back home, the man whose sneakered-foot lay along the tracks some ten kilometers away.

He tightened the straps of his backpack. When Ángela offered him some edible leaves, he turned them down. He wasn't hungry even though they'd barely eaten that day.

Their train came around the bend as Joaquín's did, except this one had a gray engine instead of a black one. He could see people already on board, lying on their stomachs with their arms outstretched to help the newcomers. Jaime took a deep breath, wishing he had gone to the bathroom in the bushes one more time. Ángela glanced his way and he saw she was just as nervous as he was—she tightened her shoulder straps as well. Somehow that made him feel a bit better. Like he wasn't weak for being scared.

"I can help you two get on. Lift you to the ladder like I did Joaquín," Xavi offered.

They shook their heads no, though Jaime wished Ángela had accepted the older boy's help.

Other people, mostly boys older than Jaime, waited up and down the tracks as well. Some looked nervous, some calculating, some as if they didn't care anymore but knew they had to keep going anyway.

Instead of appearing scared, Xavi looked determined. Across his chest he carried Vida in her double sling. She didn't fidget, just watched the train approach with her one ear cocked.

"¡Ya!" Xavi yelled over the engine's roar. They burst into a sprint alongside the train. Jaime glanced over his shoulder at the oncoming cars, being careful not to trip. The first ladder he noticed was on a tank car with a rounded top. It would be near impossible to get to the top and keep his balance. The next car was a hopper that didn't have any top. No way of knowing how high its contents reached the sides. A boxcar came next with a ladder on either end. He glanced at Ángela. This was it.

The tracks were slightly raised and the ladder started just above his head. He half jumped, half lunged for the lowest rung. The momentum jerked his shoulders' muscles, but he clung tightly, his legs dangling dangerously close to the wheels.

I. Have. To. Get. Up, he thought. He swung his legs and managed to get his inside heel on the same rung as his hands. Now he dangled from two arms and a leg. Getting the rest of his body up seemed impossible. But so did hanging on that way for more than a few seconds.

With a heaving grunt he pushed against the heel of his shoe and raised his bottom up. One arm clutching the ladder rung against his breastbone for dear life, he reached for the next rung up. Now he was able to put both feet on the bottom rung. His hands shifted up again to grab the next rung and then the next. He kept climbing until he reached the top and there was nothing left to climb. Or hold.

A boy leaned over to help him, but by that time, Jaime had made it on his own. He lay flat on top of the boxcar, his arms spread out as if he were hugging it. His head lifted and behind two boys standing near him, he saw Ángela doing the same thing on the other end of the car. On the next boxcar over, Xavi stood with Vida at his feet as if being on top of a moving train were no different from being on the ground.

They had boarded the train.

CHAPTER NINETEEN

The train went through villages and farms, open plains and mountains. At the sight of the mountains, Jaime remembered what Pancho had said: "There'll be other mountains, other volcanoes. But if you think of each different one as Tacaná, you'll never be far from home."

Home. How long ago since he'd been home? One week? Two? Jaime couldn't remember—too much had happened. For now, whether he liked it or not, the top of the train was his home.

Two boys, Lalo and Victor, also co-inhabited the top of their boxcar. They said they were brothers from Guatemala. Lalo, squat with straight hair, looked nothing like Victor, who was tall with tightly curled hair. Like Rafa, they liked to talk. Lalo of *fútbol*—he seemed to know every professional player in Latín América—while Victor's interest remained on Vida and how she was found.

"Does she bite? Will she attack anyone? Does she protect *usted*?" Victor asked, his head cradled in his arms as he looked up from his lying-down position and winked at Ángela, who returned his advance with a seething one of her own.

"She hasn't bitten anyone yet," Xavi said.

"But she was used in dogfights, so she knows how to take care of herself," Ángela insisted while keeping a hand on Vida. The dog took that moment to roll over on her back and expose her stitches in favor of a belly rub. Ángela leaned over on the pretense of checking her wound, but Jaime noted the way her eyes narrowed and the harsh tone of her voice when she spoke to them. These weren't boys she would try to mother.

"Speaking of biters." Jaime licked his finger and smudged out a line of the graffiti he was drawing on top of the boxcar with a chunk of chalk rock he'd found along the tracks. "What do you guys think of Luis Suárez?"

The conversation shifted from Vida and Ángela to the Uruguayan *fútbol* player known for using his teeth in games. When they exhausted that topic, any reference to Vida or Ángela had been forgotten.

That night they shared some of their limited food with Lalo and Victor, who only had a bag of stale potato chips and a flask of something to share in return. Victor laughed when the other three refused a swig. Its smell, like paint thinner, was enough to bring Jaime close to motion sickness. When the other boys fell asleep with loud snores, Jaime, Ángela, and Xavi took turns keeping watch from their spot atop the flat boxcar. Xavi kept reminding them about the "rules" of riding the trains: never let down your guard, never trust anyone, never look down while jumping from one car to the other, never pee into the wind, and like Ángela had mentioned while they were inside the boxcar being cooked alive, never ever take off your shoes.

Jaime insisted on taking the cold predawn watch while Ángela and Xavi slept facing each other with Vida cuddling between them like a chaperone. Lalo and Victor snored away, too drunk, it seemed, to notice anything. An hour before sunrise and the sky was just beginning to change colors. The night chill remained, giving the air a crisp fresh smell with none of the train fumes that had lingered before. A perfect, peaceful time. If Miguel could see the same color display from Heaven, Jaime knew he'd be impressed too.

Jaime rolled onto his stomach and tuned out the rumble of the train as he focused on the cows grazing with calves at their sides. One little fellow couldn't have been more than a few hours old by the way his long legs went off in different directions as he tried to scramble away from the giant iron worm.

The train passed the calf in seconds, but Jaime kept the memory in his mind. In his sketchbook he drew the calf with awkward legs as he loped back to his mamá. So quiet—this was definitely the best time to sketch. Plus, the train moved slowly enough at the moment that the wind wasn't whipping the pages from his numb hands. He'd never seen so much open space, never properly seen the sunrise. If only he had his paints. If only he could freeze this moment forever.

A huge yawn escaped his mouth. He stayed stretched out on his stomach over the boxcar with his nose close to the pages. The calf's eyes were tricky—Jaime hadn't seen them from his viewpoint above the pasture. He closed his own eyes for a second to think about it. He wanted curiosity and fear in the eyes but couldn't remember the correct shape. Did cows have big circular-type eyes or were they more like sideways eggs? What if cows laid eggs? Wouldn't it be fun to search the vast ranchland for freshly laid cow eggs . . .

"Goddamn it, Jaime, how could you?"

Jaime sat up with a jerk. The sun was fully up, and so were Ángela and Xavi. He glanced at his drawing, where his cheek had smudged the calf so it now looked like a blob with spaghetti legs.

"What happened?" he asked.

"You fell asleep, genius." Ángela looked like she was about to hit him. "And now Lalo and Victor are gone. With our backpacks."

Jaime got to his feet. The train was rocking back and forth, but he'd gotten used to the motion and could keep his balance. He looked up and down as if expecting the backpacks to have shifted to the side, but there was nothing on their boxcar except the three of them, a dog, and his sketchbook pillow. The rest of the train stretched in both directions. Other people perched on many of the other cars, and some balanced on the hinges between the cars, ready for a quick getaway. It'd be near impossible to catch Lalo and Victor. If they were even still on the train.

"I—I didn't mean to." Jaime patted his pants pocket as if the backpacks had mysteriously shrunk or were some-how sticking on him. "It was cold. I just closed my eyes for a second." He searched the boxcar again; sometimes things had a way of being invisible even when they were right in front of your eyes. His pencil had rolled over to the lip of the boxcar—but no bags. He pocketed the pencil before he lost that, too.

"How could you be so stupid?" Ángela continued in a low, angry voice. "The whole point of having someone keep watch was so this wouldn't happen. Pancho warned us to be careful trusting people. What if they had attacked us?"

"Vida would have bitten them," he said in a soft,

unconvincing voice. Last he remembered, the dog was lying sound asleep between Xavi and Ángela. But she had also spent half a day with those boys. Assumed, like he did, that they were trustworthy.

"I knew they couldn't be trusted, soon as I figured out they lied about being Guatemalan," Ángela said.

"How did you know?"

Ángela shook her head in anger. "They kept calling us 'usted' instead of 'vos.' What a pain in the . . ." She crossed her arms over her chest and swore. She stood near the edge of the car with her back to him. Twice Jaime caught the movement of her shoulders jerking.

"What did you have in the bags besides food?" Xavi asked in a voice that barely carried in the train's continual rumble.

Ángela swore some more and turned to confront them as she used her fingers to count off their last remaining possessions. "A clean shirt, a pair of socks, and underwear. Toothbrush. The cigarettes. A few pesos, for emergency. And a picture of my brother."

Xavi put his arm around Ángela; they'd told him about Miguel.

Jaime's bag had contained the same things except no pesos, and he had also had his pencil case with lead and colored pencils, a pencil sharpener, and a spare eraser. He had carried a family photo too, one taken before Tomás moved away—the only thing he had of *his* brother. At least the rest of his family were safely drawn in his sketchbook.

"And your sewing kit." Jaime slapped his forehead as he cursed himself. Why had he fallen asleep? He had wanted that early morning shift to see those predawn colors, and all he'd done was outline a stupid calf. Now when they had to use some of the money sewed into their jeans, how were they supposed to repair them so no one would steal the rest?

Ángela got a funny look on her face and then dug into her front pocket. From there she pulled out a piece of cardboard with needles, thread, and a pair of tiny scissors—all that fit in her palm. "I cut one of Vida's stitches yesterday but thought they needed to stay in a bit longer. I put this in my pocket instead of back in my bag."

"You're lucky," Xavi said. "They can come in use. It could have been worse."

"Oh, yes, needles and thread will definitely keep us alive." Ángela gave Jaime a look of annoyance and turned so her back faced him.

Jaime returned to sulking with his knees to his chest and picked the dry grass from his shoelaces. He couldn't even feel happy that at least they still had their shoes. "I'm so sorry," he mumbled.

Vida wagged her tail with her head hung low as if she were sorry too for not noticing the boys taking off with their bags. She gave Jaime a little kiss on his palm. It almost made him smile.

Xavi put his hand on Jaime's shoulder. "Don't beat yourself up about it. It could have happened to anyone. I fell asleep for a few minutes during my shift too."

"Yeah, but no one stole from us then. What are we going to eat now?" Ángela gestured at the arid vegetation. Gone were the lush greenery and tropical fruit trees of home and southern México. Now they were in open ranchlands where there wasn't even a cow in sight, just endless patches of dry grass and scattered bushes.

There hadn't been much food left in the backpacks: a half-squashed guava and avocado, some tortilla scraps, the *turrón* and water bottle Jaime had been saving. Hardly enough for one meal for one person. Still, it had been something. His stomach rumbled.

"We'll see what we can find next time we get off the train," Xavi reassured them. "We'll be fine. God will take care of us."

"I'm sorry," Jaime said again, but Ángela turned away, not ready to forgive him.

Nothing Jaime could do changed her mood. She spent the rest of the day snapping at him and making him feel like he was in the way. When they changed trains in Torreón, she wanted him to go off with Vida and leave her and Xavi alone for a while. Xavi, however, said absolutely not. Torreón and northern México were run by a drug cartel called los Fuegos. More than ever, Xavi said, they had to stick together. Jaime mentally thanked Xavi for sticking up for him. On the other hand, if Xavi weren't there, his cousin wouldn't be treating him like a pesky fruit fly.

Back home when Ángela had gone off with her friends, she had never made him feel like a little kid. They had always been equal, even when she mothered and ordered him around. He'd never seen her like this. It was as if Lalo and Victor had taken Ángela away too and replaced her with this alien.

In Torreón they kept a lookout for los Fuegos. They took turns guzzling water at a fountain in the park and found a half-eaten sandwich in the trash. There was so much *chile* on it, Jaime thought a hole would burn through his tongue. They snuck behind a grocery store and in the dumpster found a few rotten tomatoes and a loaf of sliced white bread with a hole in the plastic where mice had gnawed it. A few times Vida's hackles raised along her spine and she cocked her head to unknown sounds, but no one confronted them.

When they jumped on the train again, Ángela seemed to be in a better mood. At least she wasn't giving Jaime dirty looks. But she did ignore him as she and Xavi talked in low whispers, interrupted by giggles, as the train rolled out of Torreón. Would she abandon him? The possibility made him almost ill with fear.

He stared at the sun setting behind a mountain. The way the red melted into yellows, greens, and purples and seemed to stretch to the ends of the earth did nothing for him. What was the point of this sunset? Or any sunset? And that mountain all ugly and bare, it looked nothing like Volcán Tacaná back home. He only had one pencil left, but he didn't want to remember this moment. Nor this desolate place, where few things grew except prickly cactus and scraggly grass, where Ángela could leave him at any moment. His skin burned hot and dry from spending all day in the scorching sun.

He hated this train, hated this land, hated this trip. He wanted to go home, have a bath, eat everything in the house, and let his mamá tuck him into the hammock outside. It'd be worth facing the Alphas if it meant being home.

He buried his hands into Vida's fur, and wished Ángela would stop giggling.

"Wake up!" Ángela cried.

Jaime sat up with a jerk. Headlights from two trucks sliced into the dark night alongside the slow-moving train. A cry came from the front of the train and passed down the cars. "¡Los Fuegos!"

Los Fuegos, who made the Alphas back home seem like

annoying fleas. When they weren't trafficking drugs into los Estados Unidos, they raided cities and trains, demanded pay, and killed whoever got in their way. It was said they etched marks on their arms to keep a tally of their murders.

Four figures scrambled up the ladders of the front cars and a scream cut into the night.

"Get off, get off," Xavi urged. He tucked Vida under his arm and pointed to the ladder with his free hand. "Jump clear of the wheels."

Jaime shoved his sketchbook into the front of his pants and patted his pocket to check for his remaining pencil. Still there. He hurried down the boxcar's ladder. The ground looked hard and far away from the last rung, but he didn't have a choice. Another scream pierced the night. Glints of metal shone from the men on top of the train like they were swinging swords. Or machetes.

Jaime glanced up to make sure Ángela was above him before flinging himself to the ground. He landed on his side and rolled until he came to a stop. His shoulder and thigh hurt from the impact, but he didn't think any bones were broken. He looked up in time to see Ángela land on the ground, and a second later, Xavi with Vida in his arm.

"C'mon, let's go." Xavi dashed to Ángela and helped her up while waving at Jaime to run.

Only a few trees were scattered across the dry land. The

emptiness made it feel like they were the last people on earth. Nothing around them would offer protection.

"Run to the hill!" Xavi yelled.

In the moonlight Jaime could just make out a dark looming shape in the distance.

Bright lights from a third truck turned on directly in front of him. The contrast between the dark night seconds before and the spotlight was too much. He shielded his eyes and dodged to the side. The roar of an engine came from behind him.

"There's one of the bastards over there," a voice cackled behind him. "Let's see how fast the little turd can run."

Jaime put on an extra burst of speed. His sketchbook shifted to poke him in the stomach, but he didn't let that stop him. The headlights gained on him. There was no way he could outrun a truck. Impossible.

But you can turn faster, said a voice in his head.

He could almost feel the heat from the engine when he darted to the right. He was so close to the car, he felt the swish of air near his head and knew he'd come close to meeting a baseball bat or machete.

Behind him the truck skidded and kicked up a cloud of dust as it tried to turn.

Over there, to the left, the voice said again.

In the moment without headlights glaring at him, Jaime noticed a hole in the ground just ahead. He ran with all his might, hoping the scant moonlight wasn't playing tricks on him, hoping the truck's headlights didn't spot him before he got there.

The hole was small, probably made by a coyote or another animal. Still, he kicked his legs to wiggle in deep inside, leaving only his shoulders and head exposed. He hid his head under his arms, squeezed his eyes shut, and prayed.

If I don't look at them, they won't sense me looking at them, he repeated in his head, even though Miguel always teased him for being superstitious. That trick had worked surprisingly well when he was younger playing hide-and-seek. *Please, Miguel, help it work now.*

Even with his eyes squeezed tight, the change in darkness told him the headlights were passing over him, searching, seeking. He didn't move a hair, even with dust entering his nose. But then the truck roared off in a different direction. He blew the dirt out of his nose with a sneeze. It was impossible. The lights had been right on him. Had Miguel—

But the thought left his mind as a scream forced him to open his eyes and lift his head.

"¡Ángela!" he called out, then stopped, fearing he'd just given them both away.

If those guys dared lay one finger on her . . . He knew why everyone kept saying it wasn't safe for girls to make this journey. He knew why Joaquín pretended to be a boy. He knew what they'd do to his cousin if they caught her.

"¡Ángela!" Better they get him than hurt her.

He pushed against the dirt to free himself from his hiding place. The soft, sandy ground that had helped him fit into the small animal den crumbled and filled the gaps around him. The more he tried to get out, the more sand and dirt sifted in and the more stuck he got.

More screams came from different directions followed by revving engines and laughter. Jaime tried to turn around in his trap. The headlights from the three trucks were fading away. In the distance a steady beam of light kept moving toward the horizon. The train continued heading north without stopping.

"¡Ángela!" he said again. Nothing. The night became still with only the chirp of insects. A partial moon and the stars gave off enough light to show the empty land. Everyone else who'd been on the train seemed to have disappeared, or worse. No, he couldn't be the last one left, no.

Don't do this to me, Miguel. I need you. I need her.

He tried again to push himself out, slowly, carefully. By twisting like a corkscrew, he was able to get some leverage, until his whole chest lay flat on the ground. He extracted his legs and stood, his chest heaving to catch his breath. He brushed the dirt from his clothes.

"¡Ángela!" he called one more time. He tried to remember where they'd last been together . . . not too far from the railroad tracks, right before the truck's lights turned on and blinded them. That was where they had split up. But where near the tracks, he had no way of knowing.

Tire tracks lined the desert ground, but they were hard to see in the night and it was impossible to tell which ones were coming and which were going.

He turned in a slow circle, pretending he was Batman with night vision. It didn't work. He saw nothing but the dark shape of the large hill. Or maybe it was a volcano like Tacaná.

That was it. Xavi had said to head there. That was where they'd be waiting for him.

Jaime jogged toward the looming shape. A couple more times he called out Ángela's name, but heard no reply. Maybe the wind was carrying his voice in the wrong direction. Maybe she was afraid one of the thugs was still around. Maybe she was still mad at him. He pushed that thought out of his mind and kept jogging.

No one was at the foothill, or anywhere nearby. No Ángela, no Xavi and Vida. He sat on a rock and tucked his knees to his chest as he watched for anything that might be a shadow walking in his direction. He waited and searched. No one came. The temperature began to drop. During the day it had been scorching hot; his skin still pained with sunburn. Now the night chilled him to the bone. He pulled his shirt over his knees as he began to rock back and forth. To keep warm. To stay awake. To stop himself from crying.

What if no one came?

What if he never saw Ángela again?

What if he was all alone?

What if all of this—the lost bags, the lack of food and water, this whole trip, Miguel's death—was his fault?

CHAPTER TWENTY

Jaime woke up with the sun. He could still feel the cold that had lodged itself in his bones, but already the sun's rays were warming him up. His legs were stiff and half-asleep from having been curled up under his shirt all night.

Now with the daylight he took in the vast landscape. The scattered trees seemed more like bushes and the bushes were more spiny growths surrounded by brittle grass, all of them in various shades of brown and tan from the lack of water. From where Jaime stood, he couldn't even see the train tracks.

The only good news was that there were no trucks and no dust being kicked up—and there was nowhere los Fuegos could be hiding, waiting to pounce. Now that he could see, he had to find Ángela. She was out there, somewhere. He knew it. Just like he knew she wasn't . . . No, she was out there. He just had to find her.

He found truck tracks and followed them but couldn't be sure they were made by the truck that had been after him—he never came across the hole that had almost swallowed him. Occasionally he found footprints, but they were too scuffed up to tell him anything. There had been lots of other people who'd jumped off the train. And yet Jaime didn't see any evidence of another soul.

"¡Ángela!" He removed his sketchbook from his waist and took off his shirt and waved it over his head like a flag, even though he was still cold. "¡Ángela!"

He turned in a slow circle, focusing on every detail he could see and listening as hard as he could. He waved his shirt and called out again.

Then, there it was. A faint sound. Something moved in the distance by a bush. An animal, maybe. Didn't matter. Shirt and sketchbook clutched tight, he ran.

As he got closer, the shape took form. First black, then blue—neither were colors that belonged in the browns and tans of the desert. A call came, louder than before, but muffled in the wind. A few seconds later arms waved over her head, and there was no doubt who she was.

Ángela stayed sitting but held her arms out to him. He dived right into them.

"I'm sorry, I'm so sorry." He couldn't stop the tears that stained his dirt-caked face.

She hugged and kissed him, then kissed and hugged him some more as she cried too. "You're here, you're alive."

"I didn't mean to lose the bags," he sobbed into her shoulder. "And if you and Xavi want to be alone, I don't care. Just don't leave me."

"Who cares about the bags?" She shook him by the arms. "Don't you ever leave *me* again, you hear?"

"Please forgive me. I never meant for Miguel to die." For the first time, he let his guilt pour out as he confessed. "If I hadn't been sick—"

"Then you would be dead too, and I couldn't have dealt with that. Miguel's death wasn't your fault."

Jaime hugged her tight. She was his whole family, the only thing that mattered.

After a minute he realized there was still something wrong.

"*¿Y Xavi?*" He looked around.

Ángela shook her head. "I don't know. We got separated."

"Now that it's day, he'll be here soon," Jaime guaranteed. Any minute Vida would be leading Xavi to them. If Jaime could find Ángela in the middle of the desert with nothing more than his senses and a family-homing gut feeling, Vida could sniff them out. She knew her family too. She would find them—he knew it. "Or we can look for him."

"I can't walk," Ángela said, wincing and looking like she might start crying again. "I hurt myself last night."

Jaime glanced at her legs. A huge rip exposed her left thigh, but there was no sign of a cut. On the other leg, however, in the gap of flesh revealed between her jeans and sock, her right ankle looked double the size of the other. "Is it painful?"

She tried to laugh. "Like an elephant is balancing on it. It won't take any weight."

Jaime stood and held out a helping hand.

"You're not—" she started, then looked him up and down with the sun behind him casting a long morning shadow. "When did you get so tall?"

Jaime shrugged and teased. "Last Tuesday?"

Ángela cracked a smile. She took hold of his hand, but as soon as she put the slightest pressure on the ankle, she crumpled back to the ground.

"We should make some kind of brace," he said.

"¿Con qué? We don't have anything."

Jaime looked around. One of the bushlike trees stood nearby, but none of its branches would work. Too thin. The grass wasn't long enough, much less strong enough to weave; it crumbled in his hands when he picked it. Still, there had to be something. His eyes landed on his sketchbook lying in a heap with his shirt. If only he could draw her crutches that would come alive to help her out . . .

"Do you still have your sewing kit?"

Ángela pulled the packet of needles, thread, and tiny scissors from her pocket. Before she could stop him, he grabbed his sketchbook and tore off the front cover. The tiny scissors couldn't cut the cover, but he took one of the blades and made an incision in the middle of each side and was able to bend it until it tore in half. Then he cut a strip from the hem of his shirt and double-checked Tía hadn't sewed money into it. She hadn't.

He took off Ángela's shoe but left on her sock, pulling it up her leg; Ángela bit her lip in pain. He sandwiched her foot between the two cover halves and secured it tight with the strips of cloth from his shirt. By loosening the laces, he carefully replaced her shoe over the mock cast. It was the best he could do.

"That feels better," Ángela said. He couldn't tell if she was lying or if it really did work. She hadn't tried standing again.

Before she could, a high-pitched yip came from the south. A white-and-brown blur dashed toward them, a single ear flopping up and down.

"Vida!"

The dog greeted them with slobbery kisses while Jaime and Ángela petted and scratched her. They stared at the horizon and waited.

"Vida, where's Xavi?" Ángela finally asked the dog.

Vida lay down with her muzzle over her paws, staring at them with sad eyes.

Ángela repeated the question. "Where's Xavi?"

The dog looked away, as if she couldn't bear the awful truth.

Xavi wasn't coming.

CHAPTER TWENTY-ONE

"Maybe he and Vida got separated. Maybe he got back on the train," Jaime tried to comfort his cousin. But he didn't believe his words anymore than she did. A gut feeling told him Xavi was gone. Like Miguel. Forever.

"I'll go look for him if you'd like," he said. "Vida can help me."

"No, don't leave me." Ángela clung to his arm. He nodded. He didn't want to leave her either. He stood up and stared into the horizon as he had to find Ángela.

"¡Xavi!" Jaime called out. "¡Xavi!"

He paused, listening to the quiet surrounding them. Nothing.

"He might still show up."

But he didn't.

Finally Jaime put his arm around her shoulder, letting her cry on him like he'd cried on her. "I'm sorry. I liked him too. I know how you feel."

Ángela stopped crying and snapped. "What do you know? I've lost a boyfriend and a brother. You still have your brother."

Her words stung. For a moment the anger and resentment he had felt yesterday flooded back. Then he remembered how lost he'd felt last night, all alone. Now was not the time to argue with her, no matter how much they were both hurting.

Still, he let go of her to look her straight in the eye.

"Miguel was like my twin, a part of me that is gone forever. Don't ever think I loved him less because we had different parents." Jaime looked at the east. The sun was fully up and threatened to be hotter than yesterday, yet the cold from the night before still chilled his bones.

"We didn't know Xavi for very long," he continued, "but he was always there for us. Like family." There was still a chance Xavi would come back, right? Unless they found proof, there was no way of knowing if he was truly gone. Jaime remembered Miguel in his coffin. As horrible as it had been to see his cousin like that, at least there was no question of his death. With Xavi, nothing was certain, and Jaime didn't know if that was worse. "But last night, when I thought I'd never see you again, I didn't know if I could go on. Even if Miguel helps me, like I think he did last night, I can't do this trip without you."

Ángela collapsed into his arms. They hadn't had anything to drink since yesterday, and still her body seemed to have an endless supply of tears. After several minutes her breaths were more chokes. "It's just . . . I'm so scared."

"I know. Me too."

She closed her eyes and took a deep breath. "I barely felt the pain in my ankle last night—I was worried I'd never see you again."

"You almost didn't." He told her about the truck chasing him and getting stuck in the animal den. She told him how she'd twisted her ankle in a rabbit hole and then had lain flat on the ground, praying the bush and grass would hide her if the trucks returned.

She yanked up a handful of brittle grass before throwing it to the side. "I'm going to end up like Tía, barely able to work, having to depend on others to take care of me."

Jaime pressed his lips together. His mamá might have a limp, but she wasn't helpless.

"Mamá doesn't depend on anyone. She can take care of herself, and everyone else. You know that." How dare Ángela suggest that being like Mamá was anything to be ashamed of, that she was less of a person because she couldn't run well, when Mamá had raised Ángela like her own? "Stop acting like your life is a *telenovela*."

Ángela stared at the dusty ground and then around

the vast landscape. "I think we should go back."

With no sign of civilization between the scraggly bushes, not even a cow grazing or a rabbit searching for a nibble, Ángela had finally spoken some sense.

"Yeah. The train tracks are our best hope to head north," he said.

"No. Back home. To Guatemala."

"What?" Jaime jumped to his feet and glared at his cousin. It was one thing to think these thoughts, but to say them out loud?

Ángela hugged the knee of her good leg to her chest. "I'm tired of being scared all the time. I miss my parents and Abuela. I want to hang out with *mis amigas*. I want a bath and regular meals. I want things to go back to how they were."

More than anything, he wanted those things too. He hated that even here, thousands of kilometers away, the Alphas were still controlling their lives. He kneeled next to her. "You know we can't go back. Things will never be the same."

"But they'd be better than this here, in the middle of nowhere." She lifted her head, her dark eyes turned wild. "I've been thinking. It won't be that hard. We turn ourselves in to *la migra* and they'll load us on a bus back home."

Jaime couldn't believe his ears. This wasn't Ángela. Ángela took care of everyone. She told everyone what to do, and how to do it. But she wasn't a person who gave up.

They'd seen how *la migra* had treated that Salvadoran lady on the bus. What about everything they didn't see? There was no guarantee that *la migra* had even taken her back to the México-Guatemala border.

"But the Alphas," he reminded her. "They're sure to make us pay for fleeing. If they killed Miguel for refusing to join, what will they do to us?"

Ángela gulped and turned away. "Maybe it won't be so bad. Manny Boy is in the gang and we used to be friends. Maybe, maybe he can soften the blows."

Manny Boy? Jaime swallowed a snort. Please. He remembered when Manny Boy and Ángela were "friends." They were eight and Manny Boy would chase her around the schoolyard, trying to kiss her while Ángela screamed for him to stop. Really screamed, not teasing, playful screams. Jaime didn't want to think how Manny Boy would behave now.

"We can't go home. You know that," he said. A new determination surged through his body. They were going to continue, or die trying. No giving up. Normally he was happy to let her make the choices, but this was one decision he wasn't going to let her make. Time to be strong and brave. Like Miguel. "I miss *la familia* too, but it's for them we have to keep going. What would Tío say if you joined the gang that killed your brother?"

Ángela turned away.

He lifted her chin so he could look right into her eyes. He had to make her understand. "If we don't make it, then Miguel died for nothing."

Ángela shook her head. "But it's hopeless. I can't walk. I'll never be able to get back on the train."

Jaime crossed his arms over his chest and used the same glare both of their *madres* had gotten from Abuela. "But you think you can walk to a *migra* station? There's nothing out here. We're in the Chihuahua desert. No one's going to find us until our bones are bleached by the sun. And I'm *not* going to let that happen."

"But . . ."

"But *nada*." There was no way he could have saved Miguel—he understood that now. But as long as their hearts continued to beat, he wasn't giving up on her. "You can't always be the boss. I'm in charge now and I'm going to take care of you. I'm going to help you—we're going to keep heading north, even if I have to carry you on my back like a burro."

Ángela's shoulders dropped as she let out a deep breath. Finally she nodded.

"C'mon, let's get back to the tracks." Jaime stood up first and then offered a hand to his cousin. Ángela got up slowly but scrunched her eyes in pain the second she put weight on the ankle. This time, she didn't give up and fall to the ground. Jaime put his arm around her waist for support. By stepping on the ball of her foot, Ángela managed to stagger a bit. Without Jaime, though, she wouldn't have been able to do more than hop.

It took forever to get back to the tracks. While Vida trotted ahead of them, her paws barely touching the railroad ties, Jaime tried his hardest not to show how tired he was. He couldn't let her down. Ángela didn't complain once, just did what he said. Miguel would have been proud, of both of them.

They hobbled along while keeping an ear out for the next train. It could come in a few minutes or a few days. If it came in a few minutes, it'd be near impossible to board it; if it came in a few days, they could be dead.

As they walked, he searched for something that might help them survive in the semi-desert. He didn't have Vida's nose; the fresh, unpolluted air was more a non-smell than a scent. There was no obvious water nearby. He figured if there were, there'd be clusters of trees and greener shades of brown huddled around the water source. Maybe even the scent of moisture. Instead his nose itched with sunburn and dust.

There were various plants besides the patchy grass, shrubby bushes, and prickly cactus. Plants with little purple flowers and others a cluster of spines with a flower stalk jutting high up the middle, but he had no idea if any were edible. None of them looked the least bit appetizing. Occasionally a plastic water bottle lay near the tracks—dirty, cracked, and bone-dry.

And there was no shelter where they could rest and escape the scorching sun.

"We'll keep following the tracks," Jaime said, breaking the silence to keep optimistic. "Maybe there's a sharp turn where the train slows down enough to hop on."

But realistically, he didn't see how that would work. His determination to do or die seeped away. Even if the train slowed to a crawl, climbing a ladder to the top of a boxcar with only one leg would require a lot of arm strength for Ángela. And he didn't even want to think of how they would get off the train if los Fuegos came back.

The intense sun continued to beat down on them. It was past midday when a rutted dirt road crossed over the tracks. Vida retracted her tongue, which had practically been hanging to the ground, as her nose twitched down the road. Jaime kicked the dust under his shoes and blinked his sore eyes. *Was that . . . ?* In the far-off distance he could just make out a structure. The dry heat evaporated most of their sweat, but beads rolled down his forehead and drenched the areas where their arms were around each other. White salt stains appeared under their armpits. He was so thirsty, it surprised him that they had any fluids left to sweat.

"Is that a house or are my eyes playing tricks on me?" Ángela squinted down the dusty road as she panted.

"It's a building of some sort," he confirmed. "Let's check it out. Maybe there's water."

She leaned against him to catch her breath. "What if that's los Fuegos' headquarters?"

Jaime licked his chapped lips and took a deep breath. "Then let's pray they're sleeping and left the keys in the truck."

It was a joke, but better to think about that than the more realistic truth—they had no other choice. They wouldn't survive another hour under this sun.

They dragged their feet to the house that slowly grew closer. It was a mobile home, rooted securely to the ground with an added wooden porch, and four times the size of Jaime's two-room house. There was a truck parked in front, but instead of being sleek with oversize tires like the ones los Fuegos drove, this one was battered and scratched, a result of many years as a farm vehicle. Jaime didn't get close enough to check for keys in the ignition.

A cow pasture stood half a *fútbol* pitch away from the front door. On the side closest to the rutted track stood a metal cattle trough. Water.

Jaime stepped on a strand of barbed wire and helped Ángela through the gap without getting snagged before ducking through himself. For a few seconds they stared at the half-filled trough. A quick glance around confirmed no water spigot nearby. Slimy green and buzzing with flies, the water smelled as appetizing as sewage. Still, it was better than nothing. Vida didn't hesitate to lap up the muddy water that had seeped out underneath.

"What are you two doing? Get out of here."

A slender woman appeared at the front door a second before they plunged their hands into the water. She carried a long hunting rifle.

"Excuse us, *jefa*." Jaime used the term of respect he knew Mexicans liked. "Could we please have some of your cows' water? We've been walking for hours and have nothing to drink."

"We'll leave in a second and not bother you again," Ángela added as she hopped in place to keep her balance.

From inside the house a baby started crying. The woman groaned at the sound and lowered the rifle. "Come here, and I'll get you some clean water. That water there is not even fit for the cows. I've been telling my husband to clean that trough for months."

They hobbled toward her wooden porch, straining to climb the two steps and too tired and thirsty to be cautious.

They sat on the covered porch, not wanting to intrude in her home. The crying came from not one but two babies who'd just woken up. The woman seemed torn between letting go her rifle and seeing to the twins. Still, she set down a large jug filled with water and cups followed by a plate of vanilla-cream cookies and painkillers for Ángela before returning to the fussing babies. They drained the jug and devoured the cookies in seconds. A stitch in Jaime's stomach told him he probably shouldn't have ingested so much so fast.

We should leave, Jaime thought. But it felt nice sitting on the folding chair, massaging his stomach, out of the hot sun. If only he'd dare take off his shoes, he'd be perfectly happy.

"Thank you for your hospitality," he called into the house as Ángela swallowed the painkillers. "Is there any way we can repay you?"

"Yes," Ángela agreed. She didn't seem willing to leave either. "I can change the babies or play with them if you'd like."

The woman reappeared, bouncing the crying twins on her hips. She stared at Jaime and Ángela as if they were trying to trick her in some way until she finally nodded. "How are you, boy, with a hammer?"

Jaime straightened up, trying to look important and trustworthy. Any fatigue he was feeling he hid in his enthusiasm. "I helped my papá fix the roof last year."

She used her chin to point to the cow pasture in front of the house. "That gate is falling off and my husband hasn't had the time to fix it."

"Do you have some tools?" he asked.

The woman handed him a hammer and a paper bag of nails before rounding on Ángela. "You, go clean yourself up before handling my babies. There's plenty of soap in the bathroom. You can do the same, boy, once you're done outside."

He wasn't a carpenter or an engineer, and it took him double the length of time it would have taken someone who knew what they were doing, but in the end, he got the gate fixed. The woman, Señora Pérez as she asked them to call her, didn't mind the time it took and had another task for him once he finished.

They spent the rest of the day doing various jobs around the ranch house. Not only did Jaime fix the gate, but he tacked down the roofing paper on the chicken coop and cleaned the cattle's disgusting water trough. The smell from it curled his insides—thank goodness they hadn't had to drink it.

Ángela likewise kept busy changing the twins, putting them to sleep, and washing their diapers. Even Vida did her part by catching a rabbit that went into a stew.

The thought that Señora Pérez was going to keep them as slaves crossed Jaime's mind. It was possible. They'd done more work than the water and cookies were worth, and she never praised them. On the other hand, he didn't mind too much. It was nice feeling useful and not being on the run. Like he was worth something.

As the sun set, Señora Pérez fed them homemade bread slathered with butter and the finished rabbit stew, by far the healthiest, heartiest, and most flavorful thing they'd eaten during the whole journey. Why did they need to continue traveling? It took so long. Surely this woman would let them stay and work for her in exchange for room and board. She didn't talk much, but she seemed fair and maybe even nice.

The floor creaked under their feet as they washed the dishes, but the rest of Señora Pérez's kitchen was elaborate—she had a refrigerator as tall as Jaime and even a microwave. Next to the kitchen were worn but comfy-looking couches and a TV with a combination VCR and DVD player. Down the hall there were two bedrooms and an indoor bathroom. He'd never been in a mobile home before—they weren't safe in Guatemala with all the hurricanes—and had no idea how nice they were. It also helped that the walls were covered with photographs of the twins and the rest of the family. It felt like a home.

While Señora Pérez bottle-fed the babies, she looked around the clean house and fixed outdoor structures. Her tired face cracked into a smile. "I'm glad you came. You hear all these stories about immigrants robbing and sometimes even killing the residents."

"We hear the same thing about the locals." A sad smile crossed Ángela's face as she gave the counters a final wipe. Like her, Jaime still couldn't accept that Xavi was gone.

Señora Pérez handed them the bottles to wash and picked up the two babies. She stood rocking them, her mouth twisted as if she were debating something. After a few minutes she took a deep breath. "I need to pick up my husband near Ciudad Juárez. He drove a bunch of calves up to El Norte and has to return the trailer to another rancher. It's about a three-hour drive. Do you want me to drop you off along the way? I assume you're trying to cross."

"*Gracias*," they said together. They couldn't believe their luck. It was more than they could have hoped for. No more trains! No more traveling across México. From Ciudad Juárez they would be able to see los Estados Unidos. Now they just had to cross the border to Tomás.

CHAPTER TWENTY-TWO

Except crossing into los Estados Unidos would be harder than everything they had gone through in México. Señora Pérez said so. Back home, everyone—family, friends, newscasters—agreed.

It was night when Señora Pérez dropped them off at the migration camp on the outskirts of Ciudad Juárez. From what they could see in the dark, sheets of metal attached haphazardly made up the structures at the camp. Trash littered the ground. Her rifle lay propped next to the gearshift.

"I don't want to leave you here," she said. She reached for the door and hit the powerlocks even though she'd already done it fifteen minutes before.

"It was on the map." Jaime glanced through his sketchbook to make sure. He could feel the vibration of Vida's growl against his arm. "The map with shelters for immigrants."

"Do you know a better place?" Ángela licked her dry, chapped lips.

Señora Pérez shook her head. "I live on a ranch in the desert. I don't get visitors."

Jaime and Ángela communicated via one of their silent looks. Like on most of their journey, they had no choice. Ángela unlocked the door while Jaime kissed their driver.

"We wouldn't have made it without you, *en serio*," he said as he slid across the seat to get out.

"We owe you our lives," Ángela agreed as she set Vida on the ground.

"*Que Dios los bendiga*," she blessed them. They slammed the door shut, and in an instant the sound of power locks clicked. From the narrow cab behind the truck's main seats, the twin babies began to cry.

As soon as Señora Pérez drove away on the dusty path back to actual roads, people crawled out from the misshapen buildings like cockroaches. Young men with bulging muscles and red eyes, older men with barrel chests and untrustworthy smiles, all of them offering passage into El Norte, all promising they were the most efficient, reliable, and cheapest.

Vida's hackles raised as she growled at each man presenting his border-crossing deal.

"Twenty-five hundred dollars."

"Thirty-two thousand pesos."

"Five thousand dollars per person and I can guarantee your safety."

Jaime and Ángela told everyone who offered their services that they'd think about it. It was impossible to choose one—they didn't know who to trust, and Vida didn't seem to like any of them. Jaime remembered what Xavi had said after they'd met El Gordo, about the ignorant paying more. But even with all these different prices presented to them, every single one of the smugglers, or coyotes as they were called, wanted more money than Tía had sewed into their jeans, even with the money they hadn't paid Santos back in Lechería.

"Call your parents. Get them to wire the fee," one coyote suggested. Jaime didn't have to look at Ángela to know that wasn't an option. Their parents had already borrowed all the money they could to get them this far. Besides, in order to collect any money sent, they'd need identification. Something they didn't have.

"Have your parents send the money directly to me," said another coyote who had the small, weedy look of Jaime's former friend Pulguita back home. Jaime got the feeling that if they had money sent to this coyote, they would never see him again.

One man even yelled at them that since there were two of them, he'd only charge them a thousand dollars each to get to the border. But not to help them cross it.

They issued a flat-out "*no, gracias*" to that offer. They were already at the border—they weren't going to pay for someone to take them a few kilometers up or down to a different part of it. Especially when crossing it, wherever they were, was the most dangerous part.

"Boys, boys, let the poor runts get settled in." A tall boy not too much older than Jaime emerged from the narrow pathways of the migration camp in heavy combat boots. The coyotes vanished between the falling-down shacks and spewed litter as quickly as they had appeared. Although the boy was dressed in camouflage pants, shirt, and a wedge cap with a pistol resting on his hip, Jaime knew this was no junior law enforcement officer. Only one kind of person made crooks scurry away so fast, and it wasn't the police. This boy was a member of whatever gang controlled the migration camp.

"I'll show you where you can stay," the boy grunted. His voice sounded as if it had only changed a few weeks ago and he was still getting used to its new sound.

They had no choice but to move from the dirt track where Señora Pérez had dropped them off and follow him. Vida kept to their feet, hackles raised and turning her nose and pricking her one ear from one direction to the other. At least she wasn't growling anymore. Still, Jaime's scrunched shoulders didn't relax.

The boy left them at a shack made more out of cardboard than metal. Seven other people sat huddled inside. When Jaime asked Ángela if she thought they were safe to stay there, he received a roar of laughter from the inhabitants.

"*La migra* doesn't come here, if that's what you mean," said a Mexican man with a head that looked like an anvil had squashed it. "But that's because this area's run by the Diamantes."

Another Mexican, this one with a nose that looked like it had been broken more than once, continued, "The coyotes pay the gang a cut of the crossing fee to let them do business with us. Junior Diamantes members come by all the time to sell drugs, but other than that, they leave us alone. Just as long as you don't cause them no trouble."

Jaime and Ángela glanced at each other. They didn't for a second believe the Diamantes would leave them alone for too long. They'd have to figure out how to cross, and fast.

When Ángela didn't say anything, Jaime took a deep breath and asked the question himself. "Which one of those coyotes is any good?"

"None of them," two or three answered at once.

"I've been here four weeks," a man with a grizzled beard and South American accent explained. "And it seems half of the people these dimwits take across get caught on the other side. The others wash up downstream with a bullet in their head. If you can, go with Conejo."

"He's the cheapest of the good ones," one Salvadoran man agreed. "I paid another coyote, only to end up right back here a week later, half-dead from dehydration, and poorer than dirt. I wish I had saved more then and paid Conejo the higher price first. Conejo's clients don't get caught or sent back as often as the rest."

"That's because they're killed or die trying to cross," said a different man who came from the south, Nicaragua or maybe Panamá.

"No!" The Salvadoran slapped his fist on the dirt floor. "They don't come back because Conejo's that good."

"How much does he charge?" a Guatemalan woman asked.

"And how much is he paying you to talk him up?" the other man demanded.

The Salvadoran looked like he was about to attack the cynical man. "For that, I hope your corpse rots in the desert. The kid asked who the best coyote is, so I'm telling him, you son of a gun. He charges twenty-one hundred dollars, and that includes the drive to the safe-house on the other end. He won't take pesos."

Ángela and Jaime looked at each other as they huddled in their cardboard corner with Vida on high alert. They couldn't get over how much money that was for one night's work—it took their parents a whole year to earn that amount. But on the other hand, what choice did they have? Going with someone cheaper, and less reputable, could cost them their lives. In unison they both let out a sigh. This Conejo did sound better than the others.

"We'll check him out in the morning," Jaime whispered. Maybe, just maybe, the Salvadoran was mistaken about Conejo's rates. Because if that was what Conejo really charged, they'd never come up with the extra money.

Unlike the shifty coyotes in the immigration camp, Conejo didn't lurk around seeking business. Customers came to him.

Jaime and Ángela slept in the next morning and waited until the afternoon to follow the directions the Salvadoran man from their cardboard shack had given them to seek out Conejo. Ángela's ankle was better, but she still walked with a limp. They went through neighborhoods with decaying walls, where they felt eyes glaring at them through slatted windows; dark alleys with homeless men begging for any coin they could spare; and trash-littered streets with girls wearing very little except empty expressions on their faces. From a shadowed doorway a man came at them with a knife, but Vida bared her teeth with a deep growl and the man backed off.

They found Conejo munching on peanuts and playing pool against himself in an outdoor cantina, just as the Salvadoran man had said. It made sense immediately why this man was called "conejo." Sticking out from his pouchy lips were two large front teeth. His face was long, body slight, and legs lean. He was even a bit twitchy like a rabbit, and at the slightest noise would freeze to look at different directions. His shoulder-length black hair covered his ears, but Jaime wondered if they were large and twitchy too.

"Twenty-two hundred dollars each," he said with his back toward them before they had even reached him.

The thin desert air made Jaime struggle for enough oxygen. That was a hundred dollars more than what they'd heard last night. Each. They might as well find another smuggler because there was no way they could afford him.

Jaime tapped Ángela's shoulder to go, but his cousin crossed her arms over her chest. She stood her ground with determination he hadn't seen since Xavi disappeared. "Two thousand dollars each since there's two of us."

Conejo pocketed the next ball before his nose twitched and he jerked his attention at Vida. "Is that thing coming too?"

"*Claro*," Ángela affirmed.

"Are you paying for her crossing fee?"

Ángela put her shoulders back and glared into the rabbit man's amber eyes. "She pays her own way by alerting us if anyone is near."

Conejo threw a nut on the ground. Vida looked at the food and then at Ángela as if waiting for permission to eat it. Ángela nodded before Vida gobbled it up with a crunch. Conejo raised both his eyebrows, impressed. "Twenty-two hundred dollars each and the dog goes free."

Jaime and Ángela exchanged looks. Ángela gave him a slight nod before glancing at Vida. Jaime sighed and nodded back. Going with Conejo did seem like the best option. And there was the fact that this was the first coyote they'd met that Vida seemed to like.

"Do we have your word?" Jaime held out his hand like businessmen on *la tele* did to seal deals. "Twenty-two hundred dollars each?"

Conejo took his hand and shook it hard without breaking eye contact. "Be back here at ten o'clock sharp, any night except Sunday. With the money."

He threw Vida another nut and returned to his game, where he pocketed two balls in one turn.

"We should just call Tomás. He can come over and hide us in his car to go back," Jaime said the next morning as they walked the streets of Ciudad Juárez with Vida at their heels. They'd spent half the night thinking of ways to earn Conejo's extra money.

The downtown area, an hour's walk from their camp, seemed like a more promising place to earn money. At least the buildings weren't made of metal sheets and cardboard. But from here they saw what stood against them: the river with its cemented sides, the giant wall behind it, the armed guards, and the tall buildings of the Promised Land that was El Paso, Texas, and the rest of los Estados Unidos. All so close, Jaime could throw a stone and have it fall into the other country. But unless he were a stone, getting there was near impossible.

"And if they catch us crossing in Tomás's car, they send us back to Guatemala, and throw Tomás in jail for smuggling," Ángela said.

She was right, he knew that, but he hated having come all this way just to face a dead end. Especially when he thought about how close they were. Tía had said there was about two thousand dollars in each of their jeans. Which meant they were two hundred shy of Conejo's fee. Each. He came back to the same question they'd asked the night before: "So how're we going to earn the extra money?"

"Maybe I can get a job as a nanny," Ángela said as she noticed a dark-skinned woman pushing a stroller with a blond toddler.

"Should we talk to her?" Jaime asked. But before they could ask the babysitter if she knew of extra jobs, the pair had disappeared into the crowd.

A huge sigh escaped both of them. Hopeless. The people who could afford a nanny in Ciudad Juárez probably lived behind security-guarded gates. In his head Jaime went through his abilities. Thanks to Señora Pérez, he was better at swinging a hammer, but not skilled enough that people would actually pay him. At the *mercado* in Lechería, the merchant had paid him in rotting fruit for carrying boxes. He knew without asking that Conejo wouldn't accept squashed papayas as payment.

"If Xavi were here, he'd figure something out," Ángela muttered. Vida's ear pricked at the name. Ángela scooped up the dog and buried her face in the white-and-brown-patched hair.

Jaime stopped next to her, his hand on her shoulder. Yes, Xavi would have thought of something. He was good at taking charge. Like Miguel. What would they have done? Jaime glanced through his sketchbook at the picture of Miguel's funeral. An idea began to take shape.

Without the cover, the front sheets were bending and curling, but the blank ones toward the back were still in good condition. The old woman on the bus had paid him twelve pesos for his drawing even though she had been poor. Would other people pay him to sketch their portraits? He counted twenty sheets of paper left in his book. His last pencil was almost at its full length, but since his sharpener had been stolen with his bag, he'd have to chip away the wood by hand. Not ideal, but not impossible.

"We need to go someplace where all the *gringo* tourists walk by," he said, his eyes shining with new hope and determination.

"What do you have in mind?"

"You'll see."

They found an empty bench in the huge Parque El Chamizal with paved paths, irrigated grass, and shade trees. It was near the city center and very close to the border, and very far from their ugly camp. The day was cloudless and hot, but not too hot to keep people indoors. Jaime began to set up shop. First he tucked in his frayed T-shirt, which he'd cut to tie the brace for Ángela's ankle, and brushed off his dirt-covered jeans as best he could. Then he used the back of a used page to draw portraits in each corner of four famous people everyone would recognize—Jennifer Lopez, Jesús Cristo, President Obama, and Mickey Mouse. He held out the sketchbook with one hand and his pencil with the other.

Every time someone passed by their bench, he waved his pencil as if he were drawing in the air and pointed to his sketchbook.

"Me make you? Me make you?" he asked each person. He wished he knew more English, but that was the best he could say. Ángela couldn't remember how to say "draw" or even "paint" in English, so wasn't able to help his vocabulary. Instead she mended the large rip in her jeans—if Abuela had been there she would have been scandalized that Ángela had gone around the whole state of Chihuahua showing so much leg. Vida lay down at their feet and gave every passerby a hopeful one-ear look.

Most people ignored Jaime, but finally he noticed a group of girls a bit older than Ángela. The one in the front with long blond hair and skin browned by the sun carried a bag with the face of Frida Kahlo, one of México's most famous artists. If this blond *gringa* liked Frida, maybe she'd like her portrait sketched.

"Me make you? Make you *como* Frida?" He pointed to her bag with his pencil and then at his sketchbook.

She stopped and looked at him, then at the sample sketch of the famous people. She asked a question he didn't understand while rubbing her fingers together. That he understood. She wanted to know how much.

"Tain," he said. He wanted to charge more—the poor *viejita* on the bus paid twelve—but ten was the highest he could count in English.

She nodded and smiled as she sat down on the bench. "Sure."

He took his time outlining her face before filling in her features. Her eyes were small, but her cheekbones and smile highlighted her face, making her very pretty. He ignored the pimple on her forehead but made sure to include her beaded dangling earrings. She sat still with her chin up like a perfect model during the time it took to draw her. He couldn't have asked for a better subject and, as a result, the drawing turned out really well. He wished he could keep it for himself.

He remembered to sign the bottom with his illegible autograph before handing her the portrait. She broke into a wide grin that had him smiling back in an instant. He knew the words "fantastic" and "beautiful" and took it to mean she liked it. Then she asked him something he didn't understand.

"¿Tú años?" she asked again, and comprehension suddenly hit him. She wanted to know how old he was.

"Tain ahn tu," he said, holding out his ten fingers and then two more.

"Twelve?"

He nodded and hoped what she'd said was correct.

She carefully rolled up the portrait and pulled off a spare hair band from her wrist to hold the shape. Then she dug into her Frida bag for her wallet. Instead of the ten-peso coin he was expecting, she handed him a crisp US note, green with blue watermarks, and the number 20 on each corner.

"No, tain." He held out his hands, showing her again his ten fingers.

She shook her head no and waved him away as if it was nothing. How could anyone think twenty dollars was nothing? She had given him more than fifteen times what he had asked. She must be very rich.

"Tank you," he said. He couldn't make the "th" sound but knew she understood. He stared at the note for a second longer before tucking it deep into his pocket.

It wasn't until then that he noticed Ángela had convinced one of the portrait lady's friends to let her reattach a shirt button that had come loose. She handed back the shirt and was given a few bills in return. Once the group had left, Ángela showed her earnings. Three dollars.

"I didn't ask for any price. That's just what he gave me," Ángela explained. She tried not to look disappointed. "We must accept and be grateful for whatever we can get."

They were discussing how to get their next clients when a brown-haired woman with pale skin who had been watching stormed up to them, demanding something. They looked at each other nervously. Was she accusing them of stealing?

She let out an exasperated sigh and then pointed to Ángela's mended jeans, pinched her thumb and forefinger, and shook the skirt she wore up and down.

"I think she wants you to sew her skirt," Jaime said. "Or else she's afraid of caterpillars going up her legs."

Ángela smiled with a nod and pulled out her sewing kit.

"It's a lucky thing I still have this," she said, and Jaime knew she'd forgiven him for losing the backpacks on the train.

The new *gringa* made cutting motions with her fingers

and pointed to where she wanted the alterations. Ángela folded the skirt in position and confirmed before making the cut with her micro scissors. The lady stood there in the middle of the park, looking at her phone while Ángela tried not to poke her legs with a needle.

"Me make you. Tain dola," Jaime called out. He didn't think he could say "twelve," but now that he was changing his rate from pesos to dollars, that was good enough. People paused to look at Ángela fashioning a skirt still on the lady. An old couple stared first at Ángela, the woman nodding her approval of Ángela's technique, before turning to Jaime, who pointed from his portrait sample to them. "Tain dola."

"Five," her husband said as he pushed up his thick glasses.

"*Sí*, yes," Jaime agreed, even though the old man's gold watch implied he could pay more. Like Ángela had said, they had to accept whatever they could get.

Jaime drew the couple sitting together, the lady with a wide fake smile and her husband scowling as if his face had frozen that way years ago. The sketch turned out well, but Jaime didn't have any problem giving it up. The old man grumbled but handed him ten dollars. Maybe they figured because there were two of them, the price was five each. This time, Jaime didn't correct them. He took what he got.

By now, two children were posing for photos with

Vida—her missing ear made the children exclaim "how cute" a million times. They fed her their ice creams and pork rinds while Jaime tried not to be jealous; he and Ángela hadn't eaten anything today—everything they earned they needed for the crossing. When the parents said it was time to leave, the children began jumping up and down, whining and begging their parents for something. Jaime couldn't help but think he and his cousins back home never acted like that.

The father, who spoke decent Spanish, turned to Jaime. "My children love your dog. How much for her?"

"She's not for sale," Ángela said with a needle in her mouth.

"A thousand pesos?" The father raised his eyebrows as if daring them to refuse. Jaime wasn't sure of the conversion rate, but he knew it was a good amount toward their crossing fee.

"Absolutely not," Ángela confirmed, her eyes never leaving her job.

The father looked at Jaime to see if he would try to convince the stubborn seamstress. Jaime lifted his shoulders in a shrug as if there was nothing he could do. Secretly, though, he was glad. If Vida hadn't found them under the car in Lechería, they might have never made it this far. If she hadn't caught the rabbit, Señora Pérez might not have driven them here. No, Vida stayed.

The father sighed but slipped Jaime a fifty-peso note for letting his children take doggie selfies. A bit confused, Jaime thanked the family anyway. He couldn't get over how generous all these *gringos* were, especially when the news always said how they didn't like immigrants. True, he wasn't in their country (yet), but it was weird how they expected to pay for everything. He would have never thought of charging people just to take a picture of their dog. The customs were so different from what they were back home. He wasn't sure if he would ever get used to them.

CHAPTER TWENTY-THREE

It took them two days to earn the money they needed to cross and have enough to buy a couple tacos at mealtimes; the migrant camp offered nothing more than keeping *la migra* out. The skirt that Ángela had altered had ended up looking weird, but the lady loved it, saying it was exactly what she wanted, and came back the next day with shopping bags of clothes she'd bought that didn't fit right. When a security officer came by to inquire why a seamstress had set up shop in the middle of the public park, Ángela's client waved him away with a few dollars. The lady complained a lot, but seemed to think she was getting a good deal, so paid well.

"I never want to sew for money again." Ángela showed him her fingers, which were red and cramped from holding the needle. She had had to buy more thread, but thankfully, it didn't cost very much.

Jaime's portrait business went well, and Vida's cuteness raked in a couple extra dollars too. He was down to his last sheet of paper when they packed up for the second day. He debated whether to buy a new sketchbook. They had a little extra just in case, and he always liked having a backup. But it would be one more thing to carry while they made the crossing.

Without the money sewed into the waistband, Jaime's jeans felt strange. Ángela had repaired the stitches to perfection, but the pants were loose; he'd lost a lot of weight during the trip. Maybe the jeans felt strange because this was it, their final hurdle. If they failed now, they'd have to start all over again, but with no money in the seams.

"Remember, if we're caught, we're Mexican, from Chihuahua. We describe Señora Pérez's house as our home. That way, they only send us back here instead of all the way to Guatemala," Ángela said as she smoothed out her own jeans. They also hung low on her hips.

They met Conejo at his cantina at nightfall and hung around until ten o'clock that night. Gunshots and screams echoed through the streets. Ciudad Juárez had the reputation of being the most dangerous city in the world. Walking the streets at night with all the cash in their pockets was asking for trouble. Several times a growl rumbled in Vida's stomach as she heard one danger or smelled another. Jaime and Ángela made sure to keep her near.

There were five of them crossing with Conejo. The other three were young men, from México and El Salvador. True to his word, Conejo didn't charge extra for Vida's passage. One of the Salvadoran men only wanted to pay him half now and the other half when they were on the other side, safe.

"What if I get shot while crossing? I'm paying you to get me across safely."

Conejo's mouth scrunched in a grimace, showing off his large teeth. "If you want to come, you pay all of it now. But if you get killed, I'll return you half of your money."

With a moan the man forked over the full amount along with the rest of them. Conejo stashed the money in a plastic wallet attached to his waist.

The five of them squashed together in a tiny car and were taken a few hours away from the border city with the concrete river and the cardboard houses. City lights disappeared and there was nothing to see out the window. When they got out of the car, the river had muddy banks and looked relatively calm and unthreatening in the dark night. The other side held nothing but darkness. Jaime reminded himself that looks could be deceiving.

They crouched behind some bushes by the river while

the coyote's eyes shifted from one direction to the other to detect any lurking danger hidden in the dark. "I have two rules. Whatever happens, you listen to me. If you disobey, you're dead. If you don't listen but live and we're all dead because of it, we'll haunt you until you wish you were too. Second rule, you do what I tell you to do."

He pulled out some plastic grocery bags from his pockets and passed them around. "Take off your clothes and shoes and put them in the bags. Wet clothes will drag you down and be a dead giveaway if we meet an officer on the other side. Anyone who goes across in their clothes will be left behind." He said this to Ángela, the only girl, as he set the example and started removing his clothes.

Jaime stripped to his underwear and felt strangely self-conscious and nervous. A shiver went through him and his legs shook, more from nerves than the brisk night air. Without his clothes protecting him, he felt exposed and vulnerable. Getting caught didn't seem so bad now. Getting caught in his underwear would be a million times worse.

It could only be worse for Ángela to be mostly naked around these strange men. His vulnerability turned to chivalry when he noticed the Salvadoran who didn't want to pay the full amount ogling his cousin.

"Keep your eyes to yourself, pervert," Jaime said in a voice that came out like a growl. Vida pricked her one ear and strolled to Jaime's side with her hackles raised and teeth gleaming in the night. The man turned away and shoved his clothes in the plastic bag. The other two men didn't even glance their way.

Jaime hesitated for a second before placing his sketchbook and remaining pencil stub between his clothes. He tied the bag extra tight with a double knot. If water splashed on the bag, hopefully his sketchbook would remain safe.

Conejo crouched in the water and waved them to join him. Ángela picked up her plastic bag and tucked Vida under her other arm.

Jaime took a huge breath and let it out slowly. This was it. They were really going to cross. Into a new country, into the unknown. Everything that had happened in their journey, good and not so good, had led to this moment. He sent a prayer of thanks to Miguel for all his help and hoped there was no going back.

Rocks under the cold water hurt his feet, and he felt the slight tug of the current around his ankles. His legs continued to shake as his heart pounded. The river reached his chest when he stepped on a large rock, slipped, and the plastic bag tumbled into the water, sinking to the bottom.

"My sketchbook!" He lunged into the dark water after it.

"¡Jaime, no!" Ángela whisper exclaimed. Vida saw her chance and wiggled out of Ángela's grasp into the water herself.

"Leave it," Conejo hissed.

But Jaime ignored them, diving into the cold river, waving his arms in front of him in search of the bag. The water stung his eyes, and the dark night made it impossible to see. The coldness rattled his bones. He was almost out of breath when his fingers brushed against the lumpy plastic bag. He surfaced with a gasp and hugged the wet bundle to his face like a baby blanket. Conejo had secured a long arm around Ángela's waist to restrain her from going in after him. Vida stood already on the north bank, gave herself a good shake, and waited for them. Conejo glared at Jaime and shook his head.

"*¡Idiota!*" Ángela whispered. She freed herself from Conejo's clutches and said with another of her low-tone exclamations, "Four thousand kilometers and you almost die for a book." She kissed him on the top of his wet head and grabbed him so tight he could have popped.

Jaime wiped the water from his eyes and shook his head, sending droplets of water all over her. "It's not just a book. It's my life."

"But this life"—she poked him in the chest, hard—"is the one that matters."

"Enough," Conejo said, low and angry, as he jerked his gaze around them. "Another word from anyone, and I leave you all here."

Jaime and Ángela nodded. They knew he meant it. One hand holding the dripping plastic bag over his head and the other gripping Ángela's hand, he continued wading across the Río Bravo.

When they were almost at the north bank, a helicopter engine roared above them like a giant mosquito. A spotlight flicked on, swooping over the river. The Mexican man dove into the water with his white plastic bag clutched to his chest. The rest of them froze, watching the beam like a paralyzed mouse watches a stalking cat. If it landed on them, they were as good as caught.

Vida on dry land began going crazy, growling and barking at the "mosquito" droning over her head. A couple times she jumped in the air to try to catch it. In one of its sweeps the beam landed right on her and stayed there.

Ángela buried her face in Jaime's shoulder as if she couldn't bear to watch.

The rescued mutt twisted and turned, snapped her jaws in the air. Any second Jaime expected a gun to fire and Vida to be no more. Instead the helicopter turned its spotlight away and flew off farther down the river. The man who had been hiding underwater surfaced with heaving gasps of air.

Conejo watched as the helicopter faded into the distance, then waved an arm for them to continue wading across. But not before he gave Vida a nod of approval—the chopper had assumed she was what the radar had picked up.

Less than a minute later they were on dry land. Jaime and Ángela shivered as they looked at each other and let out a simultaneous breath they had been holding since they were first loaded into Pancho's truck. From leaving their family and everything they'd ever known, to escaping gangsters and drug cartels, extreme heat and dehydration, they'd done it. They were finally here. In the United States of America. The land of the free, where they would make their new home. But they weren't safe yet.

There was no wall on this stretch of the river like Jaime had seen from Ciudad Juárez, and no sign of armed guards, but there was a chain-link fence two or three times the height of a grown man. By a bush between the bank and the fence, Conejo had them put their clothes back on. Jaime's were only damp in a few patches, a surprise after his bag's swim. And while he couldn't tell for sure in the dark night, his sketchbook didn't seem damaged either as he tucked that into his waist. The plastic bags went back into Conejo's pocket.

"The fence is easy to climb, but it has sharp points at the top, so watch out." Conejo crouched low to the ground. His eyes twitched from one direction to the other as if he could see in the dark. "There are hidden surveillance cameras and infrared detectors scattered around this area. They send data back to the patrol offices, who can have that chopper back here in less than a minute. Once over the fence, you follow me and run or you're left behind."

Jaime glanced at Ángela. She rotated her ankle. If it still hurt her, she didn't let it show. They hadn't been told they'd need to run. Had they known, they could have waited a few more days before crossing.

"Remember my rules and pray to whatever god you believe in the detectors pick up nothing more than the dog like they did before. Go!" Conejo sprinted to the fence, jumped on it, and continued to scurry up and over in seconds.

The fence wasn't as easy to climb as Conejo said, but it wasn't impossible, either. Their toes fit in the grooves, and with a bit of scrambling they made it to the top. One of the sharp metal points snagged Jaime's jeans and cut his thigh as he swung a leg over. He winced but held on tight. Conejo had jumped from the top, but Jaime wasn't that brave. He lowered himself down some more before letting go. He landed on a graded dirt road running alongside the fence. Ángela climbed all the way down like the fence was one of the ladders on the train. Vida was small enough to slip between a post and a locked gate.

Once they were all clear of the fence, Conejo took off at a mad dash through the dry grass, dodging bushes and scrubs. This was it. Their last flight to freedom.

He gripped Ángela's hand and ran after their guide. If Ángela's ankle didn't hold up, he'd drag her one way or another. He wasn't losing her again, and he wasn't going to let them get left behind.

Obstacles came into view only seconds before Jaime was upon them. Twice he came close to colliding with a cactus as tall as him. He kept a close watch on Conejo, trying to follow his path.

He kept his ears open for the slightest hint of the helicopter coming back, but all he could hear was Ángela's jagged, struggling breath. He gripped her tighter and kept running.

Then, as if it had appeared out of nowhere, a dark blue car stood in the empty landscape. A lady not much older than Ángela with dark hair and blue eyes sat waiting in the driver's seat. She looked like she had just been to a party with her perfect makeup and dressy clothes. She acknowledged them with nothing more than a glance and a quick exchange of money with Conejo.

The trunk popped open, and Conejo motioned for the Salvadoran who had complained about the money and the Mexican who'd almost drowned to climb in. Over them he then set the hard plastic cover meant to hide the spare tire.

Jaime was sent to the backseat with the other man and Vida; Ángela was ordered to sit up front. The driver stayed put, tapping her egg-yolk-yellow nails on the dash in boredom. Jaime figured you'd have to be really bored to paint nails that ugly shade. Or completely color-blind.

The car was one of those fancy ones that didn't make much noise, and they were off before Jaime knew the car had turned on. He looked through the window behind him, but Conejo had already disappeared into the night as if he never existed.

They drove without headlights, bumping over shrubs and rocks, not even following a visible path, until reaching a paved road. Now, headlights on, speakers playing some twangy tune, they were driving along as if they were normal people in a normal car.

The tranquility didn't last long. Lights flashed up ahead. The driver swore as she slowed down. From under the seat she grabbed a silky shirt and hairbrush and threw them at Ángela.

In half English and bad Spanish she turned to each one of them.

"You." She pointed to Ángela next to her. "*Mi amiga.* You, *dormir.*" She pointed to the man next to Jaime and implied she wanted him to pretend to be asleep. "And you, with bowwow."

Vida barked back as if to say she got it. Jaime wished he felt as confident. From what he gathered, the lady wanted him to pay attention to the dog. In other words, act casual. Like they lived here. Right. Even though the driver with her blue eyes was the only one who looked like she lived, and belonged, here.

A uniformed man swaggered up to the car carrying a flashlight. As he got closer, Jaime let out a gasp. The man was short with strong arms and broad shoulders. His black hair was combed to one side, his eyes hidden in the shadow of his large nose, and his skin shone brown in the flashlight glow. He looked so familiar, he could have been a distant uncle. The nametag on his uniform said "Rivera." Yup, he could definitely be related.

"Hi ya." The lady rolled down her window and smiled at the man. She waved a manicured hand and set it down against the car as if she wanted him to touch it. "How's it going?"

Jaime couldn't stop his eyebrows from rising. He'd understood her words. And understood what she was doing. Flirting.

A low growl came from Vida's belly, and Jaime remembered he was supposed to act casual. He placed a reassuring hand on Vida's head and she licked him. She turned away from the officer and wagged her tail as if to say she had his back and could play it cool.

Jaime had no choice but to keep petting Vida. He missed what the officer had asked but heard Ángela's response.

"Yeah," she said. Just like a *gringa*. She also looked

different now with the flashlight on her. Pretty. Her hair brushed and out of the ponytail as if she hadn't gone weeks without washing it. The silky shirt made it look like she had come from a party too. She smiled at the officer like the driver had, like she used to smile at Xavi.

Whatever she had responded to was the right thing to say. The officer smiled back with a wink and waved them by.

"What did he ask?" Jaime asked as soon as the window was rolled up and they'd driven away.

Ángela turned in the seat to look at him. This time her smile wasn't flirtatious but pleased. "He wanted to know if we live here, so I said yes. Which is true. We do. Now."

CHAPTER TWENTY-FOUR

The safe-house they were taken to was in El Paso, Texas. Had there been no border to cross, no wall, no security to avoid, they could have walked over the bridge and been at the house in twenty minutes. Instead the journey had taken most of the night. But what did it matter? After all this time (weeks, or even months?) since his parents had woken him up in the middle of the night, they had finally made it.

Two stories high and impressive, the safe-house looked exactly like its neighbors on the quiet street, as if the builder had lacked creativity after the first one. Still, they must have been in a very rich neighborhood because there were no bars on the doors and windows, and each house had a small garden up front with planted desert flowers bordered by neat gravel.

Doña Paloma, a stout Mexican woman who ran the house, glared at Ángela holding Vida in her arms.

"You're not coming in here with that dog."

"But—" Jaime and Ángela started to say, but Doña Paloma shook her head.

"Has she been vaccinated? Has she been treated for fleas and ticks?" Doña Paloma raised an eyebrow, though she already knew the answers to her questions.

"So, what are you going to do? Are you sending us back?" Tears welled up in Ángela's eyes. Jaime squeezed her hand tight and hoped she understood his message: if Doña Paloma threatened to send them back, they'd run away. Under no circumstances were they getting sent back to Guatemala now that they were here.

Doña Paloma rolled her eyes and sighed. "I'm strict but not heartless. Tie her up in the back. Don't let her bark and clean up her messes."

"¡Gracias!"

When Jaime and Ángela entered the house, after a long reassurance to Vida that they weren't leaving her for long and that she had to behave, Doña Paloma lined them up behind the other three who'd been in the car. The closed door in front of them led to a shower.

"The water is on a timer for three minutes. There's lice shampoo and disinfectant soap in there, which you must use," Doña Paloma commanded. "Once you're clean, you can pick out a new set of clothes."

During his turn, Jaime scrubbed himself and rubbed the smelly shampoo into his scalp quickly before spending the remaining eighty-four seconds enjoying the lukewarm water pouring down his head. Back home, with no indoor plumbing in his house, showers meant standing outside in the rain. This really was the land of dreams and opportunity.

One room held bags of donated clothes heaped on top of a long table. Most of the things were old and frayed, but compared to what he'd been wearing during their whole journey—a shirt he'd cut to bind Ángela's ankle and the ink-stained jeans that almost fell off and had a rip in the thigh, anything "new" felt like a treat.

He picked out a red-and-white-striped shirt, a faded but intact pair of blue jeans, and some white socks that looked new. His shoes he kept; they were smellier than rotten cheese but still worked. The Batman underwear he picked was a bit tight on the waist, but sometimes you needed to sacrifice comfort for coolness. His old clothes went into a heap where they would be washed, mended, and offered to someone else.

Ángela chose mid-calf aqua-green pants, a flowery shirt, and sandals. After having worn plain, blending-in colors, she wanted something pretty.

They hadn't slept all night, but there was something else they needed to do before crashing in one of the three rooms crammed with bunk beds.

The mantra Jaime had memorized in Tapachula came back to him as he tapped his leg in rhythm. *5, 7, 5-5-5-5, 21, 86.* Doña Paloma let everyone use her phone for two minutes to call anywhere in los Estados Unidos. Jaime swallowed a few times to clear his dry throat. He could feel his heart pounding through his whole body. He couldn't do it—they'd have to communicate a different way. E-mail maybe. Something where he could plan what he would say. He had never made a phone call in his life.

Tomás's voice recording sounded foreign as he asked callers to leave a message. At least that was what Jaime guessed he said. The recording was in English, and he called himself "Tom."

Jaime licked his lips and took a deep breath to calm his nervous heart. What if Tomás didn't get the message? What if he never came? "Ah, hi. It's me. Jaime. Your brother. We're here. Me and Ángela. In El Paso. 2910 Wee-Joo—"

"You pronounce it 'Willow,'" Ángela interrupted over his shoulder.

"Ah, Wee-Lo Estreete," he corrected. "See you soon?" And he hung up quickly, his face red and heart hammering in his ears like he'd just crossed the border again.

Ángela chuckled and pushed him playfully on the shoulder. "You really need to work on your English."

They woke up at lunchtime to some very strange food. Doña Paloma had prepared sandwiches with some kind of salty brown nutty spread and sweet red *mermelada*. When they asked her what the sandwiches were, she said, "Peanut butter and jelly." Jaime wasn't sure if he liked the combination—salty, sweet, and sticky—but ate it anyway. His abuela would have been proud.

The sixteen other people staying at the house huddled around the giant television watching English soap operas and talk shows, but Jaime and Ángela spent the afternoon outside with Vida. Doña Paloma had a nice backyard with a high fence that kept out peering neighbors who might report the suspicious amount of "cousins" she always had at her house. After spending weeks outdoors, it was strange being confined inside a house that reeked of bleach and insecticide.

Jaime rescued his old holey socks before they were thrown away and managed to wad them up into a lumpy ball. Once Vida got over the fascinating smell, she learned to play fetch quickly. Every once in a while she'd leap into the air with a great twist, flash the blue belly stitches Ángela said still needed one more day, and land squarely on four paws with the sock ball in her mouth. Jaime could scarcely believe this was the same dog who'd survived a murderous dogfight, had been found with half of her innards showing, and then had been stitched up by kids before traveling across a dangerous country. It was a lot to go through, and most dogs wouldn't have made it. Most people wouldn't have either.

"I was expecting two of you, not three," a voice came from the backdoor.

They both jumped and turned to the shape emerging from the shadows of the house.

Jaime's face went from *caramelo* brown to *café* with lots of milk. Ángela went even paler.

"Miguel," she gasped.

The figure at the door smiled, one side of his mouth going higher than the other. His eyes were so dark they couldn't be seen in the shadow except for the bright white surrounding them. He brushed his shaggy hair out of his face just like Miguel used to do. Everything like Miguel.

But it wasn't Jaime's cousin.

"Tomás," Jaime whispered, but couldn't move any closer.

Vida wiggled toward the stranger with her tail wagging, licking his legs as if he were a long-lost member of her pack.

The figure stepped into the sunlight. Wrinkles scrunched

around the corners of his eyes; a scruffy beard grew on his cheeks. While in the shadows he could have passed for a twelve-year-old, now in the sun he looked older than his twenty-five years. But still it was him. Jaime's brother.

"Well, are you two going to say hi?" Tomás's smile widened to become more lopsided.

Jaime and Ángela ran the few paces to him and jumped into his arms, something they hadn't done since they were four and seven.

Tomás hugged and kissed them both, then kissed and hugged them again. "I can't believe you're here. Do you two know how lucky you are?"

Images of others flashed through Jaime's head—the Salvadoran woman on the bus, the man under the bridge without any legs.

Xavi.

He thought of little Joaquín, Eva and Ivan from the train, and even crazy Rafa, and hoped they had been lucky as well.

"We . . ." Jaime paused to look at Ángela. Mothering responsibilities forgotten, she still had her arms around Tomás, her head against his chest, like a little girl. "We had help from many people along the way."

Pancho with his sacks of used clothes; Padre Kevin, who liked ridiculous outfits; Señora Pérez. All of whom seemed to have been sent especially to help them.

Jaime glanced up, the other two following his example, and stared at the pale blue sky without a cloud in sight. They stood there, feeling eyes looking at them from above, until Vida yipped and returned them to the backyard of a safe-house in El Paso.

"I'm sorry about Miguel," Tomás said, rubbing both of their backs. "He was a good kid. Smart, good-looking. Took after his cousin."

Jaime couldn't stop himself from grinning. "Except more humble."

Tomás shook his head as if he didn't believe that and then smiled back.

"Let's have a look at you." He held them at arm's length. "Ángela, I wouldn't have recognized you, you're so beautiful. And you, *hermanito*, when did you start growing a mustache?"

Jaime bounded to the window to check out his reflection. It was faint, but sure enough, there were definitely some dark hairs growing on his upper lip.

"It's not real—I know you just drew it on," Ángela teased. Jaime stuck out his tongue at her.

"We need to call our parents. They've been so worried." Tomás put his phone on speaker and called Tío Daniel, Ángela's papá, the only one in their family with a phone. But it was Abuela who answered.

"Tomás, what is it? No, I don't want to know. Please don't tell me."

"*Está bien*," Tomás reassured their grandmother. "I have them. They're here."

"*¿En serio?*" Abuela asked in disbelief.

Tomás waved at them to speak.

"*Hola Abuela*," Jaime and Ángela said at the same time.

Abuela gasped, and Jaime heard her start to cry. He imagined her holding her heart as she leaned against the counter full of her tortillas. "*¡Gracias a Dios!* I must tell everyone. The whole family has been praying for weeks. Bless you three." And she was gone.

They stared at the phone for a few minutes after she hung up, thinking about Abuela and their parents, Guatemala, and home.

"C'mon, let's get going." Tomás put an arm around the two of them and kissed them once more on the top of their heads.

They went through the house with Vida in Ángela's arms and Jaime clutching Tomás's hand. They thanked Doña Paloma, and Tomás slipped her some extra money for taking care of his family.

They climbed into the red truck Tomás had borrowed from his boss, and they drove out of El Paso, Texas, and into Nuevo México. They passed one checkpoint, but the officer just glanced in the truck and waved them along without even asking a question.

Jaime turned to the last blank page in his sketchbook and tapped the remaining pencil stub on his lip as he wondered what to draw. Cacti covered the landscape along with flowering spiny plants. Cattle herds near the road and speckled in the distance were more common than people or houses. At one point three brown-and-white Bambis, which Tomás called pronghorn antelopes, leaped across the road. Sometimes they drove for twenty minutes without passing another car. Everything was big and sparse, and nothing like home.

During their journey Jaime had only worried about getting to his brother and safety. Now a whole new set of concerns took over. What was it going to be like to live here, where there was no one? Would he ever be able to speak English properly? What if he never stopped missing his family back home? What if, after everything, they still got deported?

Next to him Ángela stared out the open window with Vida on her lap. She turned to look at him. With wide eyes and a deep breath she mouthed, "We made it."

Jaime started sketching without realizing what he was drawing. The perspective was from behind instead of facing forward like he normally drew. He made rough lines into right angles until he had the three-dimensional image of a rectangular box. Or the bed of a truck. From there he worked on the back of the heads of each of the passengers. A shaggy, taller head on the driver's seat with one arm dangling out the window. A smaller head with shorter hair growing a mustache (even though that couldn't be seen). Next to the other window, long tresses whipped in the breeze from another head. And finally a white-and-brown-patched mutt with one ear and a flapping tongue.

"You see that mountain over there?" Tomás said. "Millions of years ago it used to be a volcano. Home is just on the other side."

Jaime looked up and smiled. It was just like Pancho had said.

In the background of his drawing a volcano appeared. Instead of being lush with foliage and half-hidden with fog, this volcano held clumps of brown-green bushes with rocks on the top that seemed to wink in the setting sun.

Together, as a family, they drove toward the volcano, and their new home.

AUTHOR'S NOTE

"Look out the window because this is the last time you'll see your country." These were the words my mother heard when she and her family left Cuba in 1960, following the Cuban Revolution and the rise of communism. My mother immigrated to the United States with her parents and siblings when she was seventeen; my father immigrated at nineteen and had to work hard to save enough money to pay for his parents' and siblings' passage. They didn't meet until they got to Miami.

Both of my parents had to leave everything behind: homes, possessions, friends, but mostly family members they thought they'd never see again. In my mother's case, it was the grandmother who had raised her and the aunt and cousins who had lived in the same house she had. They traded everything for an unknown future, a life they had to start new with only two changes of clothes and five dollars in their pockets—the Cuban government didn't allow them to take anything else.

At the time of my parents' immigration, Cubans were allowed to enter the United States legally and were granted residency, then citizenship. Sadly, legal immigration is much harder to come by these days, regardless of which country the person comes from. People desperate to immigrate today face many dangers and expenses, and still run the risk of being sent back home if caught. It's a sad, worldwide conflict that is close to me, one without an easy solution. For me, had my parents not been able to leave Cuba when they did, my life would be very different, and the opportunities available to me in communist Cuba would have been limited.

While Jaime and Ángela are fictitious characters, their story is similar to millions of real immigrants. In recent years there has been a huge wave of children traveling alone from Central America to immigrate illegally into the United States; their parents unable to leave the rest of their family behind. Many are fleeing towns where gangs are terrorizing the citizens and "recruiting" children and teens to join them, or die. To many, leaving is the only choice, the only road. If they stay at home, they will die; if they leave, they might live.

Jaime and Ángela were very lucky on their trip; most people do not have it so easy. Murder, abuse, robbery, drug addiction, loss of limbs, kidnapping, imprisonment, and deportation are all common outcomes. Some give up and return home in worse condition than when they left. Those who continue hold on to the hope of a better life and the prospect of reuniting with family members already there.

For so many Latin Americans, whether Cuban or Guatemalan, if there is no family, there is no life.

Glossary

Note to the language enthusiasts: Spanish is a very phonetic language to read, much easier than English! Here are a few basic pronunciation rules: *J* and sometimes *x* are pronounced like an *h*. *LL* makes a *y* or *j* sound, depending on what country you want to be from. *Ñ* is a bit tricky it sounds like "nee-eh." If there's an accent mark, emphasize that vowel. There are other rules, but that's enough to get you reading most Spanish!

abran las bolsas: Open the bags. Can refer to a purse or backpack.

abuela: Grandmother; grandma. Saying *abuelita* would be like saying "granny."

adentro: Although it means "inside," it has the implication of "get inside."

ándale: A command to hurry up. It can also mean "come on."

aquí: Here; over here.

ay: A very common sound or exclamation. It can mean "oh" as in "Oh my dear!", "ah" as in "Ah, I don't know," or "ouch" as in "Ouch, you stepped on me," as well as other meanings, depending on the tone and the words that follow it.

Benito Juárez (1806–1872): A revolutionary hero, he brought liberal reform to Mexico and is considered one of Mexico's greatest presidents.

bien: Usually means "good" but also means "fine," especially when following the question "How are you?"

bienvenidos: A greeting, meaning "welcome."

bruja: In its simplest terms it means "witch," but it can also signify "herbalist" or even "fortune-teller."

brujería: Witchcraft. It is not always seen as evil.

bueno: Means "good" but can also be used as an interjection like "okay." *Bueno* and *bien,* although they both mean "good," are used in different cases and are not interchangeable.

café con leche: A small cup of coffee with milk, often drunk with lots of sugar. A staple in many Latin American countries.

cállate: An order to be quiet, like "shut up."

caramelo: A caramel or sometimes a generic candy.

cariño: When Ángela says this to Joaquín, it's a term of endearment meaning "sweetie."

carretera: Highway; road.

Centro Americanos: Central Americans, or people from Guatemala, Belize, Honduras, El Salvador, Nicaragua, Costa Rica, and Panama. Mexicans are not considered Central Americans.

chapín/chapina/chapines: A slang word for Guatemalan. For a boy it's *chapín*, for a girl it's *chapina*, and *chapines* is the plural. Guatemalans often call themselves these words and they are not offensive terms.

chicle: Chewing gum.

chico: Boy; kid; guy. As an adjective it also means "short" or "small."

ciudad: City. Ciudad México means "Mexico City" and Ciudad Juárez means "Juárez City."

claro: Clearly; obviously; of course.

claro que sí: Similar to *claro* but with more enthusiasm and often the confirmation to a question, meaning "of course!" or "certainly!"

como: As a question it means "how" or implies "I don't understand." Within a sentence it usually means "such as."

compañeros: Used for companions or schoolmates but it can even be a word for buddies.

con qué: With what.

Conejo: Rabbit. Because of their illegal work, most *coyotes* will not use their real names.

coyotes: A slang word for smugglers, especially those who smuggle illegal immigrants over the border from Mexico into the United States. They get their name from the sly, cunning, and mischievous animals that live throughout most of the southwestern part of the United States and northern part of Mexico.

curandera/la curandera: Witch doctor or healer; a woman who takes care of villagers who are sick by supplying herbal remedies and can also lift evil curses that have been placed on her patients.

desayuno chapín: A traditional Guatemalan breakfast often serving beans, eggs, cheese, corn tortillas, and plantains. Other additions, such as avocados, sausages, and tomatoes, are also common.

desgraciados: An insult without a real English translation but it carries the implication of loser or scoundrel. As an adjective it also means "unlucky."

Diamantes: The name of a made-up gang in Ciudad Juárez, meaning "diamonds."

dieciséis: Ángela's pretend age, meaning "sixteen," but she's really fifteen, or *quince.*

Diego Rivera (1886–1957): A famous Mexican painter whose last name is the same as Jaime's, although they're not related.

dola: Not a real word, but how Jaime says "dollar."

Don: A term of respect added before a given name, similar to "sir." For Padre Kevin to call El Gordo "Don Gordo" is respectful, even if the padre has no respect for the smuggler.

Doña: The female form for *don* and used to show respect, similar to "ma'am" but used before the woman's first name.

dormir: When the lady driving them to the safe-house says this, she's literally saying "to sleep" but the meaning is understood to be "you're sleeping."

el chico salvadoreño: *El chico* means "the boy" or "the guy" and *salvadoreño* means "Salvadoran," so together it's "the Salvadoran guy."

El Gordo: The fatty; the fatso. In Spanish-speaking cultures being called fat is not an insult. It's just a matter of fact.

El Norte: Literally means "the north," but it is how Mexicans and Central Americans refer to the United States.

el tren se lo comió: The train ate him. Implies that the train ran over and killed him.

en serio: Seriously. Often asked as a question or when replying to a doubt.

está bien: It's fine; it's okay.

Estados Unidos: United States.

familia/la familia: Family. One of the most important things in Spanish-speaking cultures is one's family. *Familias* are always there to feed, help, and support each other.

fiesta: Party; festival.

flan de coco: *Flan* is a custard made with milk, eggs, and sugar with a caramel sauce. *Coco* means coconut, so a *flan de coco* would be a custard made with coconut.

Frida Kahlo (1907–1954): One of Mexico's most famous female painters. She did many self-portraits, and her face is often seen on merchandise throughout Mexico.

fuera: A demand to get out.

fútbol: Yes, it sounds like football, but "football" to most of the world actually means "soccer" to people in the United States.

gelatina: A gelatin dessert, like Jell-O.

gracias: One of the most useful words to know in any language, meaning "thank you."

Gracias a Dios: Thank God.

gringo/gringos/gringa: A white person or a person from the United States. When ending in an *a*, it is used for a female.

These words are not usually meant as insults, just as a way to describe someone.

guanaco: A slang word for a person from El Salvador, but most Salvadorans do not like being called *guanaco* and find it highly offensive.

ha estado allí: The formal way to ask, "Have you been there?"

habés estado allí: In Central America, because they use the word *vos*, they would use this phrase to ask, "Have you been there?"

hasta: Technically means "until," but when Rafa says it as a slang term or abbreviation, he's saying "later" as in "see you later."

hermanito: Little brother. *Hermano* means "brother" or even "buddy."

iglesia: Church. Padre Kevin's Iglesia de Santo Domingo would be Saint Dominic's Church in English.

jefa: A term of respect meaning "boss lady." The person addressed doesn't have to be your boss. To a man, you'd say *jefe*.

Jesús Cristo: Jesus Christ.

Julieta: Juliet, as in *Romeo and Juliet*.

la bestia: Literally meaning "the beast," this is the nickname that has been given to the freight train that travels through Mexico, often laden with illegal immigrants on top of its boxcars. This train is also known as "The Iron Worm" and "The Train of Death."

la migra: A slang term for immigration officers who are present all over Mexico and into the United States. Their job is to stop illegal immigrants and send them back to their countries.

la tele: An abbreviation meaning "television," like saying "TV."

lempira: The monetary unit for Honduras.

Los Fuegos: A made-up violent gang whose name means "the Fires."

malcriado: Used to signify people who are rude, obnoxious, disrespectful, and/or spoiled.

Mamá/mama: Mom; mother. Also a term of endearment like "honey" or "sweetie," often used by an older woman to a younger girl.

mamacita: A word with different meanings, depending on who says it. A boy will say it to a girl he thinks is attractive, but it can also be a term of endearment like *mamá* above. While technically it means "little mama," when Rafa calls Ángela *mamacita*, he's pretty much calling her "babe."

mamey: A tropical fruit that looks a bit like a melon but grows on a tree. The inside is sweet and orangey pink with a big center seed.

mami: Means "mommy," but when Pulguita uses it while speaking to Jaime and Miguel, he's using it as a putdown toward Jaime's mamá.

mamita: Another word of endearment like "sweetie," used toward little girls or a pet.

masa: The moist, uncooked cornmeal that is used to make tortillas and tamales, similar to dough.

me imagino: Although it technically means "I imagine," it's used the same as "I guess so."

mercado: A market composed of lots of stalls or booths, either indoors or outdoors.

mermelada: Jam; jelly; marmalade.

mi hijo: Another term of endearment, meaning "my son." It is often contracted to *mijo* and can be said by anyone, not just a parent.

mi madre: My mother.

micoleon: A small rainforest mammal of Central and South America that looks like a cross between a ferret and a monkey, even though it's neither.

mira: Technically it means "look" but it can also mean "hey."

mi amiga/mis amigas: My girl friend/my girl friends. To include both boy and girl friends, it would be *mis amigos*.

Mona Lisa: Perhaps the most famous painting in the world, painted by Leonardo da Vinci.

muerto: Dead.

mule: Someone who carries illegal things, usually drugs, on their body to smuggle them into a country.

muñeca: A doll. The term can also be an advance from a man toward a woman he thinks is attractive.

nada: In the context used, it means "nothing."

Nuevo México: New Mexico, where Tomás lives.

niños: Children.

Niñita: Little girl.

no es necesario: Literally means "it's not necessary," but when said in regards to payment, it implies "don't worry about it."

no lo toques: Don't touch him. Officers are very strict about not touching working dogs.

Norte: North.

once: Eleven.

oye: Technically means "listen" but is often used to mean "hey."

padre: Father. Can refer to a priest or to a dad.

paloma: A woman's name. Also means "dove" or "pigeon."

Pancha plancha con cuatro planchas: Part of the tongue twister *Pancha plancha con cuatro planchas. ¿Con cuantas planchas plancha Pancha?* The English translation isn't a tongue twister: "Frances irons with four irons. With how many irons does Frances iron?"

Pancho: A man's name; a nickname for Francisco. The English equivalent would be Frankie or Frank.

parque: Park. *Parque de San José,* where Miguel was murdered, translates to Saint Joseph's Park.

papi: Daddy. When Ángela says it to Joaquín, it has a motherly connotation like "sweetie."

patojos: Slang used in Central America to address friends or people. It pretty much means "you guys."

pero: But. Not to be confused with *perro*, which is "dog."

peso: The Mexican currency. Like the dollar, the symbol for *peso* is $, which can sometimes be confusing if you don't know which currency someone is talking about. Currently one US dollar equals seventeen Mexican pesos.

plumas: Feathers. In some countries it also means "pens" (from when feathers were used as pens or quills).

pobrecito: A word of sympathy, meaning "poor thing" or "poor dear."

por fa: A slang word for please and the same as saying "pretty please."

por favor: Please (another good word to know).

por qué: Why. Not to be confused with *porque*, which means "because."

Prevocacional (also called Ciclo Prevocacional): School systems in other countries differ from those in the U.S. In the case of Guatemala, a prevocational school is similar to middle school or secondary school. Many children in Guatemala do not attend school beyond sixth grade, so for Miguel to attend a *prevocacional* was a big deal.

pues: Well; so. Used at the beginning of a sentence as an interjection.

pues, con vos: Well, with you.

pulguita: Little flea. It is common for Spanish speakers to give people nicknames based on what they look or act like. Also, most gang members take on new names to keep their real identities secret.

pupusas: A Salvadoran dish made from corn *masa* and stuffed with beans, meat, and cheese, then fried.

qué: Can mean "what" or "how" and only has an accent mark when it's used at the start of a question or exclamation.

que Dios los bendiga: God bless you all.

que pena: What a shame.

querida/querido: Just like the word "dear," you can use it to start a letter, say it to someone special, or start a prayer. Ending with an *a* is for a girl; with an *o* is for a boy.

quetzales: Guatemalan money. The value of money is always changing, but at the moment one US dollar equals almost eight Guatemalan quetzales.

rápido: Quickly.

Río Bravo: Literally means "brave river" or "fierce river," and it's what Mexicans and Central Americans call the Rio Grande, the river that separates Mexico from the United States.

salchichas: Pork sausages, often eaten for breakfast.

San Francisco: Also known as St. Francis, the patron saint for children, animals, and travelers. Praying to him while traveling is said to help for a safe journey.

Santa María, Madre de Dios: Part of the Hail Mary prayer, it means, "Holy Mary, mother of God."

sálganse: An order for a group to get out.

sentate: How many Central Americans say "(you) sit down." In other Spanish-speaking countries it's more common to hear *siéntate* (informal) or *siéntese* (formal).

Señor: Mister.

si: Means "if" but is often confused with *sí* (with an accent), which means "yes."

sí: With the accent mark on the *i* it means "yes"; otherwise it means "if."

sí, soy yo: Yes, it's me.

siesta: A nap, often taken in the afternoon.

son mexicanos: As a question, this means "are you guys Mexican?" As a statement it changes to "they are Mexican".

Sur: South.

tain ahn tu: This is Jaime's attempt to speak English. He's saying "ten and two" because he doesn't know the word for twelve.

tank you: Jaime's way of saying "thank you." For many Spanish speakers, making the "th" sound is very difficult.

tanks geeveen: This is what Jaime hears as "Thanksgiving" when he sees movies about Thanksgiving.

telenovela: A soap opera known for being overly dramatic.

tenés razón: Another example of how Central Americans would say "you have reason" or "you're right." Other Spanish speakers would say *tienes razón* or *tiene razón*.

tía: Aunt; auntie. It's common to call female relatives *tía* even without their given name.

tío: Uncle. Like *tía, tío* can be used without a given name.

tíos: Can mean more than one uncle or a combination of aunts and uncles.

típico: In the context used, it means "how typical."

tostones: Like the French fries of Latin America, often served with beans. They are made from green plantains that have been cut, smashed, salted, and fried. A plantain looks like a green overgrown banana and needs to be cooked before eaten.

tú: The informal word for you, used among friends or when addressing someone younger. *Tu* (without the accent mark) would mean "your."

tú años: This is incorrect Spanish, spoken by someone who doesn't know the language. It literally means "you years" but asks the question "How old are you?"

turrón: A hard nougat made with sugar, egg whites, and almonds. Very sweet and very popular in Spanish-speaking countries.

un paso a la vez: One step at a time.

un tigre, dos tigres, tres tigres: A tongue twister that is hard to say fast. It doesn't work in English but translates to "one tiger, two tigers, three tigers."

usted: The formal word for "you," often used to show respect toward strangers or older people, although some cultures use it for everyone.

volcán: Volcano. Volcán Tacaná is the "Tacaná Volcano."

vamos: Let's go. Also can be said as *vámonos*.

váyanse: An order to go away or leave.

ven: Come; come here.

ven aquí un momento: Come here for a moment.

Vida: Life. Also a woman's name.

viejita: Little old lady. *Vieja* means "old lady."

viejo: Old man. *Viejito* means "little old man."

vos: The Central American (and sometimes South American) way of saying "you," while most other Spanish-speaking countries would say *tú* or *usted*. Verbs paired with *vos* can change in a way that might seem unfamiliar to speakers who don't typically use the *vos* form.

y: And.

ya: Now.

yo no sé: I don't know.

yo también: Me too.

Further Reading for All Ages

Picture Books:

Colato Laínez, René. *From North to South: Del Norte al Sur.* San Francisco: Children's Book Press, 2010.

Mateo, José Manuel. *Migrant: The Journey of a Mexican Worker.* New York: Abrams, 2014.

Pérez, Amada Irma. *My Diary from Here to There: Mi diario de aquí hasta allá.* San Francisco: Children's Book Press, 2013.

Tonatiuh, Duncan. *Separate Is Never Equal: Sylvia Mendez and Her Family's Fight for Desegregation.* New York: Abrams, 2014.

Graphic Novel:

Tan, Shaun. *The Arrival.* New York: Arthur A. Levine, 2007.

Middle Grade:

Ada, Alma Flor, and F. Isabel Campoy. *Yes! We Are Latinos: Poems and Prose About the Latino Experience.* Watertown, MA: Charlesbridge, 2013.

Alvarez, Julia. *Return to Sender.* New York: Random House, 2010.

Bjorklund, Ruth. *Immigration.* New York: Marshall Cavendish, 2012.

Blohm, Judith M., and Terri Lapinsky, eds. *Kids Like Me: Voices of the Immigrant Experience.* Boston: Intercultural Press, 2006.

Gonzalez, Christina Diaz. *The Red Umbrella.* New York: Alfred A. Knopf, 2010.

Lai, Thanhha. *Inside Out and Back Again.* New York: HarperCollins, 2011.

Menchú, Rigoberta, with Dante Liano. *The Girl from Chimel.* Toronto: Groundwood Books, 2005.

Mikaelsen, Ben. *Red Midnight.* New York: HarperCollins, 2002.

Ryan, Pam Muñoz. *Esperanza Rising.* New York: Scholastic, 2000.

Walker, Robert. *Pushes and Pulls: Why Do People Migrate?* New York: Crabtree Publishing, 2010.

Young Adult:

Nazario, Sonia. *Enrique's Journey (The Young Adult Adaptation): The True Story of a Boy Determined to Reunite with His Mother.* New York: Random House, 2014.

Restrepo, Bettina. *Illegal.* New York: HarperCollins, 2011.

Online Resources:

"Guatemala Facts." Nation Facts. http://nationfacts.net/guatemala-facts.

Schultz, Colin. "At Least 47,000 Children Have Illegally Crossed the Border Since October: And tens of thousands more are expected to cross before the year's out." *Smithsonian* magazine online. June 13, 2014. http://www.smithsonianmag.com/smart-news/47000-children-have-illegally-crossed-border-october-and-tens-thousands-more-are-coming-180951740/?no-ist.

Further Reading for Teachers

(Some may not be appropriate for children.)

Akers Chacón, Justin, and Mike Davis. *No One Is Illegal.* Chicago: Haymarket Books, 2006.

Bridging Refugee Youth and Children's Services. http://www.brycs.org.

Dominguez Villegas, Rodrigo. "Central American Migrants and 'La Bestia': The Route, Dangers, and Government Responses." Migration Policy Institute. September 10, 2014. http://www.migrationpolicy.org/article/central-american-migrants-and-la-bestia-route-dangers-and-government-responses.

El Norte. Film directed by Gregory Nava. 1983.

"The Facts on Immigration Today." Center for American Progress. October 23, 2014. https://www.americanprogress.org/issues/immigration/report/2014/10/23/59040/the-facts-on-immigration-today-3.

Isacson, Adam, Maureen Meyer, and Gabriela Morales. "New WOLA Report on Mexico's Southern Border." Washington Office on Latin America. June 17, 2014. http://www.wola.org/publications/mexicos_other_border.

Kahn, Carrie. "A Flood of Kids, on Their Own, Hope to Hop a Train to a New Life." NPR News radio program. June 11, 2014. http://listen.sdpb.org/post/flood-kids-their-own-hope-hop-train-new-life.

The Other Side of Immigration. Documentary film directed by Roy Germano. 2009.

Sin Nombre. Film directed by Cary Joji Fukunaga. 2009.

Torres, Olga Beatriz. *Memorias de mi viaje: Recollections of My Trip*. Translated by Juanita Luna-Lawhn. Albuquerque: University of New Mexico Press, 1994.

Urrea, Luis Alberto. *The Devil's Highway: A True Story*. New York: Hachette, 2005.

Bibliography

(Some may not be suitable for young readers.)

Byrne, Zoë. "Guatemalan Funeral Traditions: A look into traditional Guatemalan beliefs about death and funerals." Seven Ponds Blog. June 12, 2014. http://blog.sevenponds.com/cultural-perspectives/guatemalan-funeral-traditions.

Carina, an undocumented Guatemalan living in the US in a personal interview with the author, March 10, 2015.

"Central American Insomnia." *Médecins Sans Frontieres.* August 4, 2014. http://www.msf.org/article/central-american-insomnia.

Eichstaedt, Peter. *The Dangerous Divide: Peril and Promise on the US–Mexico Border.* Chicago: Chicago Review Press, 2014.

Daily Mail. "From Bribing Drug Cartels and Immigration Officials to Paying for Hotels and Train Rides: Coyote Smugglers Reveal Costs Involved in Smuggling Child Migrants from Central America to the U.S." July 22, 2014.

http://www.dailymail.co.uk/news/article-2700946/ From-bribing-drug-cartels-immigration-officials-pay- ing-hotels-train-rides-Coyote-smugglers-reveal-costs- involved-smuggling-child-migrants-Central-Ameri- ca-U-S.html.

Gordan, Ian. "70,000 Kids Will Show Up Alone at Our Border This Year. What Happens to Them?" Mother Jones. July/August 2014. http://www.motherjones. com/politics/2014/06/child-migrants-surge-unaccom- panied-central-america.

Isacson, Adam, Maureen Meyer, and Gabriela Morales. "Mexico's Other Border: Security, Migration, and the Humanitarian Crisis at the Line with Central Amer- ica." Washington Office on Latin America. June 2014. http://www.wola.org/files/mxgt/report/.

Maril, Robert Lee. *The Fence: National Security, Public Safety, and Illegal Immigration Along the U.S.–Mexico Border.* Lub- bock, TX: Texas Tech University Press, 2011.

Martínez, Óscar. *The Beast: Riding the Rails and Dodging Narcos on the Migrant Trail.* Translated by Daniela Maria Ugaz and John Washington. London: Verso, 2013.

Nazario, Sonia. *Enrique's Journey: The Story of a Boy's Dangerous Odyssey to Reunite with his Mother.* New York: Random House, 2007.

Rodríguez Tejera, Roberto. *"Prohibido Callarse."* Mira TV online video, 2:00–13:14. July 2, 2014. https://www.youtube.com/watch?v=oaNU9EnfOV8.

"Rutas a Estados Unidos." Map. Fundación San Ignacio de Loyola and Servicio Jesuita a Migrantes México. http://www.sjmmexico.org/uploads/TBL_CDOCUMEN-TOS_78_2_49.pdf.

Sánchez Saturno, Luis (photojournalist), in a personal interview with the author, July 28, 2015.

DISCARDED

DISCARDED

J DIAZ
Diaz, Alexandra,
The only road /
R2004414211 PTREE

Peachtree

Atlanta-Fulton Public Library